Ultimatum

David Gledhill

"Sometimes you can't dispel the feeling that a machine has some sort of soul."

Bill Smith

Bluebird Project Leader (2017)

CONTENTS

DAVID GLEDHILL

PROLOGUE

The Reichstag, West Berlin, August 1987.

"I'm not sure you do understand Prime Minister," countered the intransigent voice of the translator, the Russian enunciation harsh and aggravating.

Margaret Thatcher weighed up the poker faced Soviet Premier, recognising the potency behind the inscrutable stare. The man was obstinate, unquestionably, but was he immune to the pressures from the peoples of the satellite countries of the Warsaw Pact? Close by, just beyond the Brandenburg Gate and under the canopy of trees lining the showcase boulevard, Unter Den Linden, lay in wait the most pressing manifestation. The Deutsche Demokratik Republik, or DDR, was becoming a focus for unrest, the puppet Government of the post-war, satellite country barely functioning, propped up by the Soviet Union which had ruled with an iron fist since the collapse of Nazi Germany. Increasingly uncertain, was the willingness of other eastern bloc governments to continue to comply with the rigours of communism. Eastern Europe was in turmoil.

The Hungarian Uprising of 1956 was the first test of Soviet domination. A Soviet invasion, at the cost of over 3000 lives, both Soviet and Hungarian, crushed the fledgling resistance. An absence of public discussion, suppressed for years afterwards, ensured further resistance was quashed. The Prague Spring of 1968, when the reformist Dubcek sought to liberalise the adjacent, browbeaten nation, prompted further Soviet military intervention and led to brutal reprisals. New leaders and a policy of "normalisation" guaranteed that Soviet policies and values were reinstated. Most recently, in the early 1980s, the Solidarity trade union in Poland had begun to espouse anti-communist ideals as the movement sought to weaken the repressive, communist Polish government. Far from prompting invasion, and despite the arrest of 38 union leaders and the imposition of martial law under General Jaruzelski, the union prevailed.

Around the table, the mood in Berlin was markedly different from typical Cold War summits. Only the previous year, aware of the term's historical and more recent resonance, Gorbachev and his advisers had adopted "glasnost" as a political slogan. Together with the obscure concept of "perestroika", the wind of change was blowing through Red Square. The British Prime Minister could sense that transformation was inevitable but would the man across the table embrace the momentum? Might he be the conduit for that change or was the posturing a sham?

The choice of venue for the meeting, the Reichstag in West Berlin just metres from the Inner German Border, the Berlin Wall, was no coincidence and shaped the mood of the conference. Despite the fact that the seat of Government for West Germany was in the Bundeshaus in Bonn, many miles to the west, the backdrop was symbolic. The Brandenburg Gate was where East meets West.

As recently as the 6th of June, the rock star David Bowie, who had lived for a number of years in West Berlin, had arranged a concert close to the Wall that attracted thousands of concertgoers across the divide. East Berliners listened to the same music as West Berliners, the Wall a stark symbol of division. The violent rioting in East Berlin that followed would not be the last sign of unrest amongst a young population starved of contemporary heroes. Their actions spelled discontent. Just a few days later in a speech at the Brandenburg Gate, President Regan appealed to Mikhail Gorbachev to "Tear down the Wall." The status quo could not last but how change would come had yet to be shaped.

The British Premier was not easily cowed.

"I realise that you have a difficult task Premier Gorbachev but the signs are self-evident. The people of East Germany, and those in Hungary and Czechoslovakia to the South for that matter, are crying out for normal relations. They have an overwhelming desire to travel; they crave consumer goods yet the present border restrictions make that impossible. We cannot allow ourselves to be diverted by political dogma. Every citizen of this enlightened age has a right to self determination. We in the UK stand ready to support your efforts to bring Germany back together as a symbol of a return to normality in Europe. Not only would it reunite a divided people but it would represent an end to the Cold War which has placed enormous pressure on our respective economies in the relentless search for military superiority."

The translator had resumed a flat monotone diminishing the intensity of the words. A sheen of perspiration on Gorbachev's forehead, highlighting the prominent birthmark, was the only hint at an underlying tension.

"It is not that simple Prime Minister. Many of my fellow Politburo members feel I have been too lenient already. If I concede further it will be seen as a sign of weakness. That would not be healthy in my present position. I have no desire to step backwards, yet neither do I wish to abdicate my responsibility."

"Far from it Mikhail," she replied, her tone softening. "It would be seen as the mark of a true statesman. To end a division which has scarred Europe for over 40 years would be the ultimate symbol of strength not frailty. Some in my own party urge caution and do not want a united Germany, fearing it may lead to altered borders which might undermine the stability of our military power blocs. Their position is understandable and I share some of those concerns, yet it is easier to defend the status quo than to pursue radical reform. I agree; no one is able to predict how the international situation could be destabilised by such changes, nor whether it might endanger our collective security but, given the chance, we must all work within our respective governments to seize the opportunity and offer an alternative. It could still be a smooth transition and one which might benefit Soviet citizens as much as it would benefit us in the west. We owe it to the World; if you'll forgive me for being rather dramatic."

"Much as it may seem superficially attractive, you set me an impossible challenge Margaret. I cannot see how I can possibly endorse a plan which makes it appear that the Soviet Union has capitulated. Remember that millions of my countrymen lost their lives in the Great Patriotic War. Freeing the continent of Nazi tyranny was a hard fought battle and cost the lives of a generation. Many of those who survived have long memories and do not forgive easily. Allowing a reinvigorated Germany to reunite would be a step too far for many at home."

"I have confidence that your vision will prevail Premier Gorbachev," she replied, the formality returning, decorum re-exerted. "I repeat my willingness to support you in any way possible."

The Iron Lady, uncharacteristically, seemed chastened, shuffling her papers, distractedly, as the meeting broke up amid a cacophony of noise. Gorbachev rose, a press of bodies forming around him as stern faced security staff scrambled to usher their leader from the room. The delegation surged through the conference room, headed for the palatial doorway and on into the adjacent anteroom. Gorbachev paused briefly in the doorway still in sight of the British delegation and whispered a single phrase to a solitary aide, his words unheard by all but the one man. Barely breaking step he strode on towards the tall, mirrored doors at the far end of the chamber and disappeared from view.

The British Prime Minister remained seated, alone at the broad mahogany table, her aides withdrawing to a respectful distance. They knew when to allow her space, recognising the ominous, reflective mood.

Rather than initiating a peace process, the instructions which had passed from the mouth of the Soviet Premier, directed at the inconspicuous delegate in the anteroom, were reminiscent of the most hard-line politics of the Cold War. Far from adopting a role as peacemaker and conciliator, the Soviet leader had set sinister forces in play that would pose a clear and present threat to those charged with defending Britain's skies and impinge directly on her personally. Indeed, his mumbled instructions would threaten her very safety.

Only time would show the impact that his instruction would have on the people of Britain and their daily life.

His instruction had been simple:

"Ultimatum."

CHAPTER 1

Bakara Market, Mogadishu, Somalia, August 1987.

The sounds of the hustle and bustle of daily trading permeated the walls of the dishevelled building. Outside, the temperature hit a steamy 38 degrees Celsius, the humidity uncomfortably high, influenced by the warm waters of the Indian Ocean which lapped onto the sandy beaches close by.

The stunning coastline was of little interest to Dmitry Guskov, his driving desire to escape from this hell hole at the earliest opportunity. He would leave the minute he had wrapped up his business, eager to return to Moscow. Mogadishu had not been chosen by accident. Not only was the city the hub of an illicit arms trade but the rule of law was almost non-existent. The population lived by the gun and disappearances were a daily occurrence. He was sure that his masters in the Kremlin could have provided the hardware that he had been instructed to procure but his brief was clear. Traceability was everything and, should the unthinkable occur, the weapon that was now in transit would be traced back to a consignment which had been supplied to Mohamed Farrah Aidid, Somalia's infamous warlord. In such an event, his plan would have failed because the missile would have survived its terminal voyage and missed its intended target. Nevertheless, after the programmed self-destruct, pieces of the missile would be spread across the landscape, attracting unwanted attention from prying investigators. He would double his efforts to avoid such an outcome and refine the plan, that so far, existed only in his mind.

The ragged group around him had been paid, handsomely, to keep him safe on the troubled streets that ringed the market, but looking at the faces, he hoped the payoff had been generous because there was no way to assess their loyalties. Dressed in the distinctive Arab dress, the men lounged around the room smoking the foul, local tobacco and discussing politics in the unintelligible regional dialect.

The leader of the group had disappeared with his two heavily armed cohorts. As the only English speaker in the group, the common language between the Russian and the Somalis, the leader's departure from the room had triggered an anticipatory hush. Unexpectedly, and probably innocently, one of the group members asked for the time and Guskov responded without thought. The exchange had been in Russian and he cursed his mistake. Conversing in English had been his idea for two reasons. Obviously, it made the discussions between the disparate races easier but it had also provided an element of anonymity. He mistakenly assumed his fake American accent might have posed sufficient questions in the minds of the jihadists to prevent unwelcome speculation but he was guilty of underestimation. He eyeballed the fighter who had spoken, questioning his motives. It was an error which would have to be corrected at some stage. An example would be set.

His reverie was cut short by the rustling of the bead curtain, heralding a momentary breath of cooling air. It dropped back into place behind a short figure wearing the traditional macawis, a sarong-like garment worn around the waist complemented by a large red cloth wrapped around the upper part of his body. On his head, the colourful turban, the koofiyad, an embroidered cap, completed the outfit. His concerned expression, quickly extinguished, suggested that the exchange had been overheard.

His dress was in marked contrast to the sandy-coloured carrying case he held in his hand, out of place in the austere surroundings. Over two metres long, ruggedised and secured by two formidable clasps, the Cyrillic script marked it out as a piece of military hardware. Astonished at the fact that the man would have walked through the dusty streets carrying the burden with impunity, Guskov remained silent. In any other sane city, police would have apprehended him in a heartbeat. The leader of the faction followed in the man's wake, the beads of the curtain announcing his arrival before rattling closed once more.

With the traditional Muslim greetings exchanged and without further elaboration, the man opened the box, an inane grin splitting his pock-marked face, a clear subterfuge. Strapped to the inner cradle was a KBM Kolomna, 9K32, Strela-2 launcher tube, its deadly contents known in the west as an SA-7 Grail. A man-portable, shoulder-fired, low-altitude surface-to-air missile system, the weapon guided to its target using a passive, infrared homing seeker head, delivering its high explosive warhead with unerring reliability. It could function in most climates and operate in the most harsh conditions around the globe. The benign environment in which Guskov expected it to perform would be child's play. The MANPADS, as the surface-to-air missile was known, had been exported widely by the Soviet Union and could be found in virtually any area of conflict. Its prevalence suited Guskov's purposes to a tee.

Guskov unclipped the restraining straps and hefted the launcher onto his shoulder peering down the metal sights.

"Battery?" he questioned, receiving an effusive nod in response. The man retrieved two weighty battery packs from a belt hidden beneath the folds of his sarong. Without the precious power pack the weapon was useless because the battery powered the acquisition system and provided the pre-launch commands needed before the missile could begin its deadly journey.

He now recognised the variant as a Strela 2M, the enhanced model introduced in 1970 to rectify some of the deficiencies identified in the early production models. An added bonus, it conferred an improved capability expanding the engagement envelope by a considerable margin. For what he had in mind, the extra range and enhanced aspect performance would give more flexibility. Uncapping the end of the launcher tube, he stared inside at the missile, snug in the tube. Pulling off the protective cap, the glass dome of the seeker head was revealed, reflecting the light from the overhead light bulb. Small magnets in the cap had held the delicate seeker in check, the cap normally kept in place until the missile was powered up. Now it had been released from the magnetic grip, the seeker lolled gently within the transparent radome. At least it was not a dummy he reflected, watching the delicate mechanism settle under gravity. Nevertheless, he would have it checked once it arrived at its first port of call, just to make sure. Experts whom he could trust had already been summoned to give it a clean bill of health before it found its way to its destination. The arms dealer had proved reliable in the past but was not beyond suspicion and Guskov could not countenance failure.

Satisfied, he nodded his assent but the earlier exchange in Russian had posed a dilemma, heightening his caution. The courier was merely a mule, delivering the weapon for his masters who had already been paid handsomely but if he had heard the exchange with the Arab fighter, Guskov was compromised which could not be allowed. Even if not, he could be a useful deterrent. Enormous forces were at play and speculation amongst the thieves who frequented the back streets of this den of iniquity could not to be tolerated. Information might leak out. It was a risk he could not tolerate.

Guskov stepped forward and gripped the man's throat tightly. His slight body jerked spasmodically, his limbs thrashing in response to the ever increasing pressure on his windpipe as he resisted the strong grip. His hands grasped Guskov's wrist ineffectually; but it would be a death grip. His natural response should have been to take flight but, by now pinned against the wall, his fingers locked, his last opportunity to disentangle himself was vanishing.

In a final flurry, more a show for the onlookers, Guskov drew a squat knife and sliced through the carotid artery prompting a gush of warm blood that soaked the Russian's arm. Transferring his grip around his victim's upper torso, slowly the resistance subsided and the scuffle ended. He allowed the inert body to slump to the floor, an involuntary twitch demonstrating a last vestige of defiance from the stricken corpse.

"Was that necessary?" questioned the leader, his face ashen.

"One of your men heard my voice, my friend. I need to show that weakness is not a trait we accept. This man was simply in the wrong place and it proved to be a fatal mistake. Trust me though, if I hear that there has been idle talk about our transaction, I will find you and I will be just as uncompromising. And . . . . . I will not be alone. Do you understand?"

The averted gaze gave the answer, the veteran street fighter struck by a feeling of disquiet at the piercing stare and the disturbing intensity in the Russian's eyes. It was an emotion he rarely experienced.

". . . . . But he was a friend of the Jihad."

The inscrutable gaze persuaded him not to press the issue further.

"Are you happy with your instructions?" Guskov asked tightly. "Get rid of the body somewhere. I'm sure it's not the first time you've arranged an unexpected funeral at short notice."

"He deserves a proper burial," the leader muttered, trying hard to maintain ascendency amongst his shocked followers, their unrest visible. They were used to random acts of violence but the attack had been swift and unexpected in the tight confines of the room. The loss of a fellow Muslim to an infidel; an unbeliever, was contrary to their principles, the lack of a decisive response from their leader, unusual.

The tense standoff was over almost before there was chance to ponder. The nerve-racking atmosphere was broken.

"It will be arranged."

Subservience.

"Make sure the consignment is delivered, immediately, as we agreed. Let's get out of here. I have a plane to catch."

CHAPTER 2

RAF Wattisham, Suffolk, August 1987.

Graham Ashworth was a loner. A lifelong ambition to train as a pilot, nurtured in his youth by his experiences in the Air Training Corps, had culminated in an application to join the Royal Air Force. He felt confident throughout the interviews at the Officer and Aircrew Selection Centre that he had projected his commitment. He felt his aptitude had shone through, so the rejection letter, stark in its message, had come as a complete shock. The offer to train as a technician had been scant reward. He had not even been given the chance to become an engineering officer but, lacking a degree, his options had been limited.

He had accepted the enlistment simply because he had no other alternative. His life was stagnating and the job opportunities in his home town were few and far between. At first he enjoyed the challenge and his technical skills shone through during apprentice training but he harboured an underlying, albeit unwarranted, feeling of inferiority. He had intended to become an officer and fly aeroplanes but his ambitions had been thwarted by some imbecile on the Selection Board. His attitude permeated and his popularity, fragile at best, waned further. In time his frustrations turned to bitterness. In particular, he distrusted every officer he encountered which marked him as a troublemaker and his performance assessments suffered accordingly.

His marriage was a sham. Aspiration for home ownership and a fiercely ambitious wife had meant that his stay in the Airmen's Married Quarters at Wattisham, in the leafy county of Suffolk, had been brief. Ostensibly, his wife's excuse for moving away from the Station had been that she needed to be closer to her office in Ipswich. The reality was that neither of them enjoyed the claustrophobic environment on base and both had made the move into the local community with enthusiasm. The "honeymoon" was short and, increasingly, his wife's overnight stays in town for business reasons seemed suspicious. The reality was he didn't care. In fact, her absence was often a blessing because it avoided the need to sit and listen to her endless diatribes about corporate deficiencies.

His ambition to be a pilot had not diminished and he had found solace in the vibrant Station Flying Club at the busy fighter base. Set up on similar lines to the squadrons, the three Piper Cherokee Warriors and the single Cessna 152 allowed him to scratch the itch as often as his limited budget allowed. Pottering around the Suffolk countryside sharing the airspace with the Phantoms from Wattisham, the Jaguars from Coltishall and the Tornados of the Tactical Weapons Conversion Unit from Honington, he could almost convince himself that he was a part of the flying community.

The earlier rejection still stung, even after his lengthy training as an armourer. His daily life revolved around things that went bang. The main armaments of the Phantom fighter were the air-to-air missiles, the Sparrow, the more modern Skyflash and the Sidewinder, and it was his job to service them in the bay. That they shared space with the SUU-23 gunpods, armed with high explosive incendiary cannon rounds, or HEI as they were commonly known, was an added bonus. His role was to nurture these weapons and make them ready to go to war, should the need arise.

There were no weapons strapped to his Piper Warrior light aircraft but what went on in his garage at his home was another matter. He did not need much explosive material for the mischief he had in mind so, despite stringent checks on the weapons in the bomb dump, and the tight security around the Station with the constant threat from the Irish Republican Army, he had learned how to bypass the checks. The improvised explosive device he had assembled at home contained enough combustibles to cause severe damage to any target and he had ideas forming in his warped mind. He had incorporated a warhead and a solid-propellant rocket motor from a decommissioned Sparrow missile into a carefully constructed improvised device. Its destructive effects were questionable. The expanding rod warhead was designed to penetrate thin aircraft skins rather than explode in an incendiary display of force. Had he been stationed at a bomber base with extensive stocks of air-to-ground munitions, he would have chosen a different design with more dramatic effects. Nevertheless, he praised himself on his ingenuity. He knew exactly how to utilise the weapons effects to the full and drama rather than destruction was exactly what he had in mind.

Back in the present, he released the brakes and opened the throttle, the Warrior twisting slightly, veering off the centreline as the torque of the engine bit. He checked the drift with the rudder pedals and the nose wheel realigned along the runway centreline markings that began to blur as he picked up speed.

"Warhorse, on the break to land."

He watched the pair of Phantoms break into the circuit overhead, the nose wheel lifting off as he staggered into the air, the speed building through 80 knots. The bulky planform of the fighters flashed in his peripheral vision before his attention was demanded by more pressing matters. He watched the altimeter increasing slowly as he felt the wing lift in response to the crosswind. Back in a gentle climb and slowly rising into the air, he looked around, taking in his surroundings.

"Golf, Oscar Echo, expedite your turn onto 040 and call Wattisham Approach on 125.8," he heard over the radio.

"Roger, Golf Oscar Echo, turning right and climbing. To Approach on 125.8."

He switched frequency, peeved at being shunted out of the way of the Phantoms. Soon he would not be so insignificant.

CHAPTER 3

The "Q Shed", RAF Wattisham, Suffolk.

Jim "Flash" Gordon, a flight commander of No. 56 (Fighter) Squadron, one of the resident squadrons, updated the colour states on the weather board in the tiny operations room in the Quick Reaction Alert complex. The brightly coloured magnetic discs gave an immediate picture of the weather conditions the crews might face if the hooter sounded. A red disc might spell disaster if a diversion proved necessary, denoting low cloud and poor visibility. It was vital that the crews knew what they might face if thrust northwards into the inhospitable airspace around the British Isles.

Quick Reaction Alert, or QRA, was the whole reason for the Station's existence in peacetime and, charged with defending UK airspace, two Phantom fighters were positioned in adjacent alert hangars. Holding "Readiness One Zero", the crews were required to be airborne within ten minutes of a call to scramble at any time, day or night. The "Q Shed" lay alongside the southerly perimeter track at Wattisham, positioned at the head of an access track that led directly to the main runway. Once the doors opened, it was a short dash to the active.

For the flying station, tasked to hold "Southern QRA", its airspace covered the whole of the southern part of the country including its territorial waters. Any unidentified, or even worse, hostile track that penetrated the airspace south of the 55 North parallel would be intercepted, identified and, if necessary, destroyed. Procedures were practised regularly to ensure that errors were minimised but, even so, it was a massive amount of airspace to protect and mistakes could easily be made. The line of defence was spread thinly.

"Bright blue around the country," Flash announced to the three other aircrew lounging in the easy chairs around the small room, its tight confines barely big enough to stretch out horizontally. Being on Q was an intimate experience. He received scarcely a grunt in response.

On a fine day, the weather occupied less of their concern than the incessant diet of programmes that blared out from the ever active TV set in the corner of the room. Although the weather was fine locally, in the vast ocean to the north of Scotland, it could change on a whim and a scramble message sending them into the Iceland-Faeroes Gap was an ever present possibility. Operations were normally less demanding in their own sector to the south.

"Stavanger, Sola is also blue, forecast blue, but Keflavik is intermittent red in heavy sleet showers. Head east if you need to divert in the Northern area."

It was optimism that they might be called upon to reinforce Northern Q which flew from RAF Leuchars, scrambled at short notice to head north to intercept a Soviet Tupolev Tu95 Bear intruding into the UK Air Defence Region. The Soviets often tested the readiness posture of the RAF crews, sending both bomber and maritime patrol variants of the ageing airframe into the airspace patrolled by Norwegian, American and British aircrews. Despite its age, it was still a potent adversary and was still the fastest propeller driven aircraft in the world able to reach speeds of Mach 0.95, a stunning performance. The crews lived in hope but a more likely scenario was to be launched on a training scramble to intercept a Canberra from Wyton or a Victor from Marham, pressed into service as an impromptu training target, to hone their skills.

Mark "Razor" Keene, Flash's pilot, was by now one of the most senior flight lieutenants on the squadron, rapidly approaching 1,500 hours flying the Phantom. They had served together in Germany on Razor's first operational tour and been reunited many times over the years as operational emergencies had brought them back together. Flash, now a flight commander on the Squadron, was equally experienced but the burden of command had slowed his progress and Razor was rapidly overhauling his tally of flying hours. A tour as an instructor on the Phantom Operational Conversion Unit had taken its toll with pilots occupying the back seat, teaching youngsters to operate the mighty Phantom. His earlier, rapid accrual of hours during his initial tours of duty had braked to a crawl. The mental note to do better during this tour was commendable but flying could be frustratingly elusive, replaced by the pressure of endless piles of Secret files building up on his desk. The turgid reports and assessments were no substitute for the simple release of getting airborne. It was the endless rounds of confidential reports on his subordinates that held his attention now, rather than the joys of the cockpit.

The friends no longer flew together as a constituted crew, their experience dictating that they now flew more often with less experienced youngsters, the logic being to pair experience with inexperience to ensure a "competent adult" was always present in the jet. Even so, they took every opportunity to fly together, to relive old times and to enjoy the luxury of flying with someone in whom you could place the ultimate trust. With the summer leave programme in full swing, their respective crewmates had taken time off. They were simply enjoying flying together once more.

The Squadron administration clerk popped her head into the operations room exchanging banter with the two pilots, her presence and her undoubted attributes, albeit well camouflaged by the "cabbage kit", a welcome distraction from the dull routine. She handed a brown official envelope to Flash and he tore it open impatiently. It took just moments to assimilate the contents.

"Where's Jim," asked Flash, the other navigator's absence suddenly obvious. "I need to brief everyone on the content of this signal."

"He's taking a nap," replied John Sharpe, the second pilot. "I think he had a few pops in the Mess last night."

Flash made a mental note to check the young man's bar bill. Maybe he was burning the candle at both ends. A day on Q was not a day off and he needed to be sharp if he was called upon to go flying. He could save the hangovers for the weekend.

"Get him in here John and we'll chat," said Flash picking up the phone. The Boss picked up at the other end of the line immediately, the conversation short but intense.

"OK listen up; this signal is from Strike Command," said Flash perched on a stool in the corner of the tiny operations room, the other three aircrew lounging in the seats arranged around the walls. The text was typed on the flimsy, low quality paper, torn roughly from its feeder roll, spelled out in capital letters as with all signal messages.

"FROM THE UK AIR DEFENCE OPERATIONS CELL, CLASSIFIED SECRET. SUBJECT: INCREASED THREAT LEVELS," Flash read out from the header block.

"A CREDIBLE THREAT TO THE INTEGRITY OF UK AIRSPACE HAS BEEN IDENTIFIED. CELLS FROM THE RED ARMY FACTION ARE KNOWN TO HAVE ACQUIRED GROUND-TO-AIR WEAPONS WITH THE INTENT TO USE THEM. SPECIFIC TARGETS ARE UNKNOWN BUT THOUGHT TO INCLUDE KEY POSITIONS AND HIGH VALUE ASSETS. QRA CREWS ARE TO BE CONVERSANT WITH VISUAL IDENTIFICATION PROCEDURES CONTAINED IN THE FLIGHT INFORMATION HANDBOOK AND BE PREPARED TO INTERVENE WHEN DIRECTED. ENGAGEMENT COMMANDS ARE TO BE VERIFIED USING EXISTING AUTHENTICATION PROCEDURES. IN ADDITION,

CREWS ARE TO REVIEW OPERATION TESSERAL PROCEDURES AND STANDBY TO IMPLEMENT ON DIRECTION. SIGNAL ENDS."

He turned to the young navigator who looked decidedly green around the gills, determined not to show mercy for his indiscretion.

"What's Tesseral Jim?"

The youngster looked appropriately humble. The silence spoke volumes.

"It's the anti SA-7 procedures and pretty important in the face of a terrorist threat. If you don't know what it is I won't ask you any questions now. Get out your noddy guide when we're done and read up on it. We'll sit down later and you'd better know it by heart by then."

He paused as the implication of the enormity of the simple phrase . . . be prepared to intervene when directed, sunk in. When . . . . . not if!

The two pilots seemed secretly relieved, and as Flash walked down the corridor to brief the groundcrew, the TV clicked off and three noddy guides emerged from the pockets of their immersion suits. Only one of them would spend more than five minutes re-familiarising himself with the procedures.

CHAPTER 4

The Lubyanka, the Meshchansky District, Moscow.

Life had been relatively normal for Guskov since his return from Mogadishu, if life could ever be normal in the second floor office of the KGB headquarters.

Outside, the mild, late summer weather had prompted the usual flood of Soviet citizens keen to see the sights and sounds of Red Square at the heart of the capital city. Temperatures would begin to drop soon as autumn arrived but the onset of winter was still at least a few months away. The cooler air was a relief after the oppressive heat of Somalia and he was pleased to be home, albeit for a brief interval.

His morning had been spent in the usual terse exchanges with rezidentura around the world, an endless chase as he kept track of his network of agents and contacts. Despite the tempo, he was struggling to concentrate and his thoughts, repeatedly, returned to events in London. His urgent messages winging around the globe were protected by complex, cryptographic codes. The need for secrecy inevitably slowed down delivery and the exchanges dragged on. As the cogs and wheels of the cipher machines turned his plain messages into unfathomable hieroglyphics, his frustration mounted. The delay was exasperating but unavoidable and he knew that there were many analysts around the world who would give good money to read the messages in clear text. In the end, watching the machines execute their mundane task proved unbearable and he picked up the secure telephone, keen to minimise the delay. He dialled the number for the Soviet Embassy in London.

Replacing the handset in its cradle after an illuminating discussion, he switched to the internal phone system, the actions suddenly urgent. The "Dragon", as the Head's personal assistant was known was renowned for her fiercely protective custody of his diary. Challenging her legendary gate-keeping, Guskov's persistent request for a meeting yielded a five minute window in the schedule that was only grudgingly offered up. He checked his watch. Just 45 minutes to prepare himself for the discussion. His pitch had better be good because the fate of the nation relied on him getting this right; literally. More importantly, his own position on the totem pole was under threat if he got it wrong.

Rifling through the drawer he pulled out a packet of Marlboroughs, a trophy from the airport duty free shop during his recent trip to Africa, and clicked open the lid of his Zippo lighter, touching the flame to the cigarette, inhaling deeply. He picked up the planning folder with the gaudy coloured jacket and searched again through the details he would include in the briefing. This was one operation for which he needed top-cover so things had to check out. If heads were to roll in the aftermath, he was determined it would not be his own. Fingering the paper wallet containing his flight tickets to London, he once again, mentally rehearsed his pitch. It was sound.

CHAPTER 5

Erklenz, the Dutch Border, West Germany.

Two men and a youth huddled around a table, a map of England spread out in front of them, large, coloured rings denoting key geographical points. The small group felt secure in the small flat in the West German dormer town. Surrounded by similar properties, the block of flats was unremarkable and similar to many dwellings built immediately after the war, intended to house a population displaced by wartime bombing, as rapidly as possible. The neighbours were discreet and upstanding citizens, paying little attention to the infrequent visitors to the flat. The landlord gladly accepted the rent, always paid on time, but his indifference would not extend to endorsement of the carnage that was being planned from his humble dwelling. The few visitors he had met, who dropped in at random times, seemed entirely respectable.

The cell leader was British by birth but radical by nature. Clive Hammond had served briefly in the Royal Navy after attending university but his short service commission proved even shorter than anticipated. Closeted inside the claustrophobic hull of a tiny coastal minesweeper, with a tight but right wing cadre of officers, he was almost ostracised. His strident, regularly voiced, class-based politics sat badly with his peers who tended more towards the right wing of politics. As a consequence, he often found himself alone in his confined bunk space, reading of current affairs while the small vessel plied the confines of British coastal waters. After a deeply unsatisfactory and undeniably brief experience, he resigned his commission and sought out more receptive ears.

His mother was of German origin but, more significantly, she was from a family who had suffered in the immediate aftermath of World War 2. Her experiences at the hands of the British occupiers in the Lower Saxony region of Germany had been harsh but fair, yet she had fled the poverty, finding her way to the North of England where she had met Hammond's father, a radical left-wing miner from Yorkshire. Her embittered persona blended well with the man's own radical views and they had dropped easily into a web of extremism. Their influence shaped Hammond's views, leading to his selection of politics as a natural field of study when he entered Trent Polytechnic in Nottingham. Studying Politics and International Relations he had found affinity with one particularly engaging fellow student who shared his militancy. The first drinks in the campus bar had led to a torrid relationship and quickly identified a shared goal. The girl had been a member of the Red Army Faction from her early school days in Germany but blended well with the disparate radicals on campus. She quickly won him around to the cause, although truthfully, little effort was needed. When she had offered trips to Germany to meet friends he had willingly accepted, intrigued by the thought of visiting his mother's homeland. Smitten by his new friend's passion in more ways than one, he met similarly, left-leaning activists. That their method of achieving their goals was in stark contrast to the oath of allegiance he had sworn to his own Sovereign was becoming irrelevant. He swiftly became radicalised and over a series of trips to West Germany committed further to the cause.

The youngest of the group in Erklenz was an enigma as his looks belied his real age. Twenty five years old, he had already seen more strife than some would see in a lifetime yet he could still pass scrutiny as a youth, about to start university. This was fortunate because it was the role Günter Steinbach was destined to fulfil and the time to wait was shortening. He was the ultimate product of the radical group, determined, stubborn and utterly focussed. More relevant, he was prepared to die for his beliefs and Hammond had seen his potential for the task they were now planning. Although the cell was small, it could call on support across Europe and sleepers were to be found in every European country.

As the scheme crystallised the discussions became more animated and more earnest. A bystander would have struggled to link the, seemingly, unconnected locations which had been identified by the group and marked out on the map. A couple of urban locations in Düsseldorf, a British airbase in Nordrhein Westphalen and a small village on the Dutch border had been highlighted. The largest and most prominent ring, marked in red, was the most noteworthy and at its centre: London. The focal point, the British Houses of Parliament, was the seat of democracy of the United Kingdom and its most treasured landmark.

Hammond, a self confessed control freak, would no longer hold the keys to this operation once the planning was complete. Once he set the wheels in motion, events would gather an unstoppable momentum and his protégé Steinbach would be the fulcrum. For his plot to succeed a number of initiatives would need to come together perfectly. Crucially, he could not act alone and other plans set in train by the Faction would be fundamental.

There had never been a better time to make a statement; if he could only pull it off.

CHAPTER 6

Chiswick Underground Station.

John Chisholm fought his way through the crowd approaching the tube station. He clutched his briefcase tightly, conscious of the unorthodox contents. Nothing in any of the material he carried was protectively marked but he was in no doubt that having to explain its loss would be an uncomfortable experience. Welcome to his life. Chisholm was a spy.

Being back in London was fine. The place felt comfortable like an old glove. The office was fine. The "Nine to Five" routine was fine. The relatively short commute to work in the discrete headquarters building was fine. His wife was delighted at the chance to adopt an almost normal lifestyle far away from the intrigue of the security services. She was one of the few people who knew what he did for a living but therein lay the problem. He missed the excitement of living and working in West Berlin. That was where the Cold War felt warm. That was where his efforts produced tangible results every day. His internal transfer to MI5 so that his wife could get the kids into a nice school – that word again – had been warmly welcomed by his new Boss but the job was simply boring. He was long past being excited by the protective markings on documents that hinted at intrigue. The fact was there was no longer any excitement in coordinating the activity of his small team of agents. He wanted to be out on the streets doing their job, not stuck in the office monitoring and coordinating their efforts.

The crocodile of bodies ahead slowed, as it fed its orderly way through the ticket barriers. The new turnstiles were, undoubtedly, efficient as each patient commuter fed their electronic ticket into the slot but the bottlenecks were frustrating. Gone were the days of waving a travel pass at a bored underground ticket inspector and rushing through the open gate. Life was both simpler and more ordered yet more regimented. Was it progress?

Jolted back to the present, he registered a face in the crowd; a well developed skill. The man pushing through the adjacent exit barrier was familiar but why? Surely not? It couldn't be, could it? Covering his face, hurriedly, with his copy of The Times, angling the newspaper to give him a view of the man who was already accelerating away across the foyer, he confirmed his fears. He was sure. The man fast disappearing out of the tube station was none other than Dmitry Guskov, an old adversary.

Last time he had seen Guskov, Chisholm had been working the wrong side of the Iron Curtain during a covert trip to East Berlin. The man was a legend in the Cold War cauldron and his exploits had been a constant irritation to the Allied security services. Chisholm had been priming an East German chargé d'affairs in the hope that he could cultivate him, providing inside information on the workings of the East German Parliament. It had worked but the unfortunate young man's career had been cut short, the posting to sandy climes the result of his indiscretion. Rumour had it that Guskov was behind the compromise but it was never proven. There could be no mistaking Guskov's distinctive appearance but why the hell was he in London? One thing was for certain, Chisholm's new masters were not aware of his presence or the counter surveillance boys would have been all over him like a rash and Chisholm would have known. Someone as infamous as Guskov did not operate with impunity; well, at least not in London.

Forcing his way out of the queue, he acknowledged the irritated complaints of his fellow commuters with a muted apology. Once free of the suffocating throng he slowed his pace, concerned at the prospect of attracting undue attention. His quarry was a wily, old retainer. Merging back into the flow of bodies, retracing his path, there was that cold moment of dread as he briefly lost sight of the elusive Russian. Beads of sweat spawned on his brow instantly, his light jacket clinging to his arms despite the cool morning air. Calm. There were only a few possible routes leading away from the tube station and, opting for the most obvious, he searched both sides of the road for his prey. Only moments passed before he regained contact with the Russian who was already making his way along the bustling street, apparently an innocent traveller. Skilled at his art, the man would be attentive knowing that, if he had been followed from the station, his pursuers would be most vulnerable to discovery at this point. Without the luxury of a full surveillance team, Chisholm would need all his skills if he was to remain undetected. He hoped they were still up to the task.

Guskov slowed, glancing in a shop window, his tradecraft obvious, monitoring his surroundings closely as he paused. Chisholm walked on, briskly, feigning disinterest, rapidly overhauling the dawdling spy and turning off the street at the next corner. He had been careful to shield his face, glancing away at the critical moments. The next few minutes would determine success or failure.

*

Chisholm breathed a sigh of relief as the Russian operative walked, resolutely, across the junction heading into the residential streets of the suburb. His head anchored ahead, it appeared as if he had relaxed somewhat, his earlier apprehension, seemingly, overcome. His pace accelerated. Chisholm crossed the road and headed back to the corner, turning to follow his target. The briefcase, clutched in his sweaty hand, was cumbersome yet offered an element of cover. At least he looked the part of the distracted commuter, although anyone familiar with the suburb would know that he was heading in the opposite direction to the Underground station. In fact, until a few moments ago he had been exactly what his briefcase suggested; he had been a bored traveller heading along with all the other bored commuters to another boring day in the office. But now the chase was on.

As the crowds thinned out, as he distanced himself from the magnet of the tube station, it would be increasingly difficult to remain unobtrusive and he silently hoped that, wherever their journey led, the distance to their undisclosed destination would be short. Almost as soon as he had slotted back into position, the Russian, only a hundred yards ahead now, made a left turn and disappeared once more. Chisholm quickened his pace, wary of losing sight for too long. Thankfully, the moment he turned the corner he re-established contact.

The game of cat and mouse went on for a further ten minutes, Chisholm's nerves jangling at each turn, his skill fade increasingly evident. With the number of commuters thinning out it seemed inevitable that he would soon be spotted but, as if on cue, Guskov slowed, taking in his surroundings again, once more forcing Chisholm to seek refuge. The move was clumsy and he stifled a groan, his view partially obscured. Peering through the foliage, it was a relief to see the Russian open a small gate and slot a key into a brightly painted door before disappearing from view. Chisholm craned his neck to see the road sign opposite and committed the unremarkable street name to memory. After leaving a short interlude in case his quarry should be monitoring the surrounds, he withdrew around the corner and set off to find a telephone box. One of the new mobile phones would have made his life easier at this moment but carrying a heavy brick in his briefcase was still not an attractive prospect. His mental navigation instincts kicked in as he charted his progress, keeping track of the target house in his mind's eye. It was only moments before he came across a Post Office telephone box, the corporate logos plastered across the glass, defaced by graffiti. Thankful, he pulled open the door and dialled a well rehearsed number.

CHAPTER 7

The Leman Oilfield, The North Sea, thirty miles northeast of Great Yarmouth, later that night.

The man lifted his hard hat from his head dabbing his brow and wiping the sweat from his eyes with an oily rag. He hankered for a cigarette but the reflected glow of the oil stack burning off the waste gas from the well below was enough to persuade him that it was a bad idea. He chewed at the substitute, rolling the hard glob around his mouth, distractedly. His supplies of nicotine gum had run out yesterday and it was a good few days before the next delivery was due in. Hopefully, his letter had made it home and a care package would be aboard the next resupply chopper.

The sun had set and the horizon, already dark, was dotted with flares from the other rigs in the Leman field. Lying at the southern edge of the group, his rig was one of the furthest south in the North Sea, delivering streams of oil pumped from beneath the waves, coming ashore at the Bacton Oil Terminal in Norfolk. Hard work, long hours and a solitary lifestyle were only compensated by a decent salary and generous shore leave.

It was a pleasant evening but the constant offshore wind that howled through the lattice structure gave off an eerie resonance. The wave caps frothed white and flumes of spray rose into the air on the breeze. Occasionally drowned out by the clanking machinery and masked by the constant grinding of the drill bit, it was all part of the experience of life on a rig.

The noise that cut through the din was noticeable for its divergence from the norm making an instant impression on his, otherwise, dulled sense of hearing. Used to seeing the jets fly overhead, his first thought was that it was one of them but the noise was entirely wrong. The pilots would climb as they approached the rig complex and pass a few thousand feet above, constantly conscious of the risk of mid air collision with a low flying helicopter. More dangerous, was the risk of surprising a maxed-out helicopter pilot transitioning to the hover as he jockeyed with the controls, approaching for a landing. The control zones around the rigs protected the helicopters giving a modicum of confidence as they made the precarious approach towards the helicopter platform, marked out with its large white "H" on the deck. Fast jets and slow helicopters in the hover were not comfortable bedfellows.

The noise emanated from behind his back approaching from a north easterly direction, sounding like the drone of a piston engine from a light aircraft. Odd to hear such a sound, this far out to sea and at night. He swivelled his head, peering into the gloom, shielding his eyes. Despite the glare from the flare stack his eyes were adjusting to the lower light levels but his night vision was still marginal. Luckily there was little artificial light in the seaward direction. He moved his head trying to home in on the source of the noise, his brain processing the information and rejecting the ambient sounds coming from the rig. The jets were normally easily visible with their flashing red anti-collision lights, although even they sometimes flashed past in the darkness, their lights off, conducting some obscure mutual exercise. He began to doubt his senses.

As his eyes narrowed, a vague shape appeared from the dimness, faint reflections dappling the silhouette. It homed in on the rig, slowly emerging from the gloom, its pace slow but steady. The tiny aircraft turned south westerly directly overhead, the glare of the stack illuminating the underside of the tiny fuselage and stubby wings. He strained to read the registration marks but it was just too high and just too dark to make out the details. Why was a light aircraft flying at low level so far from the coast without lights? Should he report it to the Coastguard?

On its new heading, the tiny aircraft was pointing directly towards Suffolk.

CHAPTER 8

The "Q Shed", RAF Wattisham, Suffolk.

The telebrief crackled as the connection was made.

"Wattisham, this is the Neatishead Master Controller, QRA to cockpit readiness."

The message was lost on the aircrew who had already sprinted from the small ops room and even now were surging up the cockpit ladders into the waiting Phantoms, closely followed by their groundcrew.

"01 cockpit ready," wheezed the Q1 navigator, his gloved fingers already fumbling with the controls of the inertial navigation system, the red lamp flashing its urgent signal as the system aligned on the stored heading, ready for flight.

"02 cockpit ready."

Flash in the back cockpit of his Phantom in the adjacent bay cursed at being second to check in.

"01, 02 sitrep. I have a low level contact entering Charlie Hotel, heading west, slow speed," the disembodied voice reported over the secure telebrief connection. The confidence tone bleeped, annoyingly, in the background giving a slightly eerie tone to the exchange.

"Ahh jeez where the hell is Charlie Hotel mate?"

Flash whipped out his QRA map from the leg pocket of his immersion suit and stared at the tiny annotations, cursing the fighter controller for reverting to the obscure geographically-referenced reporting system. He trained his wander lamp onto the map, the red light bathing the cockpit, his finger traced the Suffolk coastline stopping on the two letter code inked onto the map.

"Just off Bentwaters, make it twenty miles off the coast."

"Roger that."

The right hand engine was already winding up as Flash pulled the lap straps tight and accepted the top straps, plugging them into the box on his seat harness with a well practised twist of the plate. Already the top seat pin for the face blind handle of his Martin Baker ejection seat had been thrust into the housing by the "liney" arming the seat. The man eased himself off the steps which grasped the intake snugly. Memorised routines took over and Flash's hands moved around the cockpit quickly, more by rote than by conscious thought.

"Neatishead, 01 we have a problem, stand by."

The call was not unexpected and the Phantom could be a temperamental partner. As Q1, callsign Mission 01, was nominated as the primary fighter to launch, if the snag proved complex, Mission 02 would take over. The potential substitution caused the usual flash of adrenaline as Razor and Flash waited for more news from the adjacent bay watching the flurry of activity under the jet as the groundcrew applied "concussive therapy" to the recalcitrant starter motor. In other words, the frustrated liney whacked the motor with a large hammer.

"01 is bent, left hand engine failed to start."

"Confirm 01 is unserviceable?" queried the Master Controller.

"Affirmative, 01."

There was no fanfare.

"Mission 02, vector 040, climb to Angels 15, buster, contact Neatishead on Fighter Stud 42, scramble, scramble, scramble, acknowledge."

"02 scrambling," responded Flash clicking the control knob on the INAS into "Nav".

"Clear taxy."

The jet surged forward in response to a handful of throttle and the nose emerged into the darkness outside. Behind them in the adjacent bay, the frustrated Q1 crew shrugged off their seat harnesses and climbed, frustratedly, from the sick jet, their anticipated sortie cut short. If the reluctant engine could not be persuaded back to life, an aircraft swap beckoned.

CHAPTER 9

The Flying Club, RAF Wattisham.

Ashworth eased his car into the parking slot alongside the squat, green-painted building and as he killed the headlights, the dispersal returned to darkness. Towards the taxiway that ringed the airfield, the sodium lights cast a dull glow.

The car door closed with a hollow clang, echoing around the empty space and he walked the short distance to the entrance to the Flying Club. As he peered at the combination lock on the door rehearsing the sequence of numbers, suddenly, he was bathed in torch light. His heart jumped into his mouth and the familiar tang of adrenaline coursed through his body.

"Out a bit late aren't we?" challenged the gruff voice as the torch lit his face. Ashworth turned and his heart lurched. Behind the harsh beam was the distinct outline of an RAF Police dog handler, his German Sheppard at his heel, its eyes trained on Ashworth. How had he missed the policeman's van?

"Bloody hell mate, you gave me a fright."

"I'm sure I did. What are you doing over here at this time of night? Not planning to fly this late are we?" the "Plod" asked accusingly, his white-banded hat reflecting the torchlight.

"No, I left something behind when I was here earlier and I need it for work tomorrow."

The excuse sounded hollow.

"Let me see some ID."

Ashworth handed over his RAF ID card and the man shone his torch on the small card flipping it over and checking the reverse. Seemingly happy he handed it back. The dog strained at the lead and pulled in the direction of Ashworth's car causing an instant adrenalin rush. He hoped the policeman didn't ask what he'd forgotten because his excuse was wafer thin and would give him away instantly. Giving in to the dog, the handler closed the short distance to the car and the animal sniffed around the wheels before stopping at the boot and showing an unhealthy interest in the seal. Ashworth's mind raced. He couldn't afford to be challenged.

"Have you got an airfield driving permit?" the Plod asked, belligerently.

"Yes it's here in my wallet," called the nervous airman, unwilling to move, considering running away but recognising the futility. Relieved, he saw the handler drag the dog back towards the door.

"Look, you must be cold. Do you fancy a brew? I can put the kettle on and I'm sure there'll be some milk left. It's bloody freezing out here."

His voice was strained, almost cartoon-like.

"That sounds like a plan mate. It's bloody ages until I get back to the Guardroom and that'd go down a treat."

The tone had changed and relief flooded over Ashworth. He didn't mind spending time with the Plod but moving inside the building was preferable to having the dog sniff around his car.

"Hang on a minute and I'll let us in and get the kettle on."

He fumbled with the combination lock, opened the door and snapped on the light.

"Come into the crewroom mate. The dog will be fine in here with us."

As he walked over to the coffee bar, he turned and watched the Plod enter the crewroom, content to see the dog following. With the bright light illuminating the small space, the face was instantly recognisable. The man had been at Wattisham almost as long as Ashworth and was a regular at the bar in the Corporal's Club. He had spoken to him on a few occasions and felt a little happier at making small talk. Fussing around behind the small counter, dropping instant coffee into two mugs as he waited for the kettle to boil, he began to unwind. The man was looking at the aeroplane pictures which lined the wall.

"Here you go. That should work."

"It's nice and warm in here. Thank God the Air Force doesn't turn off the heating at night."

"Yes but try and get a payment from allowances and it's a different matter," he replied, sharing a mutual antipathy over administrative support on the small station. The Plod nodded in response.

They chatted amiably for a short while, lounging in the comfortable easy chairs, the dog sniffing its way around the crewroom. Maybe it is just inquisitive thought Ashworth. He was pretty sure RAF dogs were not trained to sniff out explosives but if they were, it would not be long before he was uncovered. Willing the handler to finish his drink and leave, it seemed like an eternity before the man rose, put on his gloves and called the dog over, reattaching the lead.

"Are you over this side of the airfield for long?"

The question seemed loaded.

"No, that's me done now. I'll put the dog back in the van and then I have to check the HAS site before I can go back. They'll still be working so I won't be getting out. I'll just whistle around the perimeter fence and show willing."

Ashworth breathed a sigh of relief at the news.

"Make sure you don't forget what it was that you came over for."

Ashworth tensed waiting for the inevitable question, cursing himself for not coming up with an excuse. His mind raced. There was no follow up. The man turned and left the building with a cheery farewell as Ashworth slumped back into the chair, mentally exhausted.

Outside the window, headlights snapped on flooding across the dispersal as the noise of the police van cut the quiet. The beams swept across the broad swath of concrete as the vehicle headed up the taxiway out of view, en route to the adjacent hardened dispersal which housed one of the Phantom squadrons.

Drained, Ashworth sat immobile in the chair for some minutes, his mind racing. It had been too close. After a brief interval he moved into the lobby and hit the switch for the roller door, opening the adjacent tool store. Lifting the boot lid of the car he pulled out a small carrying box and made his way back to the store, carrying it tentatively. The box fitted in perfectly with its surroundings as it should do. He had chosen a generic container from the armoury and he was confident that no one would notice its presence for the short time that it would be there. It would be hidden in plain sight until he loaded it into the Warrior the next day. Satisfied, he hit the switch once more and the roller door rattled back into place, sealing off its deadly contents.

CHAPTER 10

Over the North Sea off Lowestoft.

"Neatishead, Mission 02, on frequency, heading 070."
"Mission 02, Neatishead you're loud and clear, how me?"
"Loud and clear also, request vectors to target."
"Roger maintain heading, look low. Target is dark. Last reported bearing, 070 range 50."
Flash lowered the scanner using the thumbwheel on his hand controller. The time base flicked lazily left and right, the green response vaguely soporific in the dark cockpit. The weight of his flying helmet strained the muscles in his neck as he leaned forward over the radar scope. He was glad that they were flying straight and level or the g forces would magnify its weight even further. The scope stayed stubbornly blank.
"Doesn't sound good Razor. Last reported sounds as though they're not holding it on radar. This could be a wild goose chase mate."
Silence greeted him from the front cockpit as the radar scanner projected its invisible beam across the dark surface of the sea below.
"Mission 02, looking," he replied, frustratedly, over the radio.
Stabbing the interrogator button on his hand controller, more in hope than expectation, he looked in vain for an electronic response. Any pilot who had chosen to cross the North Sea on a dank, dark night, hugging the waves at low level, was hardly likely to advertise his presence with a cooperative electronic identification from the IFF identification system. Sure enough, the scope stayed stubbornly blank.
"We know he's low or the fighter controller would be seeing him. The safety altitude is 1,500 feet in this area. Let's take it down to 5,000 feet Razor, set speed 350 knots for now. Look out as we descend; there are a load of oil rigs out here and some of them are pretty tall."

The Phantom began a gentle descent as they set the regional pressure setting on their barometric altimeters, cross checking the height between cockpits as the dial began to unwind. They would go no lower than safety altitude without good reason.

The AWG 12 radar continued to scan rhythmically, left and right, the green symbols glowing bright in the darkened cockpit. As Flash checked his pilot through 6,000 feet he felt the rate of descent drop off and the Phantom levelled at the new height. The needles stopped precisely at the demanded level. It wasn't a surprise. He expected the precision.

"More help," called Flash to the silent controller. Once more his plea was more in hope knowing that the controller on the ground would be passing target information if he was able. Neither of them could see the elusive intruder.

"Target dark, estimate range 40 miles," came the cautious response.

The scope was still blank.

"No joy," Flash muttered keying the transmit button. In the absence of a radar contact all he could do was to continue to fly down the estimated bearing.

"OK, I'm going onto goggles," he heard from the front cockpit as Razor flicked the small binocular-like devices down in front of his eyes. There was an immediate strain on his neck muscles as the weight of the device took an instant toll. In the back cockpit, Flash left his own goggles stowed in the pouch on the console. He would don them if he needed them but, in the meantime, his concentration was exclusively devoted to the radar, probably hoping for a fleeting glimpse of the target, albeit in vain. Rolling the scanner down a few more degrees, Flash hoped that the elusive contact had not crept below his radar beam, flying below the radar as it was known. A fuzzy smudge appeared on the pulse Doppler display, barely discernible from the electronic clutter. If this was a genuine contact it was very slow. It could almost be a vehicle travelling along a motorway, other than the fact that they were over 30 miles from the coastline, and even further from the closest motorway.

"Mission 02, contact bearing 075, no range, showing low level."

"Roger 02, nothing seen, investigate and report."

"Roger, investigate, 02," he replied, parroting the controller's instructions.

The needles on his instrument panel remained fixed, belying the fact that they were speeding through the air at nearly 400 knots. It was testament to the immense skill that the pair had developed over the years. He began the manoeuvre gently.

"OK, let's take it down. This guy shows well below, probably on the deck. I can't lock up yet. Come starboard 5 degrees to centre the target and descend to 3,000 feet."

The huge jet responded instantly. Flash concentrated hard on the fuzzy return as it pegged on the extended centreline, in response to his pilot's adjustments. This was the critical phase because, if there was any drift away from the centreline, it would mean the target was crossing their flight path. If it carried on straight down the centreline, it would mean that the target must be coming straight for him. Glancing out of the cockpit, there was nothing but a few stars in the heavens. At least it was a clear night. He knew that in the front, night would have turned to day, the ambient light magnified by the pilot's night vision goggles. In the back, it was pitch black, only a distant flare from an oil rig reflecting from the canopy and casting a dull glow.

This could only be an errant light aircraft so he had no qualms about locking on. There was no way a small civilian aircraft would be equipped with a radar warning system so electronic stealth was not an issue. The pilot could never be aware that above him or her, a fighter jet was interrogating his progress. If Flash could achieve a lock against such a slow target, and it was a big question mark, he would be rewarded with extra information about his quarry. More importantly, the radar would automatically track the target providing vital clues on its progress, making the navigator's task immeasurably easier.

"OK, there's no drift on this guy. He's coming right at us. I make his heading 260 and he's down on the deck. Let me try to lock up first whilst we're steady on heading. If it tracks OK we'll start to make some displacement to give us some turning room. Hold your heading and height for the time being."

Once more the needles stabilised, rock steady as the pilot fixed the flight parameters precisely. Flash moved his acquisition markers around the tiny response and took up half-action on the trigger on his hand controller. The radar paused on the selected bearing and he could see the tiny response highlighted in the velocity display. Moving the markers over the response, he squeezed full-action and the radar switched smoothly into full track mode, the tracking symbology appearing instantly on the radar scope. Breathing a sigh of relief and with the radar now auto tracking, his life was suddenly immeasurably easier.

"Good lock. Which side do you want him on?"

"Put him down the left."

Flash was not surprised. With the throttles on the left console, it was a far more comfortable approach to fly the final turn to the left and most pilots favoured this approach.

"OK come starboard 30 degrees but make it gentle. This guy is seriously slow and we may lose lock. If I lose him we'll come back onto the original bearing."

Once more the jet reacted and Flash watched the target return as it moved away from the centreline in response to his command.

"Mission 02 is Judy," he called to the controller in the Sector Operations Centre in Norfolk, letting him know that they now had control of the intercept. It was a spurious call because the controller on the ground was still oblivious to events. As the target drifted across the scope, the navigator furiously recalculated the displacement away from his own track. He was aiming for five miles, at which time he would come back onto a parallel heading, giving them room to turn gently in behind. The question now was how low would they dare to go?

"I'm showing this guy right down on the deck. Check that with the Delta H."

Razor glanced at the tiny indicator. With a lock, the small gauge showed the relative height, above or below, and an instant appreciation of the vertical displacement.

"Confirmed. On the deck."

Short, sharp.

"Are you happy to go below safety height?"

"Affirmative. I'm on goggles. Good visual with the ground. There are a few rigs out ahead but I think we'll turn before we get to them. Where's the nearest helicopter zone?"

"The southern zone is 30 miles north of here," Flash replied glancing at the map on his kneeboard, barely illuminated by the red cockpit floodlights. It was doubtful that any helicopters would be out this late but they didn't want to push their luck.

"I'm happy if you are."

"Happy."

"OK descend to 1,000 feet initially and come port back onto 080, parallel heading."

They crept slowly lower towards the dark waters below where, if the radar was to be believed, the furtive target lurked. The area around the Phantom went even darker as Razor flipped off the external navigation lights. The only illumination now was from the tiny red cockpit floodlights.

"We'll start the turn at 8 miles but I'll have to lag this target all the way around the final turn. If I pull it to the nose too quickly, I'll lose it on radar. Expect me to lose it quite soon as we enter the turn so keep your eyes peeled."

Flash knew his warning was wasted. Razor knew the score and it would be a miracle if the AWG 12 was able to track the tiny response for more than a few degrees of turn. It was simply too slow. They both knew they would be dependent on the Mark One Eyeball if they were to intercept this elusive target.

Flash pulled on his own night vision goggles, clipping the body of the device onto the mounting track on his helmet. He slapped the battery pack firmly against the velcro patch glued to his helmet and the battery gripped on, held tight in place. Immediately his helmet felt heavier. Once the radar broke lock, he would drop the goggles into place and join the visual search.

CHAPTER 11

New Scotland Yard, London.

In New Scotland Yard, the smart new home of the Metropolitan Police in the Victoria district of London, only a handful of lonely lights burned in the largely vacant offices . The souls remaining were either steadfastly dedicated or had other reasons not to head home to their loved ones.

Simon Hawkes was born a policeman. From his earliest years, he had devoured "The Bill", his favourite television programme, and there had been little choice in vocation when it had come to career interviews at school. It was a given.

By now a member of the elite, Metropolitan Police Anti-Terrorist Branch, or SO13, he was responsible for the protection of VIPs. It was a long path from his early days on the beat in East London. Contrary to the populist view, much of his work was tedious but only rarely did he enjoy the glamorous role portrayed in the media culminating in a high profile arrest. Even those were, inevitably, preceded by endless stake-outs, followed by tedious hours sifting through intelligence reports. His staple diet consisted of summaries of conversations between Irish terrorists, captured by the communications monitoring analysts or the fearless watchers who braved the streets of the lawless province. Although his role excluded the Royal Family, the privilege of a specialist section in the organisation, his span of control was simply enormous and he relied on his colleagues in MI5 to add weight to his efforts. Although the Met was well funded, the boys at 140 Gower Street always seemed to be at the head of the queue for funding. He had learned that National security was a great buzz word when the annual funding round became brutal.

He stared at the nondescript man sitting opposite. In the cloak and dagger world of espionage, individuals routinely appeared unremarkable but, usually, in looks only. This man took the trait to the extreme. That he worked for one of the most secretive organisations in the country was astonishing, for the mysterious operative was an intelligence analyst for the shadowy, Government Communications Headquarters based in Cheltenham, an organisation not even acknowledged in the open press until 1983. His life revolved around the conversations of others. On a normal day he would be found at his workstation poring over transcripts of conversations between hostile intelligence agencies and their outlying institutions or, more likely, with his ear pressed to a headset tuned into the high frequency band networks, straining to catch snippets of conversations exchanged between wary antagonists. His expertise was the exploitation of the Soviet intelligence agency the Komitet Gosudarstvennoy Bezopasnosti, or KGB, one of the most clandestine organisations in the world.

Tonight's meeting had been hastily arranged at the request of the agency and, called at short notice, must be important. With vast amounts of information to sift through, the analyst relied on tracking key words to home-in on potential areas of interest or problems. Only when he was pricked by the proverbial "needle in the haystack" would he focus on potential trouble makers. He had a number of regular suspects and the KGB rezident in London was a particular favourite, and honing his interest was the man's dubious agenda. Ostensibly a trade secretary on the staff of the Soviet Embassy, he spent much of his time back in Moscow where targeting was far more difficult. When in London, the analysts at GCHQ tagged him for special attention. The man was a magnet for classified telecommunications traffic, some of which was highly encrypted and confounded even the best code breakers in the organisation. Even the latest computer-based machines struggled with the Soviet's most advanced encryption, chuntering away for hours, trying to fathom the unfathomable. Based on the increasingly obsolescent, Intel 80286, 16-bit microprocessor first introduced in1982, the new decryption machine had eventually come up trumps. After hours of determined effort, a section of a message had eventually emerged and the content was incendiary. It contained enough detail to cause immediate alarm and the call to Scotland Yard followed without delay.

"You said you had a worrying development Carlton."

"Yes, I thought it best to bring it to your attention face-to-face," the distracted analyst replied, fumbling with the brass lock on the black, official leather briefcase which might have been in use since World War 2. He pulled a well-thumbed transcript from inside, the gaudy caveat, TOP SECRET, stamped top and bottom. Handing it over, the additional caveat was revealed, the words "Special Handling Only" surprising even Hawkes. It was not often he had access to such tightly controlled intelligence information and he suppressed the flutter of nervousness.

"I'll give you a few moments to digest the contents. I should say the message originated in the Soviet Embassy in London and was sent to a little known directorate of the KGB in the Lubyanka."

The name, at once familiar, seemed incongruous, when discussed in the familiar surroundings of his office. Thugs and organised crime were more his bailiwick than foreign spies. He devoured the details rapidly. One name stood out.

"Do we know who "Held" is? It's an odd name."

"It's the German pronunciation," answered the analyst, "pronounced Helt, with a "t". I did some digging back in the archive and I think I have a match," he continued looking rather self-satisfied. "The only time we've seen that codename was after a series of attacks on mainland Europe aimed mainly at NATO targets and personnel. It's German for hero. Specifically, a series of messages were intercepted following the last attack on 8th August 1985 when a car bomb exploded in the car park, opposite the Commander's headquarters building at the Rhein-Main air base near Frankfurt. Two people were killed in the blast. The assailants managed to gain access to the base by kidnapping and killing a serviceman the night before in a local village. When the body was inspected his military ID card was missing. Not surprisingly, it was used to gain access and showed up on the access log on the day of the attack. It had not been cancelled so didn't show any flags. Later it was established that "Held" was directly involved."

"You said they."

"Yes, it was a cell associated with the Red Army Faction."

Hawkes absorbed the implications swiftly. It was an unfamiliar enemy.

The Rote Armee Faktion or Red Army Faction, also known as the Baader-Meinhoff Gang, had its origins amongst the radical protest elements of West German universities. Almost immediately after its formation in the late 1960s, its aspirations diverted rapidly from any loyalist leanings and, increasingly, it funded its activities through bank robberies and terrorist activity. Its members hoped that, with an increasingly aggressive stance, it could persuade a malleable German Government to adopt its left wing agenda. Far from persuading the political elite, it's violent agenda rapidly lost the support of the German political left wing. Starved of resources, it sought help from other radicals elsewhere in the world, particularly in Pakistan.

At its height in the early 1970s, the Faction comprised only a dedicated core membership most of whom had been jailed by the summer of 1972. Disillusioned, Meinhoff hanged herself in her cell in 1976 and three others from the Group, including Baader, were found shot dead in their cells in 1977. Ostensibly suicides, their deaths coincided with a failed hijack attempt on a Lufthansa airliner in Mogadishu, Somalia. Their demise thwarted the hijackers' attempt to win the release of the jailed terrorists by using the hostages as a ransom. With internal friction growing the Faction split into a number of smaller but still closely aligned groups. By now their methods had shifted considerably and the group transformed yet again into its third incarnation.

Hawkes realised he had been digressing, his thoughts drifting away from the stark reality of the threat.

"Have you established any other links other than the code name?"

"I have. The directorate in Moscow is a small unit and one of the agents is Dmitry Guskov, a notorious individual who is suspected of running black operations, mostly in East Germany. That said, he has extensive links in Libya and the Arab world but cultivated mostly to support his activities in Europe. He regularly pops up in London but we assess that his main effort is in West Germany."

"I'm still not making the connection between the Soviets and the Red Army Faction. Are you suggesting they're working together?"

"I agree it's highly unusual. The organisation has morphed since its formation. The faction was formed as a radical revolutionary group, associated with other radical socialist activists. Their original aim was clear. They attacked the establishment and, particularly the military, which gains popular support in West Germany nowadays."

"But, surely, they're just an armed band of thugs. The Soviets can't be taken in by their blunt use of force."

"Let's be honest, the Soviets are not exactly choir boys. Up to now the terrorists have shied away from overt collaboration with Moscow but, all that said, they are a Marxist organisation and, whilst their immediate aims are revolutionary, their ideology is a good fit. They want a reunited Germany and are prepared to use force to deliver. It certainly suits the Soviets to foment unrest in the Soviet Bloc at the present time. With Gorbachev's peace initiatives making headlines, using surrogate agencies and organisations suits the KGB down to the ground. If Gorbachev can make it appear like a populist arising he can keep his cronies in the Politburo in check. The Solidarity movement in Poland is not going to go away any time soon but a crackdown by the KGB needs little justification, despite Glasnost."

Hawkes was quiet for a moment but the analyst wasn't finished yet.

"I'm afraid there's more and this is the real reason for my visit," the man continued pulling a second document from the black, leather briefcase. He handed over another thin leaf of paper.

"Good God," breathed Hawkes, after a swift scan. This is dynamite."

"It's not much and we're trying to decipher more traffic. That's all we have at the minute."

One codename stood out.

"So you're saying that "Vulcan" is the British Prime Minister?"

"I don't think there can be any doubt, as you can see."

"And you're saying that this terrorist group, headed up by "Held", has a plan to destroy her aircraft using a surface-to-air missile?"

"Not only that but the plan has been implemented. The cell is active and we think the personnel are moving into position."

"Bloody Hell!"

CHAPTER 12

Over the North Sea, off Lowestoft.

"OK start your turn now," Flash called as the target hit his turn key on the radar scope, watching the blip track drifting inwards towards the nose, the closing velocity winding off as the target aspect reduced. Razor had been quiet in the front cockpit but he knew that was inevitable. The pilot was working hard, struggling to peg the flight parameters as they began the final turn in behind the elusive target.

"This guy's only doing 150 knots," warned the equally harried navigator. "We'll need minimum manoeuvring speed once we're in behind."

The speed had already trickled back to 300 knots as the pilot began the gentle turn. More speed and they would rapidly overhaul the target. Allow the fighter's speed to fall, and the Phantom would be uncontrollable. With its well known vices at slow speed, Razor risked an unnerving encounter with adverse yaw, in which the nose would slice aggressively in the opposite direction to his demanded control input. It was a phenomena he had experienced during his conversion training and it was one he had no wish to revisit. Balancing the need for enough turn performance to roll in behind yet controlling the overtake on his target once visual, was a fine margin. For now he had to rely on his navigator to give him the vital target speed data from the radar because his total focus was on his flight instruments. His capacity was at its limit. The tenuous radar lock might change it all because, if the radar broke lock, reacquisition would be more luck than skill. He stared through the windscreen waiting for the elusive first visual contact. If he could see his quarry he would be infinitely better placed to complete the intercept. In the words of the old adage, "A peep is worth a thousand sweeps."

The pilot of the tiny Cessna watched the red navigation lights flick back on as the approaching fighter, once more, marked its presence. Tracking inexorably around the final turn, the anti-collision beacon flashed rhythmically, in sequence with the wing tip lights, registering a slow but steady beat. The passengers in the cabin would be blissfully oblivious to the implications of being intercepted, although the pilot wondered whether the clandestine nature of the flight hinted at darker secrets of which he was unaware. As he eased even lower, he was not even sure that they had seen the approach of the inbound aircraft and was certain they had no inkling that it was a British Phantom air defence aircraft. Their faces reflected the dull instrument lighting, their expressions bored.

In the Phantom cockpit, against normal procedure, the QRA camera stayed firmly strapped to the grab bars in the back seat, its operator indifferent to its presence. At these light levels there was absolutely no chance of photography, even if the hard working crew could stabilise alongside. Taking happy snaps was the last thing on the agenda.

Razor listened to the familiar patter from the back seat, a commentary he had heard hundreds of times before. The profile Flash was engineering was designed to place the Phantom in a close formation position but it was more suited to the more prolific intruders such as the Soviet Bears which regularly probed the UK defences. Against such a slow, light aircraft it was an uncomfortable procedure made even more so by the dark night. Although his speed was pegged at 250 knots and the range was marching down rapidly, Razor still felt comfortable. It was a well rehearsed, albeit taxing routine. For the final stages of the pass he would drop mid flap and bleed the speed back to 200 knots. Unorthodox , normally, he would only consider using this configuration on finals to land but his breadth of experience with the Phantom meant that he could take some liberties. Sufficiently confident in his handling skills, he would adapt the techniques to the situation and, hopefully, improve their chances of making an identification. He peered ahead at the indistinct shape of the mysterious aircraft that was beginning to emerge from the murky background, although not yet identifiable. He adjusted his flight parameters yet again, matching the needles to the constant demands from the back cockpit. Glancing briefly at the repeater scope in front of him, the fuzzy blip began to increase in size as Flash selected the "visident" mode and the symbology expanded, displaying the shortest range scale. They were close now and the target tracked down the centreline only scant yards ahead of the Phantom, the closure rate rapid. He knew that Flash would offset the target to the left at the final stages of the pass and, with such a high rate of overtake, they could not attempt to stabilise as they would for a normal target. The target was simply too slow and there was too great a disparity between the relative performance of the two aircraft. It would pass down the left hand side well below the canopy rail, so Razor had mentally prepared to drop the left wing during the fly-by, to give the best chance to read the registration number and identify the mysterious intruder. The manoeuvre was fraught with danger if he misjudged the closure and allowed the Phantom to drift towards its quarry. The range display changed to the lowest setting and the fuzzy blip reappeared at the top of the scope tracking downwards inexorably, the gap between the two craft closing. It was still inky black outside the cockpit and he cursed at the lack of ambient light, entirely dependent on the night vision goggles. As the flap lever clicked to the mid position, the hydraulic system groaned, the jacks moving the heavy leading edge flaps into the airflow. The jet responded almost instantly to the controls, albeit reluctantly, taking on the lumbering gait so familiar when on short finals to land but alien out here in the dark confines of the North Sea. He stared through the front windscreen predicting where the tiny aircraft would be. Despite the close range it was still almost impossible to see and his sphincter clenched involuntarily. He had no desire to hit the crazy pilot who had doused his navigation lights. As the command from his navigator to throttle back to minimum speed registered, he jinked a couple of degrees to starboard, the final manoeuvre to put the target off to the side and avoid a collision. He glanced inside one final time watching the needle on the airspeed indicator slow to 200 knots, checking the throttles forward a fraction of an inch as he did so, hoping to stabilise the pass.

In reality, the approach had been like many other visual identification procedures he had flown over his many years on the Phantom, despite the rapid overtake. He had intercepted errant light aircraft close to the Inner German Border but never at night and never in such inky blackness. Flash's call that he was "coming heads out", announced that the navigator's part in the radar procedure was complete. Two pairs of eyes would give a better chance of reading the registration number at the pass.

As his eyes searched for his quarry, the involuntary cry was unanticipated heightening the already tense atmosphere. Rather than adopting a passive role, the intruder had sprung a late trap. The planform of a light aircraft filled his windscreen, its wings at an impossible angle, further exacerbating the already rapid closure.

With his hurried assessment anticipating an inevitable collision, his natural instinct was to pull upwards away from the dark sea below. With no time to warn his navigator, he could only hope that their mutual trust would extend through the manoeuvre he was about to carry out. If not, he would be flying home solo, if self preservation overrode trust. Seconds flashed past. With collision seemingly imminent, he pushed hard on the controls; a counter intuitive response. Whether through training, judgement or luck, he held the control column rigidly central, avoiding the risk of unexpected control anomalies. Resisting the urge to feed in a bank demand that every natural piloting sense suggested he should need, he tensed waiting to see how the Phantom would respond. Time stood still. Adverse yaw, where the nose reacted in entirely the opposite sense to the control inputs, was a real and present danger at slow speed and high angle of attack and he was in prime territory. It was precisely the circumstances in which he now found himself , where the risk was greatest. With no time to ponder on hazy groundschool lectures to decide whether the automatics would protect him, he froze his movements. . . . . waiting.

The jet responded predictably despite the slow speed. He relaxed, unable to influence events further. He had given all he had to offer. Even as the planform grew bigger, filling the windscreen, the Phantom lurched downwards towards the sea, the altimeter unwinding manically. The strangled call from the back suggested Flash had been caught in the act of lowering his night vision goggles as the g had come on. The action, probably, saved them both, avoiding an unwanted outcome as the navigator's hands had been as far away from either ejection seat handle as it was possible to be.

No sooner had the drama unfolded, it was over and Razor eased gently back on the stick, arresting the rapid descent towards the deck. The height stabilised at 400 feet and the speed picked up rapidly in response to the throttles which he had pushed to the firewall, without conscious thought. The nose was on the horizon and the near collision a recent memory. He was sweating and the cockpit was silent, the hum of the intercom the only noise evident.

"What the. . . . ." he heard from the disgruntled back seater.

"Sorry mate, this guy's playing rough. I'd say he doesn't want to be identified."

CHAPTER 13

The Perimeter Track, RAF Wattisham.

Ashworth eased away from the Flying Club building, his demeanour remarkably relaxed given his close shave with the RAF policeman. The speedometer picked up slowly but he pegged the needle at 20 miles per hour, making sure he avoided the wrath of the controller in the tower. He was conscious that the yellow sodium lights that ringed the dispersal would mark his passage until he was well clear of the hardened buildings they were carefully positioned to illuminate. Convinced that, by now, the control tower would be quiet and that he should be able to avoid the scrutiny of the air traffic controllers who policed the airfield through ever-roving binoculars, he relaxed a little. Surely after hours and with the airfield quiet they would have retired to the crewroom and be drinking coffee? Even so, he did not want to try his luck by exceeding the airfield speed limit.

Threading his way through the concrete bollards blocking access to the taxiway, he rejoined the road heading towards the married quarters, passing the entrance to the officers' married patch. Glancing into a front room, taking in a scene of domestic bliss, he felt a pang of guilt, feeling like a voyeur, even though the curtains were wide open. An officer, still wearing his blue uniform, toasted his partner with a heavy beer stein, probably a memento of a previous tour of duty. Ashworth felt the familiar wrench in his gut, the tension highlighting the recurring standoff with his wife. Domestic bliss in his own case was elusive. He wondered what she had been doing tonight. Was it another business meeting in Ipswich? Would she be home when he got back? He snapped back into the present as the car drifted toward the kerb, his attention wandering. The realisation that, finally, he could not care less was a minor revelation.

The RAF policeman on the gate lifted the barrier, his concentration more on events in the Guardroom than on the passing car. Ashworth slipped swiftly into the darkened countryside, the security lights directed towards the gate receding, rapidly, in his rear view mirror.

CHAPTER 14

Over the North Sea, Approaching the Suffolk Coast.

Heartbeats and adrenaline restored to more natural levels, Razor pulled
the Phantom around in a wide arcing turn, a more respectable manoeuvring
speed re-established. With the radar aimlessly painting random areas of the
coastal waters it was down to a disciplined visual scan to try to regain
contact with the persistent intruder. The dull green glow through the night
vision goggles drenched the seascape but, other than a few barely visible
wave crests, the horizon was clear. Occasionally, his gaze passed through a
distant oil rig causing an annoying flare and a temporary loss of vision. He
resisted the temptation to pull back on the stick to gain height, glancing
instead at the flight instruments under the goggles, forcing his training and
instrument flying skills to override his instincts. The goggles revolutionised
low flying, particularly at night, but it was easy to feel as if you were flying
in a goldfish bowl. Depth perception was poor and senses easily fooled.
Gyros stabilised, he scanned the darkened area ahead, looking for an elusive
flicker against the background. The crests of the waves marched steadily
ahead of the wind but that was the only movement he could discern. One
thing was certain, he was glad to be cocooned in the warm cockpit.

In the back seat, Flash moved the sea returns, the electronic noise
reflected back from the surface, methodically up and down the radar scope
searching for a possible target. Clearing the area ahead in the turn, he hoped
for a chance radar response from the tiny light aircraft, assuming that was
what it was. Unlike his pilot he had missed the impressive planform as they
had flashed past but his neck muscles were still protesting at the sudden
evasive manoeuvre. If he had judged the roll out properly, the contact
should break out below the mass of electronic noise but only if he had
positioned the Phantom in the right sector. In reality it was a huge guess.

In the front, Razor knew it was more luck than judgement given that the pilot of the interloper was trying his best to avoid them. With its slow speed, tiny radar signature and aggressive manoeuvring, it would be a miracle if they regained contact. In the meantime, his eyes scanned, methodically, left and right.

*

As the tiny Cessna coasted-in, it merged wraith-like into the darkened countryside, the sparse lighting on the ground failing to illuminate its passage. Unbeknown to the Phantom crew, the moment he was overland, the pilot threw in yet another evading turn, introducing a dog leg, diverging yet further from the predictable track. The manoeuvre was calculated to hinder the ever searching radar in the pursuing fighter.

Unaware of the evasive turn, the Phantom crew pressed on, following their original heading, moving relentlessly farther away from the real track. Despite the help from the night vision goggles, the tiny light aircraft was soon at the limit of visual detection. It merged into the Suffolk countryside.

CHAPTER 15

Seething Airfield, Norfolk, England.

Ironically, the dark clothed figure which emerged looking slightly shaken from the cabin of the Cessna Caravan, single-engined light aircraft, was also a member of the RAF, but her allegiances were far removed from the crew of the Phantom fighter, which had narrowly missed making an interception out over the North Sea.

Heike Brandt was a member of the Red Army Faction also known as the Baader-Meinhoff Gang which had its origins amongst the radical protest elements of West German universities. After setbacks in the late 70s, the Red Army Faction hardened its attitudes, continuing its terrorist activities but splintering into a number of groups. It was one of these breakaway groups to which Heike Brandt belonged, an enthusiastic devotee to the cause. Her topographic surname was of someone who lived in an area that had been cleared by fire. If her efforts over the coming days were successful, she would live up to her name because she planned to create the perfect firestorm. The most dramatic to have been seen in years, it would ensure her name would be the topic of conversation all over the Continent. Her moment of infamy beckoned.

A small Ford Escort estate car pulled onto the short cross-runway alongside the darkened airstrip and torches flashed briefly from the interior. Recognising the pre-arranged signal, the pilot clambered out from the door set below the wing and prompted the passengers to disembark. He unsnapped the fasteners on the rear luggage compartment and the long sandy coloured carrying case was swiftly removed. Passed over to a waiting body before being hauled the short distance to the car, it disappeared from sight into the luggage area. Covered in dust sheets, the driver hoped his cover story would not be needed tonight because the military standard travelling case was hardly at home amongst the pots of paint that surrounded it.

Brandt was unaware that she had shared the journey with, what would become an inseparable part of her life for the next hours. Inevitably, her Soviet sponsor had made sure that if compromised. Brandt, and not he, would take the fall.

Hurried welcomes exchanged, the recent arrivals climbed into the back seat and the driver moved off, angling away from the Cessna, a clattering from the engine sounding less than healthy. The car made its way towards the airfield gates and on into the back roads of Suffolk before starting its long journey towards the suburbs of London. The occupants could not hear the sounds of the Cessna as it turned into wind and began its takeoff roll, lifting off and disappearing back into the darkened countryside.

CHAPTER 16

Runway 23, RAF Wattisham.

As Razor eased the Phantom off the end of the runway, picking up the illuminated centreline markings of the taxiway, he reached down and released the brake parachute handle, checking in his mirrors that the billowing 'chute had detached from the shackle in the tail cone. The canopy fluttered briefly, released from its restraint, as the jet efflux caught the fabric and it collapsed on the side of the taxiway. A green camouflaged figure emerged from the Land Rover parked alongside, the recovery crew bundling the used contraption into the back of the vehicle to return it to the brake parachute bay for re-packing. The young airman gestured animatedly, unseen by the aircrew, as the noise of the jet engines receded.

Razor breathed a sigh of relief, the tension venting from every pore, as he dumped the cabin pressurisation, flicked the release lever on the left cockpit sill forward, prompting the front canopy to shudder open, slowly extending into the night air. Closely followed by the back canopy, a cool breeze flooded into the cockpit, venting the hot air that had built up during the recovery. He kicked the rudder pedals over, the nosewheel steering responding, the huge jet tracking, unerringly, around the perimeter track. Flash quickly changed frequency checking in with Squadron Operations, advising that their mount had landed serviceable. The Duty Authoriser sounded distinctly relieved and the reason would soon be apparent.

As the jet emerged from the gloom onto the brightly lit aircraft servicing platform, the crew waved at the local controller who sat in the glass control room atop the control tower receiving a cheery response. With the station holding QRA it was not only the aircrew and groundcrew in the Q shed who would be confined to their place of work this evening. Staff in the tower would sit ready to take their part in any scramble which followed.

Hopefully, with a sortie in the bag, they could look forward to a quiet night. Well, a quiet night once the mission report had been filed, the aircraft turned around and the cocking checks completed before it was checked back in on-state.

Rolling down the centreline of the massive concrete apron they entered the parallel taxiway and headed the last few thousand feet back towards the Q Shed, the sodium lights blazing over the remote complex, turning night into day. Ahead, a scene of frantic activity greeted them. The broken Q1 jet that they had left behind was blocking the taxiway beyond the Q Shed, the amber warning beacon on the tractor flashing its rhythmic message. The replacement jet was already being pushed back into the adjacent bay to assume its vigil as Q1. Clearly the snag that had prevented the engine from starting had proved too difficult to fix in situ. It would take at least 15 minutes to get their own jet pushed back into the shed and to declare it back on state. In the meantime, the groundcrew would be busy and the skies of Southern Britain were undefended. Flash could imagine the conversations that would be taking place as the Master Controller at the Sector Operations Centre demanded an aircraft back on state, instantly. Some things were just impossible but the gap in coverage would cause friction. The replacement would have been checked over once the missiles were uploaded but the crew would still need to accept the jet and cock it ready for a scramble. It would take a few more minutes yet.

The "liney" crossed his hands above his head prompting Razor to jab the brakes and the Phantom nodded, uncomfortably, to a halt. The nose of the replacement jet was slowly disappearing back into the gloom of the Q Shed but a grazed wingtip was in no one's interest. They waited patiently.

With Q1 safely tucked away and the towing arm unhitched, the tractor moved away to the side of the concrete apron. From their vantage point they could already see the Q1 crew climbing the ladders readying the new jet. Beneath, the groundcrew made more preparations.

The torches in the marshaller's hands waved urgently, directing Razor around the confined manoeuvring area in front of the hangar. He rotated the Phantom almost within its own length, coming to a halt outside the vacant bay they had left only an hour before. A perfectly choreographed manoeuvre later, the towing arm was attached to the nose wheel and the jet, now powered by only the right hand engine, was pushed back, noisily, into the shed.

The frantic activity would continue for some time yet until each crew had accepted their aircraft once more and declared back on-state.

CHAPTER 17

Soviet Safe House, Chiswick, London.

The delivery truck pulled up outside the darkened house and, across the road, camera shutters began clicking away once again.

A smartly dressed driver emerged from the cab and moved, indifferently, towards the rear doors, extracting a long box covered in black plastic wrapping. Making his way awkwardly through the gate, he dumped the package, unceremoniously, on the doorstep.

The door bell announced his arrival, and he waited patiently for a response, immobile, a receipt pad tucked visibly into his jacket pocket. Despite the extended pause waiting for someone to answer the door, he stared rigidly ahead, his back to the curious onlookers over the street. Eventually, the door cracked open and a short exchange followed before he was allowed inside and the door closed again. A few minutes elapsed before the door reopened and he emerged clutching the same black-wrapped parcel and made his way back to the truck. Visibly struggling with the weight, his frustration was evident to the watchers. Grappling with the box, thumping it heavily onto the ground at his feet, he mouthed a number of curses before the doors opened once more, the recalcitrant package was hefted across his shoulder and returned to the van.

As the garishly marked vehicle pulled away, the watchers across the street added a few cursory notes in the log, annotating a time against each event. Had they been more observant, they might have realised that the driver was, noticeably, more cautious with the package as he placed it back into the van. His hat pulled firmly over his eyes, he was just another anonymous delivery driver making another abortive delivery. It should also have been obvious that his gait was markedly different as he deposited the undelivered item back into his van.

The truck lights snapped on and it moved away, threading its way past the tangle of parked cars, along the quiet road.

CHAPTER 18

On the A12 in Suffolk.

The conversation in the car was stilted not only because of Brandt's inherent reluctance to discuss the clandestine operation with a total stranger, whatever his loyalties, but because of a natural antipathy. The man simply did not look or feel trustworthy. As she stared out across the dark Essex landscape, a few brightly lit hamlets flashed past, breaking the monotony. She drifted into a light slumber, tired by the long journey.

The man driving the car was sullen and the few clipped, guttural, Russian vowels she had noticed were intimidating. Obviously Guskov's man, she wondered about his loyalties. Was he an Embassy man or had he been inserted, like her, for the event? He must be trusted by the leaders of her own faction or he would not be this close to the operation but trust went only so far. She could bide her time. Providing he got her to the safe house in London she could live with the tension. When it all came down to it, the ambience in the airless vehicle was not conducive to conversation.

The enforced lull allowed her thinking time, a commodity she had enjoyed precious little of since leaving the safe house in Erklenz. She thought about the enigmatic Soviet agent, Guskov. What were his motives? Could she even trust him? Why had he provided the missile? All were obvious questions but the answers were, by no means clear. There were obviously political motives behind the enforced allegiance. The Soviet Government had no interest in their cause other than fomenting unrest and heightening tensions in the West. The assistance was certainly not to further the cause of the Red Army Faction so the motives had to be more blatantly selfish and demonstrably sinister.

Fortunately, targeting the British Prime Minister suited both antagonists perfectly. The demise of the "Iron Lady" would send shock waves through the capital cities of the West; literally. Such a patent vulnerability would unsettle the very foundations of NATO. If there was any sign of capitulation after the event, the patience of the US Government might yet be exhausted and an unstoppable schism would ensue. The plan was fraught with difficulties and her own contribution depended on a number of pieces fitting together seamlessly but the goal was worthy of the struggle. The audacious plan was not without risk to her personally and there was an ever present risk of compromise. If just one person, trusted to assist her failed, thereby allowing an inkling of what she was attempting to achieve to leak out, she would be detained.

Her thoughts drifted back to Guskov. She had not met him often but she was strangely attracted to him. Ever professional and focussed, he nonetheless stirred a strange and unexpected longing and it wasn't affection. She tried to rationalise the attraction. Maybe it was the macho image he portrayed? Maybe she had deep repressed urges to bed a real spy? Maybe it was his arrogance? Maybe it was just a function of never being in one place for more than a few days and any port in a storm was welcome. Whatever the reason, she looked forward to sharing a flat with him for the next few hours and who knows?

Light was just dawning in the eastern sky behind her, as the fields of Essex gave way to the outer suburbs of the capital. Just an hour or so to go.

CHAPTER 19

A Residential Road, Chiswick, London.

Only a few short hours since Chisholm had made the panic phone call to the operations desk, a white panelled van pulled into the only vacant parking spot on the quiet residential road. The two boiler-suited technicians that emerged from the cab disappeared momentarily, re-emerging toting tool bags emblazoned with the name of a well known utility company. Casually hefting the bags over their shoulders, they headed off down the street. Hopefully, the board tucked into the window announcing that they were dealing with a gas emergency would deter any unwanted attention from the local traffic warden. In fact, their task was even more pressing than preventing an explosion.

Knocking on the door of the unremarkable terraced house, the anxious resident ushered them upstairs into the front bedroom where Chisholm was already closeted, his somnambulant facade hiding the underlying tension. The curtains were closed and the dated dressing table had been drawn away to give free access to the window. He started as they entered, a grunted welcome acknowledging their arrival. The two men began their preparations, opening bags and pulling out random items of equipment. Far from containing spanners and hammers, the gear that emerged was considerably higher tech. The long-lens camera attached to a tripod was eased into place, the discrete crack in the curtains invisible to anyone taking only a normal interest in the unassuming residence. The directional microphone trained on the door of the house opposite, was instantly ready to capture any conversations that might follow. A sighting scope joined a raft of indistinguishable devices, the pool of gadgets mounting, the bedroom rapidly resembling a recording studio.

Preparations complete, the two men settled into a pair of fold-away chairs extracted from another bundle. Chisholm began his briefing bringing them up to speed on his suspicions about who he thought was now occupying the house opposite. The why would come later.

There was a subdued knock on the door startling the men, already tense at the speed at which events had developed. Soon, the tedium of a surveillance operation would set in but, for now, the adrenaline level was running high. Their impromptu host offered her apologies passing steaming mugs of milky tea across the threshold, her apparently innocent gaze taking in every detail. She might have made an effective surveillance asset herself, given her latent curiosity. She was unable to suppress the urge to linger and would have liked to engage the mysterious visitors in conversation but their reluctance was powerful. Giving up, she withdrew, slightly frustrated at her failure to elicit any valuable scandal. The mysterious events would keep her small circle of friends gossiping for weeks to come. Such things didn't happen in her quiet Chiswick neighbourhood.

For the watchers, the rest of the day drifted into a predictable tedium, the thrill of the chase rapidly overtaken by the dreariness of a surveillance operation. Overnight, the men slipped into the customary shift pattern, attention turning to the spotting scope the moment anyone came upon the door. Not only visitors attracted attention, passers-by along the street, of which there were few, warranting equal consideration. Lights flicked on and extinguished, prompting scribbled notes in the surveillance log, although their targets seemed reluctant to show a presence. If the house had been empty before their arrival as Chisholm seemed to think, then it could only be their targets moving around inside. Frustratingly, the front door stayed, stubbornly, closed.

The sun had barely risen when Chisholm tapped out the agreed code on the bedroom door and entered. The back door to the residential property had been used more in the last 24 hours than it had been in months. Events during his absence had been awkward and his Boss wanted to identify any contacts who may appear as soon as possible. In fact he had spent the time persuading him that, although he was ostensibly the team leader, he was the only man for the job because of his familiarity with the potential targets. The reality was that he was excited to be back on the job, hands-on hunting down elusive spies who sought to make mischief. That he was on home ground meant little to him It was the thrill of the chase that mattered. The mugs of tea he carried were a blatant bribe but were gratefully received and quickly dispatched. The watchers could not have been less interested in whether he stayed or not, providing he did not get in their way.

It was still early when a long expected visitor tweaked their interest. A nondescript estate car, a Ford Escort, pulled up alongside the kerb and, for a few moments, the shadowy figures inside stayed absolutely still. It seemed almost as if they were waiting for a signal. The watcher's camera clicked away, the autodrive rattling its way through the film, capturing nothing. The second watcher tweaked the directional microphone focussing his interest on the vehicle but silence prevailed and, whoever had just arrived in the car was remarkably restrained. Anticipation rose at the prospects. This was the most positive event yet. Perhaps just a food delivery, if they were fortunate, they may be about to discover why a Soviet spy was camped out in Chiswick.

The eyepiece of the spotting scope cupped to his eye, Chisholm focussed on the passenger. Her face was vaguely familiar but he could not think why. Certainly not one of the regulars on the espionage circuit, their identities long ago committed to memory, the notion lingered. Where was it? Prone to springing "honey traps" to entrap unwary Allied servicemen, the regular players had been well known to his former colleagues in "Six" and, keeping track of the Berlin contingent had been one of his previous roles. She was definitely not one of the regulars in that fine city. As he watched, the stranger ducked her head, not out of a desire to stay out of sight but to recover something from the floor of the car. Re-emerging, clutching a knitted hat with ear flaps, the ungainly headwear was tucked into place masking her features from onlookers. It was plain that she was avoiding the risk of identification. The camera clicked obediently on cue, its target masked for the time being.

It was some time before the driver climbed out, moved quickly to the door of the house and rapped urgently, setting a well rehearsed sequence in train. There was no delay before the door opened and a distinctive face appeared, nodding at the vehicle. The passenger appeared in full view, head bowed, walking up the path before disappearing inside. Her movements were fluid, almost sinuous, her clothes mundane. This one would not stand out in a crowd. Her identity still eluded Chisholm but there was no mistaking her host. Guskov's face, the face now staring back at him from the doorway of the terraced house, was imprinted on his psyche. They were old foes.

The driver was almost ignored, seemingly a bit player in the affair, and with his departure, the street returned to suburban normalcy. Nevertheless, his face would later be compared to the Service's database and any dubious links would be followed up. His identity would be rapidly confirmed as a Second Secretary to the Soviet Trade Delegation at the Soviet Embassy.

With the resumption of tedium, Chisholm propped the pillows behind his back and made a few notes of his own. It was some time before his stuttering synapses made the connection but it was easy to see why the links had been slow to form. The woman's identity came in a flash. Heike Brandt, the Red Army Faction terrorist. Less prevalent within the exotic cocoon of West Berlin, the antics of the radical cell had little impact on his local problems but they were a thorn in the side of the military authorities in the

Bonn area. Targeting the establishment, her activities, and those of her cronies, were a regular feature in the classified intelligence summaries that had crossed his desk every day. She was a notorious player and, whilst they had yet to pin a murder on her, there seemed little doubt that she had been closely involved in a number of incidents. That she was capable of a high profile attack was not in doubt. What on earth was she doing in London and, more importantly, why was she consorting with a Soviet spy known for his prowess in fomenting disorder?

CHAPTER 20

Soviet Safe House, Chiswick, London.

Across the small apartment, Guskov watched the woman emerge from the shower, his vantage point inside the kitchen doorway partially hidden from view. Unaware of his presence, she moved over to the bed and dropped the towel, catching it before it fell to the floor, rubbing her hair vigorously. It took all of the agent's self-control to prevent an audible gasp. Her body was truly stunning. Perfectly proportioned, her shapely breasts jiggled in tune to the movements of the towel, her long shapely legs clearly honed in the gym, seeming to extend forever. Time on the beach had left the distinct lines of a tan marking where her bikini had covered her hips. There were no lines elsewhere so during her sunbathing sessions she had clearly shunned a bikini top. Unlike his stereotypical opinion of German women, her legs were shapely and clean shaven. Turning her back, still oblivious, the towel dropped onto the bed, and she wriggled into her panties, a pair of jeans following immediately. Guskov caught another tantalising glimpse of her breasts before they were sheathed in a functional white sports bra. All too brief, he could not suppress the hint of disappointment that his voyeurism was over.

Withdrawing quietly into the kitchen, he rustled a newspaper on the worktop, just loud enough to announce his presence but not enough to cause alarm. Emerging into the room expecting her to cover up immediately, he was wrong. She stared across the room catching his eye. Seemingly indifferent, she pulled the T shirt slowly over her head, flattening down her damp hair and, as their eyes locked again, he sensed the steely challenge. Rather than intimidate her, to the contrary, his bluster was matched, yet the confrontational attitude confirmed his confidence. He had chosen well. She would do fine.

Brandt had been slightly nervous when she had arrived but with time to recover and with the luxury of a shower, she was revitalised. The presence of the other men had been unsettling and her protestations were legitimate but he accepted that she also had a lot to lose. The men were co-opted from the Soviet Embassy staff and had no involvement in the plot other than to fulfil a few specific tasks. He stressed, almost too submissively, that they could be trusted implicitly. Increasing the size of the group had not been his preferred choice, and the less people who knew of what was going on the better, but it had been important for him to maintain anonymity. He had to trust others to assist and their contribution was unavoidable. He assuaged her concerns.

The quiet knock on the door, although anticipated, prompted a nervous response. It was asinine but he was on edge; nervous. The pre-briefed sequence of raps matched an agreed code and his pulse calmed a little. Moving cautiously to the door, he peered through the peephole, confirming the identity of the new arrival. Releasing the latch and re-checking her identity, he ushered her inside, gesturing nonchalantly towards the seating area. The unremarkable woman brushed past, workmanlike, depositing her bag and coat on a chair and homing onto the carrying container lodged against the wall. Her familiarity with its contents was undoubtedly obvious before she even lifted the lid.

The briefing to the German in her native language was thorough. The newcomer had been recruited by a Soviet sympathiser. A Brit with apparently indisputable loyalties, her cooperation had been secured by regular and generous payments to an offshore bank account. In her day job she was a technical analyst with the MOD and her regular place of work was in a dingy corridor in the aptly named Old War Office at the heart of the establishment on Whitehall. That she understood the complexities of the Strela missile that she had extracted from the case, was indisputable because she was a recognised expert in her field and, fortuitously, had proved to be for sale. Guskov could have arranged for his own specialist to be flown in from Moscow but at some risk. A new arrival at the Embassy would be tracked by the minders and might be a liability. He was as confident as he could be, that the payments, and a degree of hidden menace, were enough to guarantee her compliance. Even so he had adopted a simple disguise that he hoped would be enough to fool the British woman, unlikely to identify him, despite his guise as an Embassy staffer. More importantly, she could not link him to his secretive unit back in Moscow. His thoughts in the case of Brandt were more tangled.

The briefing was going smoothly and he had little interest in the technical aspects of the Strela. He had used one of these systems in the field for real and he knew every nuance of its operation. His real interest lay in the minutiae of the logistics for the operation yet he forced himself to concentrate on the conversation to verify its accuracy. Given his years operating in East Germany his German was good yet he had to force himself to concentrate, alert for any signs of deviation from the carefully crafted plan. As he looked on, the German hefted the weapon onto her shoulder, closed one eye and peered down the iron gunsight. Her ability to monitor him temporarily suspended, his eyes dropped to her cleavage hidden by the taught T shirt and encased in the functional underwear. His memory slipped back a few moments, his natural urges responding involuntarily.

The technical briefing over, the German laid the missile launcher back in the carrying case and snapped the lid home, taking ownership of the device. That would be the last Guskov would see of it until its rendezvous with its important target the next day. It would also be the last time he would see the British analyst. It had been decided that, with the importance of this project, this would be her last operation and she would be paid off before the consequences of the forthcoming venture were reported in the national press. Her flight to the Caribbean was already booked. Once she was onboard the airliner, how she chose to proceed would determine her fate. Guskov suspected she would be easy to trace if she chose to stay in the colourful holiday islands but if the operation was compromised, she had better make sure she covered her tracks well. It would not only be him looking for her but a nervous Technical Intelligence arm of the British military, keen to find out how a low paid civil servant had been able to afford to relocate to exotic parts.

As the woman excused herself, he turned his attention back to Brandt. Undoubtedly attractive, he observed his striking accomplice as she busied herself, unaware of his unrelenting attention. It would be a sin to kill her he reflected, particularly given her unique skill set. The search for a reliable agent in Germany had taken years. Depending on how well she fulfilled her part of the contract, he might well have an alternative to a messy termination. If she performed well, perhaps she might survive the encounter.

Over the road, cameras clicked, silently recording the movements into and out of the property. How Brandt performed might be the least of Guskov's problems.

CHAPTER 21

New Scotland Yard, London.

The man in Hawke's office might have been the milkman, such was his bland appearance. Schooled in anonymity, he would blend into the most urbane company yet his manner, once he began talking, quickly doused any thoughts of incompetence. His authoritative air underlined an assured self-confidence.

"What do you know about The Red Army Faction?" he opened; straight to the point.

"Not much," countered Hawkes. "It's not a faction that interests us much here in UK as they operate mainly on West German soil. I've done a little research on them, in the past but not in any great depth. Mind you, they were mentioned in a recent report."

"The stakes have been increased," said Chisholm, ominously.

"I'm assuming that's based on hard intelligence?"

"About as hard as it comes. Let me explain."

Chisholm launched into a brief résumé of the activities of the terrorist group, mentioning the recent attack on an American serviceman. His summary was brief but left little to interpretation, homing in on the hard facts. It was the final synopsis that caught Hawke's attention.

"We're been running a surveillance operation on a house in Chiswick for the last few hours and we have reason to believe that one of the key players from the German group is here in London, right now. What's more, she's being handled by a Soviet agent who is known to us. One Dmitry Guskov."

"The Red Army Faction and the Soviets working together? Seems unlikely."

"That's as maybe but it's not in dispute. We've had eyes-on for over 24 hours and they are both holed up in what we think is a Soviet safe house right now. The problem we have is that the "who" is not in question. What we don't know is the "why" and that's the reason for my visit."

"So you have no intelligence on their reasons for collaborating?"

"None at all. Nothing has come out of the monitoring that gives us a lead but I wondered if you had any reports of collusion. Something must be afoot to bring these two together and why London?"

"Nothing I can think of," Hawkes replied before something jogged his memory. "Hold on . . . . ."

He walked over to the filing cabinet and rummaged through a stack of unsorted papers in a filing tray dumped, casually, in the top drawer. Unable to find what he was looking for he dragged the tray back across to the desk and continued to rummage.

"Something came in yesterday. It looked odd but I couldn't make the connection but what you've just told me may explain at least some of it."

Finding the loose minute that he had been searching for, he handed the crumpled paper across the desk. Chisholm scanned the military mission report, his face inscrutable, the disjointed themes suddenly crystallising.

"So we think a light aircraft dropped off an unknown player in Norfolk at night? Jeez, add the hard intelligence from GCHQ to this and we might have a link between the two players. So we have a potential threat to the Prime Minister but, thank God she's tucked away in Downing Street. What with the potential IRA threat, I guess she's safer there than anywhere in the world."

"You've not been keeping up with the news have you?" the policeman countered.

"To be frank, I've spent the last 24 hours locked up in an old lady's bedroom with two hairy blokes, so no."

The grubby image drew a grimace.

"She's in West Berlin for a meeting with Gorbachev and has been for 24 hours. She flies back home tomorrow."

The two men exchanged a glance, concern growing and realisation dawning.

"We need to move," replied Chisholm. My problem is I have no authority to intervene. I can watch but I'm toothless."

"From what you've told me I think we have enough potential cause to have a judge sign off on a search warrant," countered Hawkes. "I'm sure Brandt has a Europol arrest warrant issued against her and that's cause in itself. If it is her, and I have to rely on you for that fact, we can get a team together quickly. We need to talk to her before we hand her back to the Germans."

"How soon?"

"We'd need to go in at night so a few hours would do it. I could bring in the hooligans from Hereford if I need to but my own team from SO19 should be able to work this. It is, after all their home turf and they might be miffed if I handed it off to the military."

"Last I saw before I arrived, suggested those two were not heading out anywhere soon but we shouldn't dawdle."

"Give me an hour and I'll have a team ready for briefing. Can you give me everything you've got?"

Chisholm rifled in his briefcase assembling a few papers. Hawkes picked up the phone and began dialling.

CHAPTER 22

Outside the Soviet Safe House, Chiswick, London.

The team commander beckoned to his two section leaders who hurried over, their blacked-out faces out of place under the dull light cast by the sodium street lights. There was a hasty conversation. From the start point around the corner, the front door of the target house was obscured but that was irrelevant at this stage. The script for taking down a residence was choreographed and every member of the insertion team was carefully briefed on the layout of this particular house. Nothing would be left to chance and, once the doors were breached, the plan would unfold like clockwork. Only the response of the terrorists inside would determine how the players, on both sides, would leave the house when it was over.

The leader muttered his last minute orders and the three men split up, returning to their pre-briefed start points. Looking back at Hawkes, the beads of sweat on his face were testament more to the unseemly haste to set up the take-down than to nervousness.

"On your call."

The clipped radio call heightened the apprehension. Hawkes experienced the familiar jolt of adrenaline, anticipation ripe. It was not the first time he had been in this situation and certainly wouldn't be the last and, if he was honest, he thrived on the buzz. There was no need to consult up the line. Delegated authority had been given and it was his call when to move. Even so, he took one last look at Chisholm before giving the order. His enduring thought was that the man's face was inscrutable.

"Go!"

CHAPTER 23

Chiswick High Road, London.

The garishly marked delivery truck, apparently operated by a major logistics company, pulled alongside a vacant parking bay on the busy main artery out of London. The driver stepped down, pushing a pre-positioned traffic cone aside, before returning to the cab and easing the truck into the empty bay. To all intents and purposes it was just another routine delivery.

Emerging from the cab, the driver opened the rear doors and scanned the surrounding pavements before moving towards a black VW Golf in the adjacent bay. Conveniently parked pointing in the opposite direction, the boot popped open, silently, as the car doors were unlocked. Even if the driver's actions were being recorded, the unremarkable carrying bag that was transferred between the vehicles was barely visible for more than a few moments, its anonymity hardly likely to raise comment even from the most curious bystander. The transfer complete, the driver closed the boot lid and disappeared into the back of the truck closing the doors.

Some minutes later a black-clad body emerged, secured the doors, climbed into the Golf and drove away. Although the body resembled the van driver in stature, the garb was entirely different.

Further along the road and just out of sight, the traffic warden adjusted the hat on his head trying unsuccessfully, to wipe away the sweat that was forming around the band. The heavy coat he wore was totally unsuited to the weather conditions. He cursed the high visibility markings and the stupid high visibility jacket he was forced to wear. Damned health and safety regulations. He was more likely to die of heat exhaustion than be run over by a bus. In the past, he had been able to creep up on unsuspecting motorists and would have the ticket written before they even knew he was around. Nowadays, he stood out like a sore thumb and, invariably, he was spotted before he got anywhere close to his formerly, unsuspecting prey.

The black VW Golf had looked promising. The driver had put only an hour on the parking meter and, if experience was anything to go by, once the driver got tangled up in the seething masses of humanity along the High Street, he would overrun the allotted time. Ambling along, trying to appear disinterested, the warden approached the bay. Disappointment flooded over him as he realised the Golf was gone, replaced by a nondescript Vauxhall Cavalier.

The cones in the next bay were interesting though. He had meant to check with control to find out which utility company had placed them but it had skipped his mind. They had been pulled away and now lay, haphazardly, in front of a yellow painted delivery truck belonging to one of the large logistics companies. There was no sign of the driver and the engine had been shut off. The engine was still ticking as it cooled down. Glancing at the meter, it still had a few minutes to run but he was minded to give the driver a break. They had an impossible job around here trying to find places to pull in, out of the traffic flow, while they dropped off the parcels. Providing they didn't stretch the point, he would normally give the professionals a break. Like him, they had a job to do.

Cross checking his notebook, the tight script listed his record of potential tickets. The registration number of the Golf was plainly marked with the time he had checked its position and the time of expiry for the meter. Disappointed again, he realised that it had moved only minutes before its allotted time was up. The driver of the VW had been lucky he mused. There would have been no mercy shown in that case. The book snapped closed and dropped back into the pocket of his warden's jacket.

Five minutes after the Golf had pulled out into traffic, a uniformed delivery driver unlocked the truck, climbed into the driver's seat and consulted a delivery schedule, apparently intent on identifying his next drop-off. The van engine burst into life and it steered away from the kerb, knocking over a bollard in its haste to depart. It quickly merged with the heavy traffic.

As it disappeared, the traffic warden followed its progress, unclipping the radio and checking in with control. The conversation would yield nothing and the controller seemed entirely unimpressed at the presence of a few random traffic cones on Chiswick High Street. They really should take more interest in this security conscious age. Diverted, the warden omitted to mention the presence or the registration of the VW Golf. Maybe he would relate the tale to his mates as he clocked off. It was another "one that got away" story to report. The ostentatious BMW saloon on the double yellows, however, was too good to miss.

CHAPTER 24

Soviet Safe House, Chiswick, London.

"Nothing!"

Hawkes and Chisholm exchanged puzzled glances, neither able to work out how, or when, the erstwhile residents had slipped the net.

"What; the place is completely empty?" he queried, mystified at the escape trick they had seemingly witnessed. The black-suited operative seemed equally perplexed.

"No people but it's obvious that someone has been there for some time. There's evidence of occupation. Food cartons and the sort of stuff that you'd use for daily living are strewn around. They weren't exactly house-proud," he added, the indignation the polar opposite of the stereotypical attitude that either of the hard bitten men would have expected.

"There's also a big black, plastic covered box that looks suspicious. It's heavy but I've told the guys to leave it be until we can have the bomb disposal people check it out. It looks like something was shipped in so there may be some trace evidence that the techs can isolate. There's another thing you should see too."

He beckoned to another of the team members who approached the huddle carrying a large military looking container by the handle. The sandy coloured box was marked randomly with unusual characters that were instantly recognisable to Chisholm. He had played with the former contents of the container many times over the years. During intelligence briefings the technical details had been laid bare and he had even watched the contents being used for their intended purpose on an Army firing range in Wales. His muttered expletive was perfectly descriptive. As Hawkes inspected the container, the connection still not fully formed, he watched Chisholm closely, waiting for the revelation.

"We've got a serious problem", Chisholm muttered. "That's the transporting case for an SA-7 Grail surface-to-air missile . . . and it's empty."

The elderly resident across the road in Number 22 peered through her curtains as the team climbed back into the dark blue Ford Transit van. Life had taken on a dramatic turn this last 24 hours and she was revelling in the intrigue. Such things shouldn't happen in Chiswick she thought but, nevertheless, her false indignation aside, she could not wait to tell her story to the ladies at the Women's Institute.

*

Back at Scotland Yard some hours later, his conversation with the analyst Carlton still fresh in his mind, Hawkes pulled open the upper drawer of the drab grey, official filing cabinet and drew out the maroon folder. Returning to his desk he pulled out the single entry, only vaguely aware of the special handling caveats emblazoned across the header and footer. I really should take more care of this stuff, he thought idly, the true reason for the caution evading him. The coarse paper had yellowed quickly, despite the fact that the information it carried was barely days old. The typewriter had punched the characters into the surface and, given the sensitivity of the content, this would be one of only two copies. The other was held, safely, in the analyst's office in Cheltenham.

Hawkes glanced down the tightly grouped list of names. Something was bugging him; an itch that refused to be scratched. Red Army Faction stood out bold in the title, the list of names exclusively German. The infamous gang had taken up more than a good deal of his time recently, but the revelation of the potential threat to the PM had heightened his concerns, and strengthened his intention to shut down their plot. There was nothing startling about the names that stared back at him because they were typical of any that he would find in today's copy of the Bild if he chose to read it. On the reverse, each name was broken out in turn and snippets of detail showed the recent movements of each of the conspirators. Mostly centred around the gang's headquarters, the summary was unremarkable. Day-to-day comings and goings of an irrational, radical faction. What was he missing?

As he mused over the contents, the name Heike Brandt pushed to the fore, nagging his memory cells. Suddenly, the significance dawned on him. A recent report from an undercover source embedded within a group of dissidents in London had flagged up the very same name, suggesting that she was about to visit the city. The report had been unusual in that the Red Army Faction and the subject group in London had little natural affinity and their goals were radically different. He had thought at the time that an allegiance was odd. The association was more than worrying as the presence of the terrorist on his patch could only be damaging. Her presence was guaranteed to cause him grief.

Moving back to the cabinet and pulling out another file, he scanned the summary of known trouble makers who had passed through immigration control at the London airports over the last week. Brandt's name was notable by its absence. Had the immigration officers missed something? If she was now running around the streets of Chiswick, how had she got into the country?

The snippets of information had been culled from a collection of sources and it took him some time to make the link. Suddenly it was shouting at him from the document. The missing link was a report from MI5 of a sighting of Dmitry Guskov. Not one of the regular Soviet Embassy agents, so far no one could cast any light on why he might be visiting London but nothing the man did was by accident. With Guskov, there had to be a good reason why he was here because he did not concern himself with trivial operations. With his reputation, something substantial was underway and the find at the safe house had to be linked. The identity of the mysterious face at the door of the house in Chiswick was all of a sudden obvious.

The pieces fell rapidly into place once Hawkes knew what he was looking for. Guskov had arrived a few days earlier, flying in from Berlin Schönfeld on the daily Interflug flight and been logged through Customs and Immigration on a diplomatic passport. Since his arrival at the Soviet Embassy he had gone to ground and the MI5 minders had lost contact. That was until he appeared in Chiswick at Number 21.

He leafed swiftly through the reams of intelligence reports, searching for the elusive link. Pausing on a report from an oil rig off the Norfolk coast in which an oil worker had flagged up a mysterious plane operating at night without lights, he drew it out and soaked up the detail. Planes working in that area were a nightly occurrence, but not at low level and certainly not propeller-driven light aircraft. The Phantoms from Wattisham were regular visitors over the rigs but there could be no confusion over the noise they made.

An air defence mission report, or ADMISREP, had just been filed from a mission by an RAF fighter jet last night in which the crew had been vectored onto an unidentified slow moving contact in the same area. To be here in his file was extremely unusual as his office wasn't on the normal distribution list but its presence was fortuitous. The sighting had been put down to potential drug runners but, maybe, the analysts had been too quick to draw conclusions? This might have been how Brandt had arrived.

Now where was she and could there be a link between the Soviet agent and the shifty terrorist?

A potential chain of events was coming together. Suddenly a disturbing picture formed.

CHAPTER 25

RAF Wildenrath, Nordrhein Westfalen, Germany.

Helmut Neumann pulled up at the security barrier at RAF Wildenrath, the fighter base nestled amongst the pine trees in the German countryside, close to the Dutch border. Today was like any other day as he lowered his window and exchanged a cheery greeting with the RAF security guard on the gate. Offering his identification card, he was confident in the knowledge that it would pass scrutiny because it was genuine. The German national had been working on the base for years and was a well known face to the security staff that manned the barrier. He made his usual comment about the life-sapping drizzle that seemed to invade every pore in this part of the country, knowing how much the Brits liked to talk about the weather. How they must revel in the dank climate of Nordrhein Westphalen. It was a national pastime and every conversation seemed to begin with a lengthy analysis of every single detail. Today did not break the norm.

To his left, the security lights lit up the face of the single storey, green washed guardroom where the first signs of movement showed through the windows, as the duty corporal fussed around inside. Soon the daily rush would begin as the morning shift began to arrive to prepare the fighter jets for another days operations. Neumann was relieved to see the security mirrors stowed alongside the wall of the piquet post, not yet readied for use. The telescopic devices were simple but effective, allowing the guards to inspect under a vehicle for signs of improvised explosive devices. With the IRA threat to personnel and vehicles, the checks were rigorous and it would be a major public relations coup for a vehicle bomb to be detonated within the confines of the base. The fact that he normally arrived ahead of the crowd was no coincidence. At quieter times, such as now, the guards tended to be more relaxed and checks were less frequent. Only occasionally would he be stopped for a cursory check of his car. After all, he was not the target of the fanatical Irish terrorists. A check was rare and with the kit still stowed, today he would be waved through unmolested. On this occasion, that suited his purposes precisely.

Today, however, was not like any other day. When the activation signal had arrived in the mail he was stunned. Neumann was a sleeper; an East German agent infiltrated into the West by the Stasi, the East German Secret Police. When he was recruited back in Magdeburg, it seemed like the perfect arrangement. His handler had reassured him that he would be placed at the base but that he would only be called upon if the unthinkable occurred. Although the power blocs of East and West faced each other across the Inner German Border, the thought of a nuclear conflict seemed unlikely. The mutually assured destruction that would be the inevitable outcome seemed too apocalyptic to contemplate. He had become complacent and had expected to live out his life in comfort waiting for the call that would never come. Unfortunately, it had come and he was in no position to refuse the call. The secretive organisation had too much "dirt" in his file for him to even contemplate a refusal. In the hidden compartment in the boot was a vehicle tool kit sitting snugly alongside the mandatory warning triangle and first aid kit that every vehicle carried in West Germany. Rather than tools, however, today the box carried a small parcel neatly wrapped in brown paper and addressed to a house in the suburbs of London. His task was to deliver the parcel to the Air Movements Terminal.

Trooping flights flew into Wildenrath every Monday, Wednesday and Friday and into Dusseldorf on Tuesday and Thursday, bringing new families to Germany at the start of their tours of duty. On the homeward trips, similar families returned to their regular lives in UK at the end of their tours, although normality was elusive in the military community. Operated by Britannia Airways, the Boeing 737s were a regular sight at the toned-down fighter base, standing out from the camouflaged jets which shared the hard standing, resplendent in the gaudy livery of the charter airline.

Neumann was a baggage handler, one of the ranks of locally employed civilians, taken on by the MOD as a sop to the local residents. It was good to have the local population dependent on the base. Anti-war sentiment ran rife amongst the increasingly eco friendly Nation of West Germany and a level of dependency reminded them that the RAF was the largest employer for the residents of the local villages and towns.

Neumann's instructions were simple. He was to add the parcel to the mail sack which was carried on every flight back to UK. It would be a relatively risk-free task as the sacks were stowed unattended in the baggage room prior to loading. On a normal day, he passed the sacks numerous times and he should be able to add the package without attracting undue attention. Full of letters home, today's shipment would contain a message of anger not affection.

Neumann snapped back to the present, realising that he had been day dreaming. Apparently indifferent, the guard handed back the plastic identification card and hit the button, prompting the security barrier to rise, gently, upwards. Neumann pre-empted its ascent, accelerating down the long straight road towards the Air Terminal before he attracted any further attention. Just another normal day at the office.

CHAPTER 26

New Scotland Yard, London.

Back in his office, Hawkes fought an uncommon urge to panic. A natural optimist, the feelings were alien but, if his suppositions were correct, his nightmare scenario was coming to pass. A hitherto irrelevant group was active on his territory and seemed hell bent on mischief. What was more chilling was that only he, and a handful of other people, had even the slightest inkling that the plot was developing. If he lost his nerve now, cataclysmic events would unfold that would threaten the very stability of the democratic West. He had no idea how to respond as yet.

The raid had been a disaster. Chisholm, through a great deal of good fortune had merely framed the problem. He would carry on investigating the few remaining leads but it was doubtful if he could track down the origins of the missing surface-to-air missile from the few stencilled markings on the carrying case. It was not Chisholm's job to arrest a known terrorist loose in London. That fell to Hawkes; good old fashioned policing would be needed, and he would have to use every sneaky trick he could muster; and more than a bit of good luck.

His first call had been to GCHQ, to Carlton, the analyst who had broken the news of the threat against the PM. The regular targets had been, remarkably, quiet but rather than seeing this as good news, Carlton was worried. Normal traffic had ebbed and his analysis had been that something big was afoot. What that might be he would not say, but he had been insistent that his senses were telling him that an operation was underway. What he added was that Guskov, who by now had been designated as a target of prime interest, had rented a vehicle and was on the loose in the suburbs. The listeners had identified the rental company and the model of the car but the details did not match the vehicle, a Ford Escort estate car, that had delivered Brandt to Chiswick. What the new vehicle was to be used for was not yet obvious. To Hawkes it was readily apparent that Brandt would have to get around the capital city, so a rental car was the obvious mode of transport. If Guskov was supporting her, knowing the number plate of the rental was vital. If he could track down the car it might lead him closer to the core of the plot. He would need surveillance as soon as he had the details.

The agent at the rental car company was, initially, nonplussed at speaking to a policeman but when he demanded to speak to her Boss, announcing his credentials, she became instantly cooperative. Perhaps the threat of a charge for hindering a national security investigation had helped? The subsequent conversation elicited that the vehicle, a black VW Golf, had been rented from a small agency office in Tower Hamlets. The pickup location seemed entirely unconnected with other events and, apparently, random. It had been rented for five days and would be returned to Stansted airport at the end of the rental period. It was a start but how to track it down?

ANPR, or auto number plate recognition, was invented in the mid 1970s by the Police Scientific Development Branch and, by 1979, early prototypes were deployed on the A1 motorway and at the Dartford Tunnel. By 1981, the technology had proven sufficiently reliable to be used in evidence after it detected a stolen car. Still not widely used but rapidly expanding, cameras had been set up on the main arteries into London for precisely the purpose Hawkes now envisaged. Introduced to counter the threat from Provisional IRA terrorists to the key installations in the Capital, the system of cameras and checkpoints was becoming known as "The Ring of Steel". If he got lucky, he may be able to find and track the rental car. A BOLO, or "be on the lookout for" warning was the most likely solution to his dilemma. Bored cops in traffic cars might yet come to his rescue.

He entered the vehicle information into the database and leaned back in his chair considering his next move. He needed to speak to the crew of the Phantom which had intercepted the light aircraft. The air defence mission report had been stark and couched in military jargon but maybe they could cast a light on where the light aircraft may have landed. Knowing the simple fact may not move the investigation forward because the end result had been Brandt's arrival at the Soviet safe house in Chiswick. Even so, it might yield a snippet of unexpected information. Until the answers to his queries began to come in it was a trip worth making.

RAF Wattisham sat in the heart of Suffolk a few miles northwest of the town of Ipswich. If nothing else it was a pleasant drive.

CHAPTER 27

The Operations Room, QRA, RAF Wattisham, Suffolk.

As Flash walked back into the operations room the phone was already ringing. He tugged at the hefty, rubberised zip that bisected his chest diagonally, allowing the heat that had built up in the bulky immersion suit to dissipate. With the insistent phone demanding his attention, the promised trip outside the confined building, where he could have regulated the oppressive overheating, would have to wait. As he flopped into the easy chair, picking up the intrusive handset, he realised that the sweat he had generated in the confined cockpit was already cooling, his undergarments cold and clammy, as his body cooled down rapidly. The Boss's strident tones almost burst his eardrum.

"What the hell went on out there? I've had the controller at Neatishead on already. How long before the jet is back on state?" The questions came thick and fast with no break in the flow to allow Flash the chance to respond.

"At least ten minutes Boss. The troops are finishing the turnround now."

The pause in the tirade was imperceptible. A cup of coffee appeared on the table in front of him. He flashed a grateful thank you to the Q1 pilot who grimaced at the tirade. Sometimes it was good to escape the clutches of the squadron.

"I'm expecting a visitor and I need you down here soonest. Get the Q1 crew to cock your jet whilst you're away and you can hold state from down here. Make sure you have the pager with you and you can hold 10 minutes from my office. From what he's told me, this is important stuff and you need to hear it now. He has some questions for you about the sortie you just flew. Hanged if I know how he got your ADMISREP so quickly. I'll talk to the Master Controller and let him know what's going on. Declare "Mandatory" if you need to."

The phone clicked off and he stared at the silent handset.

Did the Boss never sleep, thought Flash.

CHAPTER 28

The Guardroom, RAF Wattisham.

Dawn had broken as Hawkes pulled past the traditional, ornate wrought iron gates at the entrance to the darkened airbase. A Lightning fighter posed, majestically, on a plinth next to the road, made an instant statement, its presence cementing the pedigree of the airbase. A long succession of fighters had operated from the Suffolk flying station since World War 2 and the Lightning had only been replaced by the more capable Phantom in recent years. Retired from service, the gleaming, burnished aluminium surfaces reflected the emerging rays of the sun. Pulling into the visitor parking bay he hefted his body from the car, enjoying the relief as the tension eased in his cramped muscles.

A military guardroom was a manifest change from his normal routine and he chatted, amiably, with the airman on duty. He glanced around the slightly depressing space as he waited for his access pass to be written out, his eyes taking in every detail. Even at this hour, the early morning flood of local tradesmen, eager to sell their wares or ply their trade at the busy base, had begun. The dingy green paint on the walls was, strangely, reminiscent of how he imagined a wartime fighter station to have been and he was transported to a past era. That it seemed more "Dad's Army" than high technology would soon be rectified when he arrived at the flight line. In the meantime, "Passes and Permits", as the drab section was known, seemed set in a bygone era. Signing the ledger, he retrieved his warrant card and was rewarded in exchange with a typewritten pass that would allow him access to the secretive airbase. With orders to place a vehicle pass on the dashboard, he re-emerged and sauntered back over to his vehicle, a depressing, grey, Ford Escort. The door echoed tinnily but by now he was immune to its "pleasures". The car had got him here, after all. The engine fired up on cue, belching fumes into the calm Suffolk morning air and, with a grinding of gears, moved off.

Previous visits to RAF bases had taught him that one of the best breakfasts in the County waited for him in the Officers' Mess dining room. He could talk to the crews at their leisure, on the Squadron, once they emerged after their spell of duty in the Q Shed. Before then he would satisfy one of his more mundane urges; his stomach growling a warning. He was unaware of the mayhem he had set in motion just a short distance away in the huge imposing hangar on the flight line.

The road threaded its way around the front of the attractive 1930s building, its elegant white, Georgian-style windows allowing a welcoming glow to spread out across the ivy-clad entrance. Flanking the triple-arched porticos, the windows gave a tantalising view into the elegant ante rooms, already dotted with officers enjoying a post breakfast cup of coffee. He made his way towards the main entrance, his passing annoyance with the car forgotten, his stomach echoing its warning once more. He could get used to this lifestyle he decided. But for a few terrorists, hell bent on getting rid of the Prime Minister, life was just peachy.

CHAPTER 29

The Flying Club, RAF Wattisham.

The sun had barely risen as Ashworth made his way across the airfield towards the Flying Club. The rays of the rising sun shone briefly in his eyes as the car swung around the perimeter track, the tyres clicking rhythmically over the joints in the concrete hardstanding. His thoughts ran over the coming day's events as he rehearsed each move in his mind.

The rubber fasteners were cold and resistant to his efforts as he struggled to release them. Eventually free, he pulled the rubberised fabric of the temporary hangar clear, opening the way for the light aircraft that sat, patiently, on the chocks inside. Fortuitously, his mount for the day had been positioned at the front of the hangar with the towing arm already attached to the nosewheel. It was a welcome discovery as there was nothing more frustrating than a double shuffle to release the aircraft from its parking slot. Glancing briefly inside the cockpit, making sure the switches were safe and the brakes were released, he dragged the chocks clear of the main wheels. The Warrior was predictably reluctant on the first tug but eventually, inertia overcome, it began to roll forward in response to his persuasion, emerging from the hangar into the dawn light. The short distance to the parking slot was covered rapidly once he had coaxed it into action and he swung the nose around to position the tail over the adjacent grass. He made a final check, sure that the prop blast would be directed clear of the buildings, venting over the grass fringes once he started the engine. Removing the tow bar, he ambled back into the hangar and tucked it back inside, resealing the doors.

Beginning his walk round, he methodically checked the airframe and services until he was happy that the small aircraft was ready for its sortie. Clambering up and over the wing, he dropped onto the seat and eased over into the left hand seat and began his pre-flight checks, methodically working through his checklist. Complete, but still wary after his close encounter with the RAF policeman the previous evening, he scanned the approaches to the squat building. There was one last task before strapping in. Climbing back over the wing, he pulled open the small door to the luggage compartment.

A quick sprint across the tarmac to the club building, he returned clutching a shrouded device snugly in his arms. At this stage, the device was inert but his caution was understandable given the explosive power he was clutching. Moving straight to the waiting light aircraft, he tucked the device securely into the rear baggage compartment making it fast with tie-downs and snapping the door closed. A final check to confirm he had not been observed and he relaxed. It would be out of harm's way, and more importantly out of sight, for the first leg of the flight before it was fixed into its final position.

Heading back into the small ops room he had a few final tasks before getting airborne. He would sign out for the sorties, do a final check on the weather conditions and pass the movement to Operations Wing. Thankfully, he was a self-authoriser and able to approve the flights himself. Explaining his slightly non-standard plans to a supervisor would have been a minefield and he had enough to worry about this morning.

The clock was ticking.

CHAPTER 30

The Flightline, RAF Wattisham, some hours later.

Hawkes nursed the substantial china mug full to the brim with strong tea, the owner's name emblazoned on the side in shiny gold script. The drink was offered by a genial officer the moment Hawkes had walked into the crewroom. He had gratefully accepted. A glance at his watch and he settled into one of the comfortable armchairs, a few minutes to wait before his scheduled appointment with the Squadron Boss.

It was impossible not to listen in to the conversations around him. The coffee bar, its facade trimmed with polished mahogany and adorned with the Squadron crest, was a magnet in the room and attracted anyone who came in. It was doubtful that the magnificent edifice had been commissioned by the MOD, more likely a labour of love of, perhaps, a closet craftsman amongst the squadron members. Across the rear wall behind the bar, a rack of mugs, similar to the one he was clutching, furnished a rough head count for the squadron. He strained to read the names from a distance. Failing dismally, he worked out that about 30 mugs hung from pegs, their owners temporarily absent, the names mostly routine, but peppered with a clutch of bizarre call signs.

The vibrant conversation amongst the aircrew clustered around the coffee bar, seemingly recounting the first sortie of the day, was surprising given that it was barely 9 A.M. To have already completed the first mission was impressive so early in the morning. As he watched, a second crew pushed through the outer door, allowing the noise of distant ground support equipment to intrude, briefly, on the tranquillity. The newcomers joined their colleagues at the bar, one disappearing behind, the impressive structure, drawing water from a cantankerous water boiler to top-off steaming cups of coffee. Visibly adrenalin fuelled, an informal debrief of their sortie had already begun, even before they had ventured into the briefing room. Hands flew animatedly, recapturing a distant air combat engagement over the North Sea. Hawkes listened, spellbound, albeit the banter amongst the aircrew might have been exchanged in a foreign language. What in hell's name was a high yo-yo?

Glancing around, he looked across the short manicured grass in front of the squat hangar annex, to where a line of Phantoms ranged across the dirty concrete apron. Umbilical cords plugged in beneath the fuselages, would soon urge the jet engines into life. Boiler-suited bodies darted between airframes preparing the jets for flight, their movements urgent but structured. Hawkes sensed that life might not always be this calm. Another Houchin external power set sprang into life, audible through the old fashioned, secondary glazed windows on the outer wall of the crewroom. The inserts rattled as the power set revved up to full chat. Still riveted, he watched a technician sprint up the ladder into the cockpit of the waiting jet. In the absence of the navigator, he could only speculate on the problem the technician was trying to fix. As he dropped into the rear cockpit a second technician hefted a black box onto his shoulder and followed the first man up the ladder, resting the box on top of the airframe. In short order, the box disappeared into the cockpit exchanged for a similar looking item which retraced the journey. It was a world away from the dogged routine of police work, Hawkes reflected, wondering at the complexity of the rugged war machines he was studying.

Another officer wearing a blue working uniform but lacking a flying brevet, wandered through from the operations room. Immediately the butt of banter from the congregated aircrew, Hawkes surmised that the new arrival was the engineering officer. His witty retort spawned muttered, uncouth responses from the assembled aircrew. Clearly used to the challenge, the newcomer held his ground. Bating over, the energetic conversation around the coffee bar returned to flying matters.

Yet another officer hunched over a low table, leafed through a thick volume of technical notes, his youth hinting at his lowly status on the Squadron, presumably still working up to operational status. The furrowed brow suggested that the absorption rate of the substantial written material ranged in front of him was less than rapid. He uttered the occasional disconcerted groan.

Hawkes slowly formed impressions, the air of the crewroom shaping the questions he planned to pose to the wing commander. A voice over his shoulder intruded.

"The Boss will see you now Chief Inspector."

*

The Squadron Commander ushered the policeman into his small, austere office and they settled into the gaudy armchairs, the colourful disruptive pattern at odds with the functional surroundings. A small conference table fought for position with a filing cabinet and bookcase, the impression one of purpose over aesthetics. The door opened and a corporal, his trousers pressed to a razor sharp crease and his toe caps shined to a mirror finish, set two steaming mugs of tea down on the side table.

The senior officer chatted amiably filling time, waiting for the arrival of his aircrew, the conversation polite as they bounced off the weather, his drive up from London and the Phantoms that were visible through the grimy window.

A knock on the door heralded the arrival of the two aircrew who entered, snapping a smart salute, before removing their hats. After brief introductions, Razor and Flash took the proffered seats, the group arranging themselves snugly around the small table in the corner, a slightly unpleasant whiff emanating from the green-clad bodies. The temperature in the small room was already rising and it was readily apparent that the flying kit had been in use for at least 24 hours; the effect powerful. The close proximity added to the already claustrophobic atmosphere, prompting Hawkes to dive in, keen to keep the meeting short.

"Gents, you'll appreciate that I can't go into sources but that's something you'll be familiar with on the Squadron. Let me just say that they're of impeccable quality."

Three inscrutable expressions fixed him, prompting him to plough ahead, feeling oddly nervous. He recognised the poker faces opposite.

"We've been tracking the movements of a group of terrorists based in West Germany. You may be familiar with some of their activity given that their principle targets are military. One member in particular, Heike Brandt, has been seen recently in the German town of Erklenz. You may have heard of it?"

Razor and Flash exchanged glances, their interest peeked at the mention of the small dormitory down, close to their former base at RAF Wildenrath.

"We have reason to believe that she has entered the country, possibly without authority, bypassing Customs. If so and given her background, I doubt her motives are honourable."

The Squadron Commander tapped his index finger on the desk, immediately drawing everyone's attention.

"Why the link with us?"

"I need to ask a few questions about a mission report that you filed last night. I believe you intercepted an unknown track off the Suffolk coast?"

"Yes we launched late in the evening and it was already dark. The merge occurred about 30 miles offshore but it was as black as a witches tit out there," replied Razor, undiplomatically.

"You reported the contact as "unidentified"; why was that?"

"Too dark to see it," replied Flash, unnecessarily irritably. The stresses of 24 hours on duty were showing. "It really is black once you get clear of the ambient lighting on the coastline. Apart from the odd light from oil rigs or burn stacks, it's almost impossible to see another aircraft. Add to that the guy turned his lights off so there was no chance of a visual pick up."

"So you have no idea about what it might have been? Weren't you wearing night vision goggles?"

"It came from the northeast at low level. It had to be a light aircraft as it wasn't doing any more than about 180 knots, maybe slower. Probably a large single or maybe a light twin at that speed. What I can say is that he didn't want to be seen and he was really hard to track on the radar. He was flying lights-out and threw in some pretty aggressive evasion manoeuvres. The goggles have some limitations. It's not as straight forward as it might seem."

"Any idea of what he did after you intercepted him?"

"He coasted in about Aldeburgh on the Suffolk coast, at a guess. After that he could have gone anywhere. It's quite secluded around there but the town itself is well lit so it's a good navigation feature and an obvious coast-in point. If he was trying to avoid detection, the countryside in the vicinity is sparsely populated with the nature reserve at Orford Ness just to the south. With the airbases at Bentwaters and Woodbridge just inland, my guess is he'd have to head northwest or jink south into Essex. There was no moon worth talking about, so if he was going to land at an airfield at night he'd need someone to light up the strip for him. Without night vision goggles he couldn't land unaided."

"Did you follow him overland?"

"No, if we couldn't get him out over the sea there would have been no way to follow him overland at those speeds, even using night vision goggles," admitted Razor.

"Can you tell us what this is all about?" asked Flash, his eyes locked onto the policeman. There was a brief stand-off. Hawkes was adopting the same poker skills. No reaction, just a stony stare. He weighed up his response.

"I have credible evidence of a major plot against the Government. What I'm about to say must stay within these four walls."

His gaze shifted around the room, receiving tacit approval to continue, his audience transfixed.

"We have reason to believe a cell is directly targeting the Prime Minister and the weapon may be a shoulder launched, surface-to-air missile. If I'm right, you may have been within a few miles of both the weapon and the potential perpetrator."

The pause was loaded, allowing the implications to sink in.

"There's not much we can do on "Q" against a SAM threat in a Phantom, Chief Inspector. Surely that's down to the Army or The RAF

Regiment, to close down any potential launch site," fired back the Squadron Commander.

"That part is true but I wouldn't discount the possibility that you'll be involved in some way. I suspect we'll find out quite soon but only if we can piece together the jigsaw. If this thing is going off, it's already underway so we won't have long to wait. Let's just hope I can flush this woman out or she'll have an unopposed shot at the PM. God forbid. . . . ."

The knock at the door interrupted a gathering despondency.

"Sir, sorry to intrude."

The normally confident NCO wilted under the hostile scrutiny.

"Yes, Corporal Higgins, what is it?"

"Message for Mr Hawkes from his office Sir. He's needed back in London as soon as possible. The lady seemed quite insistent."

CHAPTER 31

The Officer's Married Quarters Patch, RAF Wattisham, later that day.

"What did you make of the discussion with the policeman?" Razor asked, swilling his beer, reflectively, around the heavy beer stein. Flash flipped a burger as he adjusted the air inlet on his Weber barbeque, tamping down the surging flames with water from a strategically placed bottle. The burgers and sausages sizzled on the open grill, rapidly approaching charred oblivion. On the lawn, Flash's wife Julie chatted, animatedly, with the latest of Razor's random conquests, a pretty blond from a local village, the topic anything but flying.

"I guess the risk has always been there, my old mate, but it's brutal when it's explained in such stark terms."

The revelation of the risk to the Prime Minister had caused both men to contemplate the moral dilemmas posed by their, sometimes, onerous duty. It was not a topic they considered every day. To an outsider, sitting alert with a Phantom armed to the teeth with its deadly load of air-to-air missiles, might seem glamorous. Reporters appeared frequently at the "Q Shed" armed with cameras fitted with enormous lenses, and the following day an article would appear in the press, glamorising random contacts with prowling Soviet bombers. Even the crews could be swept up with the publicity on occasion. Despite the hype, If called upon, the missiles, ostensibly for defensive purposes, might need to be used for a more sinister purpose.

"There's not much guidance in the books is there?" Razor countered. "I'm not sure how I'd react if it came to the crunch. Could I really do it? Could I shoot down an airliner full of people in cold blood and still live with myself? The fact it might be the PM just magnifies the problem."

The sausages joined the burgers on a plate as the hamburger buns dropped onto the grill to face the same charcoal inferno.

"You would, and you probably wouldn't even think about it at the time."

"I'm not an automaton Flash!"

"Nor me, but it wouldn't, actually, be our decision. If an airliner was declared "hostile", it would be someone on the ground that would be making that decision and you can bet that it would be a lot higher up the chain than the mate on the control console at Neatishead. They'd be making that decision based on way better information than we would have in the cockpit."

"Without a doubt. A decision condemning 300 people to an early death would be something that would reach the Prime Minister."

"It wouldn't be an easy decision. Glad it wouldn't be my call. I'm not sure I could live with that responsibility but I guess I'll never be the PM."

"That's for sure. It might make for an interesting exchange on the frequency, but that's nothing compared to the weight of responsibility for whoever needs to decide. It would condemn a lot of innocent people to a nasty demise."

Razor slugged the remnants of his pint and pulled another can from the cooler, recharging the stein.

"Think positive, it would be a joint decision," said Flash as he pulled a brace of singed buns from the flames.

"How do you figure that out? I'd have to pull the trigger," replied the sullen pilot.

"True but a Sidewinder, probably, wouldn't take down a big airliner and the gun is probably even less effective other than as a warning. It would need a Skyflash to do enough damage and that would mean a radar lock so we'd be in it together. We'd both be pulling the trigger."

"That doesn't make me feel a whole lot better."

The look on the navigator's face made it obvious that neither did the sentiment cheer him up either. They both knew that the recriminations, if it ever came to pass, would come later. As they carried the plates of food towards the patio table where the girls continued to chat, each adopted a forced air of joviality that neither felt.

Tomorrow was another day and they were back in the Shed for another stint of QRA. If events moved as fast as expected they might face their worst fears sooner than they imagined.

CHAPTER 32

Gerderath Village near RAF Wildenrath, the next morning.

The taxi drew up outside the anonymous German house and the driver busied himself waiting for his passenger. The front door opened and a trim blond waved briefly before disappearing back inside. A few minutes passed but he was indifferent to the wait. Although the meter was ticking, it was irrelevant as the real taxi driver was still at home, persuaded to start his shift late today. The number plates on the taxi were also fake and the nondescript VW Passat would not register on any known database. The driver's friends who had paid the man a visit yesterday could be very persuasive and the taxi driver, a Turkish gastarbeiter, was keen to stay on in his new home country. The discussion had been short and he had been well paid for his silence.

With a flurry of activity at the door, a young man emerged, his parents following. The father dressed in a blue military uniform exchanged a rather formal handshake before the mother wrapped her arms around the youth and smothered him in kisses. The exchange was inaudible to the driver but he took the cue to climb out and open the boot prompting the embarrassed youngster, dragging a small wheeled suitcase behind him, to head for the taxi. The driver relieved him of the case as he waved goodbye for a final time before climbing into the back of the cab. The cab had barely pulled away the door of the house before it closed and life returned to normal. Almost.

Gerderath was a remote village set in the forest and the taxi had barely begun its journey before the driver pulled into a small passing place behind a similar looking VW. Fumes emerging from the exhaust pipe were visible in the crisp morning air, as the engine idled silently. Apart from local residents there was little traffic out here and the spot was ideal for the driver's purposes. Two men emerged from the car ahead and moved quickly towards the waiting taxi. The rear door was pulled open and, protesting noisily, the youth was manhandled from the vehicle. A bundled rag stuffed into his mouth cut off the sounds of protest as a hood dropped over his head, his arms twisted roughly behind his back and secured with a large zip tie. Bundled forcibly towards the waiting car, his now mumbled objections were barely audible.

The young man who emerged from the back seat bore a striking resemblance to the youth whom he would replace and the similarity was no coincidence. Despite the fact he was German, his English accent was flawless and his cover expertly rehearsed. He would assume the identity of the serviceman's son without a problem. The youth, ostensibly, was taking a pre-arranged trip to visit his grandparents in the UK and had arranged to visit a couple of universities ready for his degree course next year. Those plans had just changed.

The taxi resumed its short journey to the nearby RAF base. In the back seat the imposter picked up the carry-on bag which had been left on the seat and placed a small radio inside. Günter Steinbach knew that the radio would have a key role to play later in the day.

CHAPTER 33

The Central Berlin Air Corridor.

The VC-10 airliner levelled at Flight Level 100 the maximum height allowed within the tightly controlled airspace to the west of Berlin. Three tentacles radiated from the capital city entering West German airspace in the area of Hamburg in the north, Hannover in the centre and Kassel in the south. A mere 20 miles wide the corridors operated under strict agreements between NATO and the Soviet Government allowing access by air to the isolated city. In a deliberate snub to the former belligerent, West German airlines were prohibited from flying into the ex-capital city.

The climb-out from the RAF airbase at Gatow in West Berlin had been uneventful. Checking in with Berlin Air Route Traffic Control Center, the refined British tones of the VC-10 Captain, Squadron Leader Frank Newman, enriched the frequency, befitting his role as a Captain on the "Shiny Fleet", as the prestigious Royal Air Force transport force was irreverently known within the Service.

"Ascot 4386 is level Flight Level 100, heading 270, Centre Route 2, estimating Elben at minute 32, Hotel Lima Zulu next," he intoned.

Once the white-liveried airliner passed over the Hehlingen VOR beacon, denoted by its three letter indicator code, they would be back in West German airspace and able to climb to a more fuel efficient cruising level for the flight back to London. Their progress was being tracked on radar but the surfeit of information was for the benefit of Soviet air controllers who mapped each and every flight along the corridors, comparing the flight path with details passed in the flight plan. Any deviations from the plan, or heaven forbid flying outside the corridor, would attract unwanted attention

It was not unknown for the Soviets to jam radio beacons using a technique known as meaconing. To ensure a smooth passage, the crew had been religiously comparing the inertial navigation data with the bearing from the VOR beacon. The co-pilot had, unusually, drawn out a pre-prepared low flying chart from his document pocket, carefully marked with the routes along each of the three corridors. He diligently thumbed along the map cross-checking progress against features on the ground. It had been some years since he had last used a low flying chart in the confined cockpit of a tiny Jet Provost trainer.

The MiG fighter, which unbeknown to the crew was rapidly closing on their track, had launched from the Soviet base at Mahlwinkel in East Germany some minutes before and, after clearing the air corridor to the south, had followed a lazy orbit and now tracked parallel to the southern limit just metres from the boundary. The Soviet fighter controller passed precise headings, heights and speeds to fly and the pilot of the Mig complied implicitly. He was not party to the hushed discussions which had gone on in the operations centre that morning, nor was he aware that his quarry, on which he was closing rapidly, carried the British Prime Minister. His task was precise. Intercept the airliner, remain clear of controlled airspace but make sure that his presence was evident to the crew onboard.

"Ascot 4386, you have a stranger, bearing 150, range five miles, closing, any contact?"

Newman peered from the side window of the cockpit but his view aft was limited and the glare from the bright blue background dazzled his eyes.

"Negative, 4386."

"Contact closing, shows same height, now range three miles, closing rapidly."

As he dragged the throttle back in response to the fighter controller's command, the Soviet pilot eased the MiG closer towards the shiny fuselage, the red, white and blue roundels just visible through his dark visor. He wished he could ease in closer but his brief had been specific. He was not to infringe the corridor under any circumstances.

He had flown into Berlin many times but this was the first time Newman had been intercepted and that could be the only reason for a track converging so rapidly. The presence of his VIP passenger down the back did little to calm his rising apprehension. As the controller continued to call the aggressor, the range tracking down inexorably, the pilot stared out from the cockpit window, his neck craned around. It was a most unfamiliar pose in the cockpit of a "Shiny Fleet" airliner. Suddenly, a silver shape hove-to alongside, separated by about a mile before it began slowly to drift in towards the VC-10. Tracking precisely down the centre of the corridor, it was obvious that the move was meant to intimidate. The MiG had to be inside the corridor.

The Soviet pilot settled down into loose formation cross checking the navigation data from his RSBN navigation system. At this speed he would be alongside for only a few more minutes before he was "hauled off". This was as close as he could go and already he was pushing it. When his track was plotted post flight, he would have some explaining to do. Nevertheless, penetrating West German airspace was an episode he was keen to avoid, having no wish to discuss his flight under those circumstances with members of the Soviet security services once he landed.

"Ascot 4386, Berlin Centre, I see you approaching the border, call me overhead Hotel Lima Zulu."

Newman glanced over his shoulder at the MiG that had been tracking his flight path. The swing wing fighter, readily identifiable as a MiG-23 Flogger Bravo, the air defence variant of the supersonic fighter, showed a distinctive planform as it peeled away. The manoeuvre had significance. Under the visual identification procedures promulgated to all airmen, it meant "you are clear to proceed". He could only speculate at the diplomatic repercussions had his progress been interfered with in any way. His VIP passenger was not used to being thwarted.

"Berlin Centre, Ascot 4386, willco, requesting further climb to Flight Level 290."

"Roger Ascot 4386, once overhead Hotel Lima Zulu start your climb and call me levelling."

Glasnost may have been blooming but Cold War tensions were not yet a thing of the past. In the cabin, the Prime Minister, oblivious to the tense atmosphere in the cockpit, leafed through today's "Red Box" which had been flown out aboard the VC-10 that morning, along with the morning newspapers. By the time she arrived at the door of Number 10 she would be fully briefed for her first appointment of the day.

As she glanced out of the oval cabin window she sipped her coffee from the bone china cup. The silver-liveried MiG fighter jet had stayed at a distance but just close enough to make out a red star on the tail fin. It was hard to identify the features from a distance but how kind of Mikhail to arrange an escort, she thought abstractly.

CHAPTER 34

The Flying Club, RAF Wattisham.

Ashworth pulled onto the active runway, a blind radio call alerting other pilots to his presence. Although air traffic control was manned for QRA, there would be no one in the tower at this ungodly hour. It had been his intention to depart before the first wave of Phantoms taxied for takeoff at 08.20 but he was a few minutes behind schedule. Discretion had been necessary to make sure he would not be seen as he had loaded his unorthodox payload.

His flight plan, seemingly innocent, was strapped to his kneeboard, showing a short leg to a minor airstrip in Essex, before pressing onwards through the heart of the London Control Zone to the former Battle of Britain fighter station at Biggin Hill. The route he had chosen was no accident as it would pass directly over yet another historic site, RAF Bentley Priory, the Headquarters of No. 11 Group, formerly known as Fighter Command and famous during the Second World War. The Officers' Mess was an iconic building on the North London skyline.

"Golf Alpha Sierra Oscar Echo, ready for departure."

The continued silence on the radio was no surprise and his calls were for information purposes only, should another pilot be transiting through the Wattisham Control Zone at this early hour. The first Phantoms of the day had yet to start engines. He dabbed the brakes bringing the Piper Warrior to a halt just beyond the cable that stretched across the runway. Designed to stop a Phantom in an emergency, the heavy steel cable, supported by rubber grommets, would easily rip the undercarriage from beneath the tiny airframe. Needing only a few hundred yards to get airborne, the vast expanse of asphalt that stretched ahead of him was a luxury. Running quickly through the pre takeoff checks, he ran the engine up to full power, checking the temperatures and pressures one final time. The engine responded perfectly and, releasing the brakes, he corrected the torque with rudder as the aircraft slowly picked up speed, the repetitive thump of the nosewheel on the recessed lights reverberating as he tracked down the centreline. The airspeed built rapidly and, at 65 knots, he eased the reluctant bird into the air, the runway falling away rapidly, the wings responding to the back pressure on the control yoke, dipping gently in the morning gusts.

"Golf Oscar Echo, airborne to departures."

His rendezvous with destiny was set and, by the end of the day, he would be notorious . . . . . in one way or another.

CHAPTER 35

The Movements Terminal, RAF Wildenrath.

Günter Steinbach felt isolated, surrounded, as he was, by hordes of military personnel, their blue uniforms a source of irritation. Using a civilian flight had been the preferred option but with heightened tension at the regional airports, mostly prompted by his own group's terrorist activity, security had been tightened and the metal detectors that had been installed in the airport security halls, lessened the opportunity to secrete explosives in his hand luggage. Less ostentatious, the security at the RAF base was geared more towards safeguarding military personnel and their families and offered an easier, albeit, taxing option. For him to adopt a temporary identity would rely on his ability to assume the persona of the young dependant who by now, would be enjoying a temporary respite in Erklenz. Within the group they had discussed ways to get a team of hijackers aboard the flight but had failed to come up with a viable plan. Eventually, Hammond had, reluctantly, agreed that Steinbach should attempt the hijacking alone. If he was honest, he would have preferred the help of others to assist in the seizure but he would have to resort to guile instead. He was alone. He hoped the package he had been promised had made it onboard.

Steinbach's motivations were deep rooted and, as a child, he had been captivated by pictures of three hijacked airliners at Dawson's Field in Jordan. Trumpeted in the West as terrorists, in his mind the flights had been detained by Palestinian freedom fighters who then made the ultimate statement to the world's media.

On 6 September 1970, Trans World Airlines Flight 741 from Frankfurt and Swissair Flight 100 from Zurich were forced to land at Dawson's Field where the passengers were held hostage. Later in the same day an attempt to hijack an Israeli flight operated by the National airline was foiled and one hijacker was shot and killed. Leila Khaled, a member of the Popular Front for the Liberation of Palestine, became famous overnight when, during the attack, Israeli sky marshals killed a colleague before, eventually, overpowering Khaled. She was subdued and handed over to the British authorities in London. The Boeing 707 and the Douglas DC-8 were instant attractions to a fascinated media unused to acts of terror. Pictures of the stranded airliners taken against the sandy backdrop of the Jordanian desert appeared on front pages across the world but the hijackers were not yet done. A Pan American Jumbo Jet was seized and flown first to Beirut and then to Cairo offering more headlines to the copywriters. On 9 September, a final airliner, British Overseas Airways Corporation Flight 775, a VC-10, from Bahrain, was hijacked by another terrorist and landed at Dawson's Field parking alongside the others. Seemingly related, the latest seizure had been intended to pressurise the British Government to free Khaled.

Many of the passengers were freed but the flight crews and a number of passengers were held hostage, specifically all the Jewish passengers and a number of American diplomats from the three flights. The standoff went on for six days before, fearing reprisals from increasingly desperate governments, the hijackers blew up the airliners. Captured on film by the assembled press, the airliners burned leaving charred hulks as a reminder that the Middle East crisis had entered a new phase.

By the end of the month, a rattled Jordanian Government agreed to an exchange of hostages leading to the freeing of Khaled and three co-conspirators from prison. Ostensibly a stalemate, the Popular Front for the Liberation of Palestine had struck a major blow and done so in a blaze of publicity.

The incident had been a formative time in Günter's life and an inspiration for his own statement to come. He steeled himself for the next phase, unconsciously touching the makeshift weapon that he had by now secreted in his waistband. Avoiding eye contact, he willed his frenetic thoughts to slow down. The security checks may be less rigid than at Düsseldorf but the staff were trained to watch for signs of nervous passengers, even if their motives might be more to ensure a calm flight than to thwart an attack.

He glanced around the lounge sizing up his fellow passengers assessing them as potential opponents. The majority were families, arranged in distinct groups on the garish bench seats. One or two stood out from the masses, their neat blazers and old school ties marking them out as officers. One had been in deep discussion with the duty movements officer and had, noticeably, been nominated as "Senior Passenger". With his handlebar moustache, Steinbach had him marked as an RAF fighter pilot from one of the RAF bases in the area. A few were athletic youngsters, well built and obviously fit so he would watch, carefully, as they boarded and hope that they were not seated in his immediate vicinity. Once he made his move, the last thing he needed was a futile intervention from a well intentioned airman.

The tannoy crackled into life, the movements officer announcing that boarding was about to begin. Like any other announcement at any civilian airfield around the world, the flight was called in seat rows and a few excited children tugged at their mother's clothing anxious for the adventure to begin. The fact that their adventure would turn sour was of little consequence to Steinbach. There were far greater forces in play than the nightmares of a few service brats. He watched as the first passengers made their way across the departures lounge to the exit, the ramp where the Boeing 737 waited, clearly visible beyond. As the door was pulled open, the intrusive noise of the auxiliary power unit rang through the lounge, quashing any further efforts at communication. A breeze blasted through the departure lounge prompting most of the assembled travellers to shiver a little, despite the heat.

The tannoy rang out again asking the next batch of passengers to board. A small line was already snaking across the tarmac towards the waiting airliner, heading for the passenger stairs tucked against the side of the fuselage. Busy groundcrew were preparing the flight for departure, plugging communications leads into umbilicals under the jet. Looking at his boarding pass, he waited for his seat row to be called, relaxing for the first time. The duty movements officer had fussed around him given that he had been nominated as an unaccompanied minor. The attention had been unwelcome although anticipated and, so far, his baby faced demeanour had stood him in good stead. The same man was now making a beeline for him, his manner edgy, an RAF Police corporal in tow just a few feet behind. The intense look and his furrowed brow did little to calm Steinbach's nerves. What could have gone wrong? Had he been compromised?

"Ryan Holmes? muttered the man, his eyes searching Steinbach's face, seemingly challenging the nervous German.

"Yes," he replied, apprehensively, scanning his surroundings, searching for an escape route. The main exit was blocked by a burly serviceman. There was no easy way out.

"You'll be boarding on the next call. I'll escort you out to the aircraft."

The relief was palpable. Fussing with his carry-on items, anxious to avoid further eye contact, he readied himself. His apprehension had been too obvious and he prayed that he had not given himself away. A nervous swipe mopped the sweat from his brow. He needed to be more confident when he made his move.

CHAPTER 36

Over Essex, en route London.

Ashworth tracked along the path of the A12 heading towards London, his groundspeed a steady 120 knots. The speed made his mental arithmetic easy covering the ground at a stately two miles a minute. The Cherokee Warrior had easily enough fuel to make Biggin Hill in one hop but he had balked at the thought of launching from Wattisham with his improvised device strapped beneath the light aircraft. Better to drop into a minor airstrip where prying eyes would be less likely to question his actions and where volunteers staffing the control tower were less attentive than the professionals at Wattisham. As it was, the place he had selected was even more discrete and there was no control tower.

His first stop would be at the airstrip attached to Sanctuary Farm just outside the village of Little Baddow. Lying just south of the A12, the tiny grass strip was ideal for his purposes. The farmer had been remarkably cooperative when he had called, the £5 landing fee an absolute bargain, and Ashworth had been delighted to know that the farmer had no intention of meeting him on landing. His own reassurances that he would not need fuel and that he would only be on the ground for ten minutes to drop off a parcel to a friend, had been met with cheery indifference. As he diverged from the reassuring scar of the dual carriageway, he peered ahead, searching for the lead-in features he had identified to set him up for the approach. The small village of Little Baddow was easily visible, the minor road running south into the village marking its presence. The farm was a mile east of the settlement and the landing strip ran east-west. Flanked by a wood to the west and surrounded by ploughed arable land, he hoped the strip would stand out easily. Sure enough, he passed directly overhead the grass strip adjacent to the farm and turned downwind. Checks complete he turned finals, throttling back, dropping the flaps and stabilising at approach speed plus ten knots. As he fine-tuned the finals turn he felt positively elated. The Warrior settled over the hedge and dropped onto the short strip, the airspeed indicator precisely on the numbers, the stall warner advertising its displeasure as the aircraft settled onto its undercarriage. But for his sinister mission, his flying instructor would have been proud of his efforts.

As anticipated, the makeshift airfield was eerily quiet as Ashworth taxied back to the upwind threshold of the strip before shutting down. He drew the Warrior to a halt and pulled on the parking brake, immediately chopping the engine. His instructor would have chided him for not running the engine lean for a few minutes to clear the plugs but he would be underway almost immediately and felt comfortable with the risk. Given the plan he had in mind, time on the ground was a luxury that he could ill afford. The alleged "friend" would never appear and his package would never be delivered and had a much more deadly purpose. The farmer may yet make the link with his mystery visitor if he watched the evening news but for now, he was simply an unwitting pawn in Ashworth's plan.

CHAPTER 37

Aboard Britannia Airways Flight Number 24 over The Netherlands.

As Steinbach readied himself for the challenge ahead, he glanced across the aisle, startled to see Clive Hammond, grinning across at him from the centre seat. How the Brit had managed to secure a place onboard was beyond Steinbach but he had clearly exercised some influence; maybe using his former status as a Royal Navy officer. However he had succeeded, it was irrelevant but, paradoxically, his smug expression somehow grated. Nevertheless, Steinbach could now use his co-conspirator's presence, and his considerable expertise, to advantage. There was, however, a nagging doubt that he was under inspection.

Stepping back through the contingency plans they had rehearsed, fortuitously they had considered using a team of two so his revised plan would need little adaptation. Throughout the rehearsals, Hammond had coached his every step so could slot into the support role with ease. This meant that when Steinbach made his move, he would have someone watching his back in the cabin covering against the potential for rebellion amongst the passengers or cabin crew. It was a reassuring back up.

Steinbach relaxed, waiting for the precise moment they had agreed.

As the airliner approached British airspace they would make their move.

*

Aboard the VC-10, some miles ahead, the Prime Minister nodded absently, as the military steward topped up her elegant coffee cup. She had a strange fondness for the old airliner, harking back as it did, to a lost age of elegance in passenger flight. It's fading glory was a fine advertisement for classic British engineering, designed and constructed at the Vickers Aircraft works at Weybridge in Surrey. Intended to operate in hot and high environments, its excess of power meant it still held a transatlantic speed record for crossing the Atlantic, only beaten eventually by the Concorde. Its classic sweeping lines and four rear mounted engines still turned heads at airports and it was, without doubt, one of the most distinctive passenger aircraft ever built.

The cabin today was far from the standard that ferried troops to distant parts of the world. Courtesy of "The Shiny Fleet", this flight was fitted with the "VIP pack", the seats comfortable leather armchairs, a far cry from the functional blue cousins that normally filled the cabin. If she had glanced out of the window, she would have noticed that the world was travelling by in the wrong direction. In a sop to flight safety, the RAF had mounted the seats facing backwards to improve survivability in the event of a crash. Entirely logical, it took some adjustment to the altered reality as bemused troops boarded the airliner. It was a nuance lost on the PM as she attacked her paperwork.

The "Red Box" contained the usual diet of official papers and briefings. The latest fighter project in the Ministry of Defence was causing concern, mired as it was in international politics. Years behind schedule, specifications for the equipment had still not been issued and, in their absence, work had slowed to a snail's pace. To make matters worse, not only was the Company delaying the project, the Germans, to meet their own political agenda, had decided to rebrand it as "Eurofighter 2000", slipping the in-service date by another 4 years by default. In justification, unintelligible descriptions of why this aircraft design was different had baffled her at the last meeting with her own Government officials. "Top Down", meaning that they were starting from what the aeroplane would have to do to meet its wartime role, meant that the components would be of a radically different design, with each black box providing many operational functions. It sounded sensible but the company had better start offering better value for money for the billions of tax payer funds being lavished on industry by the staff in the headquarters in Munich.

Whatever the scheming, she would call the Director of the Eurofighter project across to No. 10 again as soon as she was back in the office. It was time to apply some pressure and get the hugely expensive development back on track.

A weighty briefing on the latest round of negotiations to finalise the Conventional Armed Forces in Europe (CFE) Treaty, fell victim to her renowned ability to "speed read". It was the cornerstone of the policy to bring down the "Berlin Wall" and, if Gorbachev was to be persuaded, the initiative would have to offer him a visible prize. Intended to eliminate the Soviet Union's overwhelming numerical advantage in conventional weapons in Europe, it would set limits on the amount of tanks, armoured combat vehicles, heavy artillery, combat aircraft, and attack helicopters that NATO and the Warsaw Pact could deploy into the Central Region in the event of a conflict. The apparent neutralisation of the Soviet advantage was, in reality, advantageous to both sides. For too long, citizens on both sides of the artificial divide in the centre of Germany, had lived with "Tripwire" strategies that guaranteed mutual destruction. An apparent offensive from either military pact would see the first use of nuclear weapons on European soil in an inevitable defensive response. It was a strategy, as evidenced during Exercise "Able Archer" in 1984, that was unsustainable. The risks were simply too high.

The treaty, if agreed would come with stringent and unprecedented weapons limits and a robust inspection regime, which would provide an unparalleled degree of transparency in monitoring each side's military arsenal. Talks had been slow as she had just witnessed, with a cautious approach from both sides but there were signs that officials, who worked tirelessly in the background, were starting to make progress. A "bells and whistles" announcement was still some way off but a few reassuring noises would help. She would chat to the Press Secretary and see what could be done.

The briefing papers for her meeting later that morning with the Spanish Ambassador were last on her agenda. Admitted to the European Union in 1986, Spain and Portugal had swelled the numbers to twelve. Coming at the same time as the Single European Act was signed, providing the basis for a programme to sort out free-flow of trade across European borders, the move would create what was known as the "Single Market". With her renowned love of free trade, it was a radical prize that would offset the increasingly, busy-body approach from the bureaucrats in Brussels. That said, Spain and Portugal were vastly different economies to the major EU contributors and it would be a challenge to integrate them into the infrastructure. She hoped that their admission would not create more tensions in the financial markets as a run on the Pound was the last thing she wanted to be tackling. It was timely to have a chat, as the Spanish partners had joined the Eurofighter project and were useful allies despite the tensions over Gibraltar. French and German dominance in Brussels could be tedious at times and some careful lobbying might gain useful traction with the new member. The military coup in 1981 had been quashed and Spain had entered a more stable, democratic era, with the King acting as a bridge over his country's political factions. Support from other European nations to aid his efforts was extremely important. She would extend an invitation to the King and Queen of Spain to make a Royal visit. There was nothing like a little pomp and ceremony to curry favour.

The rest of the papers were deposited, unceremoniously, back into the Red Box and the lid snapped shut. A warm, inviting plate of food was placed in front of her, the steward fussing with the cutlery, the enticing smell of the great British breakfast assailing her nostrils. It was an indulgence but one that she would happily give in to on this occasion. Let the EU ever try to take away her back bacon and Lincolnshire sausages she vowed. Now, as a resident of Grantham, that would provoke a firm response from the Iron lady!

"Prime Minister, ladies and gentlemen, this is the Captain. We will shortly be commencing our descent into London Heathrow. The weather in London is set fair with blue skies and light winds. Traffic in the holding pattern is building up but I will ensure that we are given priority to begin our approach. In the meantime, enjoy the breakfast service and I'll speak to you again before we touchdown. I estimate we should be on the ground at Heathrow in 35 minutes."

The Prime Minister enjoyed a rare moment of relaxation as she gazed out over the white wing that stretched out towards the blue horizon.

CHAPTER 38

New Scotland Yard, London.

"Is that Chief Inspector Hawkes?"

"Speaking."

"Sir, Detective Miller here from the London Traffic Security Coordination Centre. I understand you have a tracking request on a black VW Golf, registration number . . . . ."

She rattled off the number plate that already was ingrained in his mind. His breathing slowed.

"Yes; you've had a sighting?"

"Yes Sir. It was seen 20 minutes ago on a camera on the M4 near Hammersmith. We have pretty good coverage on that route because it heads out towards Heathrow Airport. The car was stationary in heavy traffic because of an accident on the carriageway and at the minute nothing is moving. Once the traffic clears, if Heathrow is its destination, it'll take about 20 minutes to reach the terminals."

"Do you have a helicopter in the area? Any chance you can get surveillance on it?"

"We do Sir but there's no way to get a car anywhere close to it. The hard shoulder is blocked with a broken down lorry. Nothing's moving. With this mess the timings are up in the air."

She giggled at the weak joke.

"What authorisation do you need?" he asked, cursing at the thought of paperwork stopping him getting to his prime target when he was this close. "Trust me, this is about as high a priority as it gets."

"Nothing Sir, the helo is already on task monitoring the snarl-up and I can ask it to keep a watch on the vehicle for you."

"You're an angel," he almost shouted as the line went quiet for a moment.

"Thanks Sir," she replied, almost gushing. "Consider it done."

"I'm getting in my car now and heading out that way. What's the best way to avoid the congestion?"

She rattled off a string of road numbers all of which were familiar to the London cop as he mapped the route in his mind's eye. He prayed for once that the accident was slow to clear.

"I'll get to the junction at Brentford and sit on the slip road and check in on the local traffic police frequency once I'm there. Can you update me on the vehicle's progress via that frequency?"

"Will do Sir and hope you get to chat with the driver."

"Oh so do I," replied Hawkes as he dropped the phone back in the cradle and bolted for the door.

CHAPTER 39

Sanctuary Farm, Little Baddow, Essex.

Ashworth took in his surroundings hoping that his research had been accurate and the makeshift airfield really was deserted. Satisfied that he was alone, the fasteners on the rear luggage compartment unsnapped easily and he pulled open the small door, removing a number of items. From a small tool chest, he extracted an electric drill and snapped the battery into place on the handle. Placing a paper template against the airframe under the wing, marking each position with a pen, he carefully drilled a series of holes into the thin metal skin. Crawling out from underneath the Cherokee, he delved back into the luggage compartment and withdrew a long metal rack that he had fashioned in his workshop at home. Within minutes, self-tapping screws secured the contraption to the structure and he had a makeshift bomb rack hanging below the wing. A lanyard attached to a shackle provided a simple release mechanism. He tugged firmly a couple of times watching the jaws on the rack snap open and closed. It was rudimentary but it worked.

Only now did he pause to consider that the Cessna 152 at the flying club might have been a better choice. With its high wing, the bomb rack would have been easily visible from the cockpit and the lanyard would have routed directly to his position at the controls. As it was, fitted under the low wing of the Cherokee Warrior, the rack would be invisible from his seat and he would have to route the lanyard around the leading edge and through the small access hatch into the cockpit. Hopefully, the circuitous routing would still allow the jaws to operate freely. He cursed himself for his lack of attention to detail but there was nothing he could do to change it at this point.

The next item was somewhat more delicate and he was much more careful with the contents of the final box. Lifting the lid, he looked almost lovingly at his creation. The snub-nosed warhead lay on the cradle, the crudely fashioned nose cone and fins vaguely reminiscent of a First World War bomb. The contents and technology in this payload, however, were decidedly 20th Century.

Crawling back underneath the wing, he offered up the device to the rack and gently withdrew a spring clip forcing the resistant jaws apart. The device slotted neatly into place and hung menacingly below the wing. Should he do one final test now that it was fitted? The risks whirled in his mind as he contemplated his handiwork. The extensive testing in his workshop should have been enough but, erring on the side of caution, he opted for one last check.

The device dropped rapidly into his hand and he was, momentarily, surprised by its weight as his elbow twisted under the strain. The device skewed crazily and he thought that it would fall from his grasp. If it detonated the deadly shards from the expanding rod warhead would rip into him. Any thoughts of an onward trip to London would be moot and, at best, he would face an onward trip in an ambulance.

The device wobbled ominously before stabilising precariously in his palm.

As he clipped it back into place on the rack he became aware of the beads of sweat that had formed on his brow and the sigh of relief was earnest. He had not yet withdrawn the arming pin and there could have been no way the device would have exploded but logic was sometimes outweighed by predicament. Had he thought more rationally, it would have been apparent that the simple safe and arm mechanism he had designed, required the device to separate from the aircraft before it was primed for detonation. His apocalyptic thoughts had been wasted.

With the device safely attached to the bomb rack he dropped heavily onto the grass and breathed deeply. He would have to be more rational over the next hour.

As he loaded his tools back onboard, he hoped his carefully designed, albeit jury rigged system, was up to the task. His long planned goal depended on it.

CHAPTER 40

Aboard Britannia Airways Flight Number 24 over Belgium.

Steinbach glanced across the aisle at Hammond who nodded briefly. He still had no idea how his accomplice had managed to secure a seat on an RAF Trooping flight but it was immaterial at this stage. All he needed to know was that he had back-up. His brow furrowed nervously as he rose from the seat, making polite excuses to the elderly woman who had set out her stall in the aisle seat. Why was he being so polite when he was about to do something that would shatter her very existence?

As he stretched his legs in the aisle, free of the restrictions of the narrow confines of the tightly packed seats in Economy Class, he took in his surroundings. In his peripheral vision he could see his co-conspirator watching him as he made his way towards the forward galley where a knot of cabin crew had gathered. As he approached, a burly but obviously gay, male steward barred his way. He suppressed his inbred homophobia. He had hoped for a female stewardess but, despite his girth, the man was hardly intimidating and posed little threat. He suddenly hoped his attractive, youthful looks might be something he could turn to his advantage but he was to be disappointed. The man's demeanour suggested confrontation not compliance. No matter, brains not brawn would prevail.

"Sir, I must ask you to return to your seat. We're about to start the meal service and I must insist on the aisles being clear."

The belligerent attitude made his task easier. He pushed his hand into his jacket pocket, gripping the butt of the makeshift pistol he had secreted into his carry-on bag, lifting it out just enough to allow the man to see it. There had been another reason to avoid metal detectors. The firing pin was metallic which had meant he had not had to reassemble a fiddly firing pin.

"Please remain calm," he instructed. "This is not a drill and, hopefully, you'll be smart enough to follow my instructions. To the letter!"

The act of menace was explicit, his piercing look daring the female stewardess to react. Her gaze faltered and she responded in fear.

"Don't touch anything. If I have any suggestion that you are trying to alert the flight deck crew I will instruct my friend in the cabin to detonate a device in my checked baggage in the hold. He is also armed by the way."

The look of confusion in the steward's eyes was telling. He looked down the cabin but failed to register anything amiss. Steinbach held his gaze, inscrutably, and he capitulated immediately. The first psychological barrier had been broken.

"When I tell you, and not before, I want you to call the flight deck and tell the Captain his meal is ready. I know you feed them separately so don't try to be clever. When the door opens, stand aside or I will shoot you. And if you think I won't, this gun is loaded with low velocity rounds modified to break up on impact. They will cause massive injuries, from which you would probably not survive, but they will not puncture the aircraft skin. If you'd care to prove my theory, please try. I will shoot without warning"

His cultured English accent gone, replaced by a guttural German accent that magnified the threat, any pretence at being the son of an RAF corporal was over.

What the cabin crew would not know until much later was that the gun, that was proving so intimidating, was a plastic facsimile. The breech mechanism and trigger were real enough and may have registered on a scanner but the tiny projectile that would emerge from the barrel would cause a nasty bruise but little else. The gun was by no means lethal. They had decided that even the rudimentary scanners at RAF Wildenrath would have picked up a real weapon and the risk of rupturing the delicate skin of the airliner was too great. It was a means to an end; a way to intimidate and to secure access to the cockpit. It need not be deadly assuming the cabin crew were reluctant to test his mettle.

"Is the meal ready?"

He received a confirmatory nod from the male steward. His colleague had gone deathly pale and tottered slightly, bracing herself against the coffee machine, blanching at the effect of the hot surface. It brought her immediately back to the present. The male steward picked up the intercom, his words measured but innocent and the hijacker heard the door locks on the cockpit door click open.

As he began to move forward he spoke quietly; his tone menacing.

"Don't do anything stupid. That will make my colleague nervous and, remember, he has a detonator in his pocket."

The warning was a ruse. The real trigger was nestling snugly in his own pocket and would accompany him into the cockpit where it would be unassailable.

He abandoned Hammond to his own fate and stepped forward.

CHAPTER 41

On the M4 Motorway, West of London.

Hawkes gunned the powerful 4.2 litre engine of the unmarked Jaguar XJ6 saloon. The car was more normally to be found in the diplomatic car pool ferrying Government ministers to and from important meetings. It had been the only vehicle that gave the remotest possibility of getting ahead of his quarry before she arrived at Heathrow, or wherever her plans dictated. Hawkes had gladly accepted it, fearing that he might have faced another trip in the dismal Ford Escort.

The blue lights pulsed behind the grille at the front of the car, prompting the majority of drivers, stuttering along the traffic-packed road, another daily commute well underway, to pull over hurriedly. The way ahead cleared momentarily, the traffic still mercifully light but there was always one dumb driver to provide a distraction. A few cars ahead, resplendent in a flat cap, his head pinned rigidly ahead on his shoulders, the man dominated the centre lane as he approached a set of traffic lights. Seemingly out of control, the car drifted drunkenly, straddling the two lanes, blocking progress. Hawkes cursed loudly willing the man to move over, switching on the siren as he bore down on the hapless motorist.

Nothing. No reaction whatsoever.

The tiny, town car remained stubbornly in position straddling the white line, forcing Hawkes to screech to a stop. The wail from the siren apparently having no effect, prompted foul curses but the head of the dim-witted driver ahead remained stubbornly immobile.

Hawkes invented a few more curses, hauling the wheel over, almost ripping the wheel from the steering column, moving the big Jaguar into the oncoming lane. More astute, the driver of a car heading in the opposite direction moved instantly to the side, mounting the kerb and leaving the way ahead clear. Hawkes pulled around the errant driver shaking a fist as he passed, the blue lights and siren blasting out, the miscreant still blissfully unaware of his blunder.

Progress resumed, Hawkes eavesdropped as the radio sparked into life, the driver of a patrol car reporting in with a visual sighting of the target vehicle. The dispatcher, quick off the mark, urged caution, the instructions to monitor but not to apprehend. It was precisely the directive Hawkes would have given had he been able to fathom the array of dials and switches on the handset. It was only a matter of time until the knots of tension rose again, prompting the familiar twinge from his incipient stomach ulcer. It would bite back later.

Only five minutes to the rendezvous point.

CHAPTER 42

Sanctuary Farm, Little Baddow, Essex.

John Hargreaves slowed to a stop and switched off the engine. He glanced back at the razor sharp furrows the plough had drawn up behind him, admiring his work. The new GPS technology that had been proudly displayed at the Suffolk Show looked promising and, if the reports were to be believed, before long, satellites in the heavens would be guiding the tractor to make sure that the ploughing was precise. Despite technology, he thought, smugly, that he could match any electronic gizmo as his trophy cabinet proved.

The noise of a light aircraft cut the still, morning air preceding a Piper Warrior that emerged over the hedge, climbing out from the farm strip. It must be the young man who had called from the flying club at the RAF station over the county border. A nice chap, he mused. Hargreaves was an enthusiastic advocate of the armed services and had only asked for a few quid to allow the lad to land at the farm strip. He did not need to make a profit but the small donation would keep the vicar happy. The church roof needed fixing again and the odd landing fee found its way into the church's roof fund.

The tiny craft banked gently, passing almost directly overhead, the engine at full throttle, clawing for height. Offering its belly, the pilot was hidden from view but Hargreaves, a qualified private pilot himself, knew precisely what would be going on in the cockpit. He had not asked where the lad was heading to after his drop-off but he had been delivering a package to a friend he had said. Funny, but there had been no cars passing along the lane. It would be impossible for a car to approach the airstrip without being seen from the fields. Very odd.

He took another look at the underside of the plane as it climbed away, something striking him as out of the ordinary. The small appendage that hung beneath the wing was outlined against the sky as the aircraft receded into the distance. If he didn't know better he would have thought it was carrying a bomb but it was a Cherokee.

Very strange he thought as he fired up the tractor again and began to cut the next furrow.

*

Safely airborne and established once again alongside the A12, Ashworth flew steadily onwards towards the Capital. His plan to deliver his payload against the old headquarters building at Bentley Priory would mean routing northwards quite soon. Keeping the navigation simple, he would follow the route of the M25 that would lead him effortlessly, albeit in a roundabout fashion, to his destination near Watford. An alternative began to form in his mind that would require even less effort to achieve. He had an even more high profile alternative that would certainly attract national headlines. He looked down at the map on his kneeboard, his mind making a few silent calculations.

*

Hargreaves pulled into the yard, closed down and walked, briskly, into the kitchen. Rifling amongst the scribbled notes strewn across the telephone stand, he looked for the particulars of a recent contact. He had spoken to a detective a few weeks ago when his red diesel storage tank had been raided and the thieves had got away with nearly 500 gallons. That had set him back a pretty penny. He doubted the police would ever catch the offenders but he was damned if he was going to let it slip by unreported. The detective had been really quite helpful despite the comparative insignificance of the crime. Baddow Farm was not the only one to have been targeted in the district so the more people who reported these minor thefts to the authorities, the more chance the gang might be caught at it. At some stage they would make a mistake. There it was. . . . .

He picked up the phone and dialled the Colchester number, the ringtone barely registering before the detective picked up. Exchanging the usual pleasantries he outlined the sequence of events.

"Probably nothing but I'm sure you would want to know," he rationalised, the hush at the other end of the line suggesting otherwise.

"Do you need any more details?"

"What was the registration?" the obviously harassed detective responded, his tone subtly suggesting that it was a waste of valuable police time even to file a report. He scribbled down the details as he spoke.

"I'm sorry Mister Hargreaves but I need to rush. I have another case that I have to follow up and I'm going to have to go now. Why is this really worrying you?"

"Listen, I'm reasonably attentive when I'm ploughing. Not much else to keep me busy, drawing lines in a field. Here's the thing. I'm sure I saw something hanging under the wing and I know enough about aeroplanes to know that a Piper Warrior shouldn't be carrying anything that looked like that. I'd say there's some mischief afoot."

As he replaced the handset, he hoped his caution was warranted. He'd seemed like such a nice chap, the young pilot.

CHAPTER 43

Aboard Britannia Airways Flight Number 24.

As the stranger entered the cockpit, the Captain was left with no viable alternative other than to accept that his aircraft had been compromised. He cursed the cabin crew for their lapse. Security protocol stated, explicitly, that the cockpit door should never be opened under duress. Better the bluff be called and the hijacker contained in the cabin than to lose control of the airliner. It was too late now.

His hand moved down instantly to the IFF box on the centre console, flicking the digits on the selector to 7600, the universal squawk signifying a hijack. Instantly, alarm bells began ringing in every air traffic control centre within range of the electronic box.

Over the Captain's shoulder, Steinbach gripped the seat back steadying himself in case the Captain was foolish enough to try to manoeuvre the airliner to dislodge him. He instantly spotted the selection which he had been warned to watch for. His first action was to reach down and select the mode switch to standby, cancelling the warning squawk. Not only had the emergency warning been silenced but the action prevented the IFF box from communicating at all. From now on, the ground agencies would be relying on a response from a primary radar system rather than the electronic challenge and response offered by the secondary radar system. It would make their subsequent movements much harder to track leaving the civilian air traffic control agencies powerless. Had the electronic warning been seen?

His next words were measured.

"Captain, I have assumed command of this aircraft on behalf of the Red Army Faction. I intend to make a statement to your Government that will be hard to ignore."

"You realise that you will not succeed, do you not?"

The Captain maintained a steady scan across the instruments, shielding his eyes from the bright light outside. He sounded pompous even to himself but he accepted that his options were extremely limited.

"Leave me to be the judge of that Captain," replied the terrorist, ominously.

"The Government does not negotiate with terrorists so your actions are irrelevant."

"Again, leave me to decide on whether that is germane."

"What are your demands?"

"In the first instance, I want a headset with a transmit function and then you will find out soon enough, along with the rest of your countrymen. You should know I am armed and there is an explosive device in the hold which I will not hesitate to use if necessary. I have the trigger in my pocket and a colleague in the cabin has an equivalent device which will be used should he detect anything untoward. Please be under no illusions that we are prepared to die for the cause if you fail to comply with instructions."

The First Officer reluctantly pulled out a headset and passed it to the interloper. The gun trained at his head ensured obedience, at least for the moment.

CHAPTER 44

The Air Defence Operations Centre, Headquarters Strike Command, RAF High Wycombe, Buckinghamshire.

The Duty Air Defence Commander, Wing Commander Phil Boyd, glanced at the master tote on the wall, an almost identical copy of the display that the Master Controller at Neatishead would be using. An experienced aviator, Boyd's flying career had ended when a medical condition prevented him from flying on "bang seats", as the Martin Baker ejection seats were fondly known. Rather than transfer to the comfortable cockpit of a transport aircraft such as the VC-10, he had elected instead to remain in the air defence arena and had transferred to the Fighter Control Branch.

His rank elevated him to the lofty heights of command and he had spent much of his recent working life in the darkened Command bunker at Headquarters Strike Command. Spending much of his time in the darkened, subterranean control room, rather than the cockpit of a Lightning fighter, he often questioned the wisdom of his decision. Around him, he had so called experts to assist. Meant to fill in his lack of knowledge of how the parts of the integrated air defence system fitted together, he often questioned their expertise. None of them had experienced the cockpit environment and often asked the pilots and navigators to attempt the impossible in the air. He was certain that few would understand the pressures that the aircrew faced in making decisions in the ruthless airborne environment. Technicians on the ops floor made sure the complex display totes worked correctly. Controllers who interacted with the sector operations centres and the wing operations officers, made sure he had assets, the buzz word for people and machines, to scramble if the need arose. Today, however, he felt isolated and, given the rapidly unfolding turn of events, he was uncharacteristically hesitant.

Used to leading a formation of Lightning fighters into the merge, his tactical air picture, despite the rudimentary radar in the Lightning, was second to none. More importantly, as a former fighter pilot, he had the fundamental skills to think in three dimensions, unlike some of his ground-based brethren in the fighter control world. Despite his skills and experience, he was struggling with the developing air situation.

His day had begun badly with the bombshell delivered at the morning intelligence briefing from the Air Intelligence Officer. He still found it hard to believe that there could be a threat to the Prime Minister from some obscure terrorist cell based in West Germany. What could possibly be their motives for expanding their campaign outside the German border? Whilst he recognised that attacks on American servicemen in Germany could be justified as a throwback against the "occupying power", to threaten a Head of Government in such a blatant manner was, in his mind, a step too far. It was madness. No doubt, if they succeeded, they would be hunted down mercilessly but, by then, the damage would have been done. Allowed to succeed, their actions would shake the establishment at its core. The analyst who had delivered the briefing, the dull monotone barely doing justice to the content, had made it clear that there was current and credible evidence of a plot to bring down the PM's plane. Intelligence officers did not make such firm claims without strong evidence. Whilst his delivery might have left a lot to be desired, there could be no doubt that his sources would be impeccable and highly believable. Boyd knew that the officer was read-in to information of the highest calibre, collected by people and systems that would never be made public. To do so would compromise the sources and that was anathema in the intelligence community. He satisfied himself that what was unfolding was based on strong evidence.

Given the potential risk to the PM, Boyd had considered providing a close escort for the VC-10 once it re-entered UK airspace but to what end? There could be no fighter threat to the transport once safely back over British territory. Only Nation states operated fighter aircraft or naval vessels able to deploy offensive missiles. The presence of a fighter alongside, whilst reassuring for the VIP passenger, would add little extra security.

In his mind, logic dictated that there could be no risk of a bomb onboard as the security at the airbase at Gatow would have been watertight. A quick check had confirmed that the VC-10 had been refuelled in UK for a return trip and that food and beverages had been loaded for both legs at RAF Brize Norton so nothing would be allowed onboard during the turnround in Germany. The RAF technicians who carried out the post and pre-flight servicing were above suspicion and local civilians had been, specifically, excluded from the dispersal where the jet had been serviced between flights. The crew would have stayed onboard restricting access to a minimum. It was established procedure. The process was watertight providing everyone followed protocol.

Boyd was unaware that his day was about to become even more bewildering. Overhead Mike Charlie Six, a reporting point on the Flight Information Region boundary over the Southern North Sea, a Britannia Airways Boeing 737 crossed into British airspace. Its brief passage across the reporting point unremarkable, the non-event was marked by the clipped tones of the Captain announcing the transition to his air traffic controller. Today there would be no jaunty announcement welcoming his passengers home to UK waters because, onboard, a tense standoff had ensued, the numbers in the cockpit swelled by the presence of interlopers. So far, their intentions were unclear but trepidation amongst the crew was rising. Boyd's first clue was brief jangling of the alarm bells in the operations room. The alarms were only triggered under specific circumstances such as a "Mayday" call or receipt of the electronic signals denoting a hijack or an emergency. His gaze slewed around to the tote.

Many miles ahead, the VC-10 carrying the British Prime Minister began a slow descent to lower altitude. Boyd was about to be tested to the limit.

CHAPTER 45

The Outer Suburbs, East London.

The pencilled track on Ashworth's flying chart moved off at a tangent skirting the London Control Zone to the north, routing over the famous Fighter Command Headquarters near Stanmore to the north of the Capital. There was an easier way to thread through the controlled airspace, by heading direct across the centre of the city through a narrow height window between overlapping zones but it was fraught with risk. Whilst it looked impenetrable on a chart with different sectors of controlled airspace overlapping laterally, when viewed in three dimensions, small height gaps were evident between the adjacent zones. That said, one slip in setting the altimeter and he would infringe at least one zone and air traffic controllers were notoriously unforgiving of transgressors. In planning the trip, he had opted instead, to skirt around the busy airspace keeping lateral separation. In reality, Biggin Hill had never been his primary destination, the line on the map more a subterfuge had his flight been scrutinised by anyone in authority at the Flying Club. What was more important was his interim waypoint. The Chief Flying Instructor was an ornery old man and arguments with him were rarely won. Luckily, the early departure had avoided a risk of intervention. The explosive device hanging under the wing was a further statement of intent, yet he would not achieve his goal by releasing it over a former Battle of Britain fighter station, no matter what its heritage. That would merely alienate his intended target audience in the military. His real target had to be much more prominent and he had a much better option. Striking at the leadership would make his peers sit up and listen. His name would be mentioned in the corridors of power, even if it cost him a spell in Colchester jail.

It was then that a fundamental flaw, which he should have noticed during his planning, suddenly became glaringly obvious. If he was to make a blatant demonstration, and his chances of avoiding retribution were limited, why not go the whole way?

Drawing a new track on the map, the line not quite true given the cramped cockpit conditions, a better option became clear. Estimating a rough heading to his new target, he scribbled the figures onto the chart using a chinagraph grease pencil. It was all very rough and ready but accuracy at this stage was not essential. The feature he had in mind stood out distinctly from its surroundings and he would have no trouble identifying the lead-in features. He studied the surrounding topography on the new track, committing them to memory. Hopefully, the next time he saw them in glorious technicolour rather than as flat features on a chart, he would be close to his goal.

What he would do after he had delivered his deadly payload would depend on conditions at the time. It may be that heading for Biggin Hill after all would give him some thinking time. In the confusion following his attack, he may be able to lose himself amongst the ground clutter of the suburbs. If he could land at a less populous airfield, he might be able to ditch the Warrior and make his escape. He would see.

Decision taken he picked up the new heading. Fifteen minutes to the target.

CHAPTER 46

The Sector Operations Centre, RAF Neatishead, Norfolk.

Like Wing Commander Boyd, Flight Lieutenant Jim Dewar was
struggling to understand the tactical situation. The tote in front of him on
the floor of the Sector Operations Centre was puzzling and unlike anything
he had ever experienced in any of the synthetic training exercises his Bosses
were so fond of. Why was this happening on his watch? Newly qualified as
a Master Controller, he had been thrown into the mêlée without warning
and it was only a question of time before the Duty Air Defence
Commander at Strike Command would be on his case. He needed to be
certain of his analysis of the air situation before recommending a course of
action. There would be only one shot at this. His first response had been to
pull out the classified "noddy guide" containing the plethora of contingency
plans, carefully pre-scripted for every eventuality. A hijack was right at the
top of the list of possibilities; a scourge of the times.

Britannia Flight 24 was tracking steadily, its electronic tag moving
systematically along the airway, closing on the Kent coastline. Due to land
at Luton airport, ostensibly a routine trooper flight from Wildenrath in
West Germany bringing service families home to UK, that it should be
hijacked seemed unthinkable. He hypothesised, ineffectually, over a
possible reason. Was it a false alarm? The 76 identification code had been
transmitted only briefly and then stopped. Could it be a disaffected
serviceman who had taken the law into his own hands or was it something
more sinister?

Speculation was useless and in the meanwhile, the absence of chatter on
the air traffic frequency was a good sign. He had asked for an update from
London Control but, so far, nothing. Let's hope the situation would be

resolved without drama and they would joke about it in the bar later when the facts emerged.

Suddenly a tag on the tote left nothing to the imagination. Even though the squawk had illuminated only briefly, a red symbol had been allocated to the Britannia flight by the civilian air traffic controller denoting a hijack in progress. A new call on the direct line to the London Centre controller at West Drayton alerted him to the developing situation. He was still coordinating the incident and so far, there had been no contact with the airliner but his first action had been to alert QRA and get a Phantom airborne. As soon as the crew came on frequency he, Jim Dewar, would be in the hot seat as he manoeuvred the fighter into close formation on the hijacked airliner. As the decision maker in the military Sector Operations Centre, it would fall to him to deal with such a crisis. The Master Controller might intervene but the civilian authorities lacked the primary radar coverage to track the airliner in the absence of a secondary radar return. Although fine in theory, his long range sensors were trained over the North Sea, configured to counter a Soviet attack. They were not optimised to track airliners over Kent. Furthermore, if deadly force was needed, he alone had the necessary communications to deal efficiently with the matter. Such decisions in peacetime were way up the food chain and fell to politicians not military men. Even so, launching QRA, as a precaution and of his own volition, had seemed a sensible idea.

The timing could not have been worse with the PM's VC-10 transiting his airspace but at least it was starting its descent into Heathrow. Normally, a VIP movement would have deserved his exclusive attention but suddenly, the priorities had changed. He wondered, idly, whether the PM was in the decision chain, because if not, her deputy in Whitehall was about to earn his keep.

"Neatishead, Mission 01."

"Mission 01, Neatishead, loud and clear, standby."

He stabbed the comms button for the direct line to the civilian agency.

"Drayton, Neatishead, QRA is on frequency, send Britannia 24 across to Fighter Stud 45. Break, break." He did not wait for a response.

"Mission 01 Neatishead, check your state," he barked, adrenaline flooding his system, the familiar buzz of the chase heightening every one of his senses.

"Neatishead, Mission 01, Charlie Four, Four Plus Eight, Tiger Fast 60," responded the clipped voice of the Phantom pilot over the radio frequency.

The Phantom was armed with four Skyflash, four Sidewinder air-to-air missiles and a fully loaded gun pod and, thank goodness, the sometimes unpredictable AWG12 radar was working. All options were open.
Hopefully, the "tiger fast" call was redundant, denoting the fighter's ability to fly a supersonic intercept profile. If it came to that, a supersonic intercept

over London was the least of his worries. Or was it? He could only imagine the carnage a supersonic shock wave would wreak over the Capital.

The Boeing tracked, inexorably, westwards closing on the outer reaches of the Capital. So far it was following its flight plan, but the point at which it should veer north towards its destination was rapidly approaching. If it failed to turn, the short leg beyond the reporting point stretched directly into the centre of London. It had been only a few months since his training course to become a Master Controller. One of the scenarios had been an apocalyptic attack on the Capital and, with a chilling resonance, an airliner had been taken over and used as a missile to attack the Houses of Parliament, the intent of the hijackers being to raze the seat of democracy to the ground. The parallels with the developing situation were not lost on him.

The airliner had been cleared to descend to 10,000 feet and the tiny numerals on his radar scope wound down slowly as it approached its cleared height. Decision time was approaching.

The buzzer, announcing an incoming call, sounded on his console. The Air Defence Commander. He steeled himself for the discussion ahead.

CHAPTER 47

Chiswick High Road, London.

Brandt dipped the clutch as the light turned red and coasted to a stop at the traffic lights. With the recognition of the enormity of her mission building, her mind was crammed with haphazard thoughts. She chided herself at her lack of concentration, trying to stay focussed on the task ahead. Now was not the time to weaken.

Looking at her reflection in the rear view mirror, she wondered at the path she had followed to this moment in time. None of the bystanders who threaded their way across the pedestrian crossing in front of her, could have an inkling of her mission or, indeed her motivation. As a German national she looked identical to any of the white Caucasians around her who were going about their daily rituals. It was her radicalism that set her apart; her willingness to take innocent life to further her cause. How had she got to this point?

Her family life had been unremarkable and neither of her parents could have been accused of extremism. they were fine, upstanding, respectable citizens, albeit blighted by the stresses of post-war West Germany. They went to church on Sunday, brushed the pathways, kept the windows clean. They were loyal denizens of society. Her defining chapter had been her spell at Dortmund University where she had been swayed by the militant views of her fellow students. Once she had been awarded her undistinguished degree, dropping into the comfortable but tenacious activist cell in Erklenz had seemed as natural as breathing. Even so, she would struggle to identify the point at which idealism had turned to terrorism because that, demonstrably, was the course she had now set herself.

There had been about a dozen members of the group, split equally between the sexes. It could hardly be described as a cosy alliance and the competition had been relentless. It was just how it was; maybe that explained it? Was she simply seeking to outclass the others? Was she that shallow? Was the event she was now embarked upon, merely a way to establish her place in the hierarchy? Maybe she had a secret apprehension that if she failed to outshine her peers, she would mysteriously disappear into the background noise? There were certainly no "ex" members of the Red Army Faction. The only way out seemed to be martyrdom and she had no desires on that score.

The harsh blaring of a car horn behind broke her train of thoughts and she realised that the traffic light had turned green. How long had she been brooding? A glance in the mirror at the belligerent motorist behind prompted darker thoughts. Given the carnage she was about to wreak, she considered how she could spoil his day.

Enough, she reprimanded. Focus.

The car eased away, a perverse feeling of satisfaction replacing her dark thoughts as the erstwhile complainant stalled at the lights, his face now apoplectic as she receded into the distance. Up ahead, the blue motorway sign beckoned her to join the M4 motorway.

A steely calm replaced the uncertainty.

CHAPTER 48

The UK Air Defence Operations Centre, RAF High Wycombe, Berkshire.

"OK Jim, what have we got?"

Boyd tried, desperately, to exude an air of calm, much against his instincts. He was as nervy as the youngster who had just picked up the handset.

"It just got ugly Sir. A Britannia Airways flight, inbound to Luton has just squawked 7600. It's the daily trooper flight from Wildenrath."

The young Master Controller was evidently rattled, his breathing laboured, obvious even over the static that distorted the phone line. Boyd fought to maintain the equilibrium.

"What's the position of the VC-10?"

"Just coasting-in, Sir, and about to start the descent for Heathrow. The PM is due to land in 20 minutes and there'll be the usual fanfare on her arrival. Doors is at minute 45."

"Hang the doors time. We do what we need to do to make sure she gets back on the ground. If we need to divert the flight we do just that."

"Copied that Sir, I'll note that in the log."

Boyd scowled, his rebuke delivered silently. He couldn't fault the young controller. He had to protect his position with the stakes so high. It would all be on Boyd.

"What have we got in the air?"

"Mission 01 is airborne and vectoring to join the Britannia flight right now."

"Position?"

"Rolling in astern. He's about two miles behind and closing."

"Where's the airliner. What's his callsign?"

"It's just passed Mike Charlie Six inbound to Dover. Britannia Flight 24."

"I see it on the tote."

"Instructions . . . . . Sir?"

"Switch Mission 01 to the VIP flight. The PM is number one priority. Get Mission 02 airborne; direct vector for the hijacked airliner. I want someone alongside to catch their attention. Have they issued any demands yet?"

"No Sir, still waiting."

"OK I'm going to patch into their frequency so I can listen in. Who are they with?"

"They just switched to London Mil. Stand by, Sir."

The microphone stayed open and the senior officer listened quietly as the Master Controller issued the scramble instructions.

"Wattisham, Neatishead, alert Southern QRA."

"Neatishead, Wattisham Wing Ops, alert Mission 02."

"Mission 02, vector 240, climb Angels 15, Gate! Scramble, scramble, scramble, acknowledge."

There was silence in response. At the first sign of the connection on the telebrief, the crews had leapt for the remaining Phantom, coffee cups and magazines scattering in their wake. They had probably only just returned to the crewroom after the first scramble. It would be a few minutes until they plugged into the intercom system in the Phantom and communications were resumed.

"I got that," replied Boyd, his own adrenaline levels responding to the familiar message. He might have been medically grounded but the thrill of a scramble never waned. The codeword "Gate" meant that the Phantom would pass through Essex at high speed. He braced himself for the noise complaints. It may even cost a few broken windows.

"I'll call you when he's airborne, Sir."

"Thanks. Bring Q3 up to Readiness 10."

"Already on it Sir."

The line clicked off.

As the scene unfolded Boyd considered his options. He would have liked more than one Phantom on each target but it was a luxury he couldn't afford. He was already stretched and until the spare Q jet was declared on readiness he had no more assets. He hoped that the Squadron didn't take all of the 60 minutes they were allocated to check in on readiness. He had an idea that he may need Q3 before the scenario had unfolded.

A new irritant was this other light aircraft. Who the hell is "Golf, Oscar, Echo" and why was the pilot still pressing on into controlled airspace? The controllers would rip the moron apart when he got on the ground. Already re-routing traffic to avoid his meandering course, if he kept going he would pass right through the arrivals lane for Heathrow and who knew what disruption was possible? If he came close to the PM's plane it would cost him his licence. Why no radio calls and what was he thinking?

On a normal day he would have put a Phantom onto him to interrogate the track and find out what was going on. Today he had bigger problems to resolve. He just hoped the light aircraft didn't get in the way of the VIP flight. If it did, he would personally interview the pilot.

CHAPTER 49

London Military Air Traffic Control Centre, RAF West Drayton, London.

"Station calling London Military, say again."

"London Military, this is Britannia Flight 24. You have no need to know my identity but you will comply with my instructions."

Steinbach's calm tones should have been the first warning.

"Britannia Flight 24, stand by."

The flustered controller immediately hit the button on his communications station. A veteran controller of 25 years experience, the unfolding events were way beyond anything he had ever experienced in the past. The normal fare in LATCC Mil was military jets crossing the airways before descending into one of the low flying areas. That he could handle. Hijacked airliners were way beyond his comfort zone. He needed top-cover and he needed it quickly.

"The hijackers have made contact."

The supervisor appeared almost instantaneously, beads of sweat already dotting his brow.

"What has he said?"

"Nothing yet, that was first contact."

"Stall him. I need time to get a hostage negotiator down here."

"Britannia Flight 24, say again your request."

"I have no requests, only demands. This aircraft is now in the hands of the Rote Armee Faktion and we will be making a straight-in approach on the westerly runway to London Heathrow. The next voice you will hear is the Captain but he has assured me he will do nothing stupid to jeopardise the safety of his passengers. There is a device onboard and I will have no hesitation in using it to bring this airliner down if I am pressed. Confirm you understand my intent."

"Britannia 24, affirmative. I copy your intentions and will give every assistance. We, presently, have a 10 minute delay in approach clearance. I will vector you into the Biggin Stack to hold before clearing your final approach to London Heathrow."

"Negative; no hold. You will clear us for immediate descent and a straight-in approach to Runway 28 left."

"Roger Britannia 24, I will attempt to clear your descent immediately, stand by."

"Did you hear that?" the jumpy controller queried.

Behind him, the supervisor nodded, the back of his hand mopping away the sweat from his eyes.

"I'm on the line to the crisis cell now. I think this may well go straight to the top and, by that I mean No. 10! For goodness sake keep him happy. Clear him into the stack for immediate descent if you have to. Make it sound convincing. I need time."

"You know that the approach from the east takes him straight down the line of the Thames, don't you?"

The supervisor's expression made it all too clear that he had absorbed the implications only too clearly. Britannia Flight 24, if cleared for an approach to London Heathrow would fly over the heart of the City and past the seat of Government.

CHAPTER 50

The Brentford Junction Over the M4 Motorway.

Hawkes checked in on the local police traffic frequency and listened to the short, sharp messages from the dispatcher. The staccato instructions directed the unseen drivers of the mobile patrols into key positions along the motorway, ready to intervene. Hawkes mapped out the unfolding jigsaw in his mind's eye.

Pulling his unmarked police car over to the side of the slip road left him with a clear view over the westbound carriageway. Cursing the fact that he had forgotten to pick up the binoculars that were still tucked away safely in his desk drawer, he strained his eyes to monitor the traffic flowing past. He scanned each car looking for the elusive number plate. There was a police patrol three junctions ahead and others were moving into place behind him on the London side of the approaches.

The frequency stuttered into life with the calm tones of the dispatcher announcing the progress of the Golf, steadily closing in on his location. By his reckoning, it was now only a few miles east of his position, reinforced by the fact that he could hear the clatter of the police helicopter in the background, steadily monitoring the target's progress. Its presence aloft meant he had eyes on the target even though the tiny machine was invisible to him, even from his elevated position on the slip road. Surely success was guaranteed, providing the terrorist didn't try anything stupid? Reassured, misgivings lingered and, with foresight, he realised that he should have called up an armed response vehicle in support. Too late now.

The helicopter pilot's methodical commentary reinforced the picture in his mind's eye. The Golf was approaching the junction. In a perfectly timed response, he fired the big engine of the Jaguar XJ6 into life. Far from the image of a typical police cruiser, the vehicle suited his needs perfectly and was more than a match for the Golf, providing he could use the big V8 engine to his advantage. He coasted down the slip road looking over his shoulder for the black car. From the calls, it was tucked into the middle lane, lodged in a tightly packed column of vehicles, travelling at about 40 miles per hour. The traffic still dense, there was little leeway for manoeuvre as he slotted into the flow of traffic about three vehicles back from the target vehicle. Perfect! He accelerated to match the speed of the surrounding vehicles, easing forward towards his quarry but his progress was slowed by the tightly bunched cars. Jostling aggressively, he tucked in behind the Golf in the centre lane, squinting at the registration plate.

Not his target! How had that happened? He thumped the steering wheel in frustration.

A mile behind, Heike Brandt eased up the exit slip road at Brentford junction and turned left down the A4, the Great West Road, heading towards Osterley. She was blissfully unaware that she had avoided interception by the narrowest of margins.

CHAPTER 51

Approaching the English Coast.

Almost as soon as Steinbach had forced his way into the cockpit, the metallic thud of the cockpit door echoing around the enclosed forward galley, the passenger in the aisle seat on the first row recognised the predicament. Had he been more sure of himself he may have intervened but the moment had passed and the youthful looking traveller had disappeared, now hidden from view behind the stark barrier between the cabin and the cockpit. The heated discussion between the flight attendants told him all he needed to know.

Heather flicked through the magazine in her lap happy for some quiet. She glanced along the row of seats at her young children, both quietly reading books. It was a rare moment of peace. The youngsters were growing at an alarming rate and it was rare for tranquillity to win over energy.

Tom craned his neck over the seat back in front, squinting to focus on the overhead screen. He adjusted the ear buds, pressing his right ear to refine the elusive sound track. The movie was reaching its climax but the words were barely audible. He fought the urge to rip the intrusive device from his ear but there was little else to do to while away the time, trapped in his temporary jail, his knees pressed against the seat in front, preventing any reasonable movement. He would have to take the movie out on loan from Blockbuster when he got home.

Fred rolled down the aisle, steadying himself by clutching the headrest of an adjacent seat. He muttered a brief apology to the irritated traveller who stared back, annoyed by the temporary intrusion. Fred registered the occupied sign on the bulkhead ahead, muttering a silent curse. He wished now that he'd excused himself from the restrictive seat a little sooner. He hoped dearly that his bladder would hold out. The alternative would be hugely embarrassing.

Jim rolled the beer around the plastic glass pondering. He was finally homebound but it was not a cause for celebration. As a single soldier, he had enjoyed the last few years enormously. The sense of camaraderie at the Army base at Paderborn, close to the Inner German Border, had been incredible. Separated from normal life in UK, the isolated military community lived by a simple code: "work hard, play hard". And he had. Life had been lived at breakneck speed and it had been exhilarating but what the future held, he had no idea. The posting to the Regimental Headquarters on administrative duties had come as a shock. He was a soldier. He lived in the field. Yorkshire was pretty but hardly a substitute for Paderborn. Rolling the beer around the cup once more, he slugged it back. That was another thing. Gone were the days of duty free booze. His weekly pay check would take a big hit if he kept on at the rate he had been enjoying life for the last few years. Hitting the call button, he placed the discarded vessel on the tray table. There was time for at least one more before they began their descent into Luton. Thank goodness this was a civvy flight and the RAF movers had not banned booze onboard.

None of the travellers could have any inkling of the drama unfolding just a few miles behind them.

The shrill utterance from the man in the front row to his fellow passengers was neither subtle nor restrained and, overheard by those in the row behind, a ripple of disquiet began its inevitable journey rearwards. Relaxed expressions were replaced by looks of concern.

*

In the cockpit things were marginally calmer but that was about to change.

"Britannia Flight 24 this is London Military. I have a message."

"London Military, please go ahead."

Steinbach was amazed at the pilot's, seemingly, unruffled response. It was not only the Germans who were inscrutable. It was almost as if the exchange was scripted.

"Britannia Flight 24, London Military, I am under instructions to relay this message verbatim."

"Go ahead," snapped Steinbach, his response aimed at the back of the Captain's head, his patience suddenly tested.

"This message is from the British Cabinet Office. The British Government does not, repeat not, negotiate with terrorists. You will not be cleared to make an approach into London Heathrow under any circumstances. An interceptor aircraft is closing on your position and has orders to intervene and escort you to an alternative destination. You are to acknowledge his orders and follow his instructions precisely. Please indicate that you understand."

Unexpected. The script was changing. This was new ground. He had to react decisively. The challenge was intended to test his will. He hit the transmit button.

"You understand the implications of your actions? People will die because of this."

How could they place so many lives at risk? He was in control of this machine and his intent would prevail. Idiots!

The radio remained stubbornly silent.

It would be a battle of wills but he had a fitting response in mind. Where was the interceptor and how had they positioned it so quickly? He craned his neck searching the empty blue skies around the airliner, careful to keep the weapon away from the pilots. He knew exactly where the alternative destination might be.

CHAPTER 52

Overhead "Sandy" reporting point, Southeast of London.

"Mission 01, Judy," called Flash as he took over control of the intercept from the ground controller, locking the radar to the fuzzy green blip on the scope.

"Centre the dot Razor," he called watching the lively steering dot move quickly into the centre of the steering circle as his pilot followed his command. The move put the target on a collision course.

"Looks like he's heading 310, check his height."

The pilot glanced at the tiny instrument on the panel that would give him the target's relative height.

"Delta H shows five above."

"OK, take out the height, climb to two thousand feet below and hold the speed at Mach Point 8. Final turn will be to starboard."

The mental gymnastics were already underway in Flash's head as he worked out the displacement he would need to give them enough turning room in the upper air. The Phantom was an ungainly beast at height and he needed to give Razor the flexibility to make the turn, leaving performance in hand.

Glancing down at his en-route chart on his knee he moved his finger outwards over the reporting point which sat on the coast between the coastal towns of Kent. Sure enough, the radial extended north-westerly along the airway towards the reporting point at Detling, a mere 25 miles from the London Control Zone. The radial for the airway, marked with the annotation "311", stared back at him. The figure matched the heading he had calculated.

"Look like he's following November 57 Razor," Flash explained, identifying the airway on the chart. "We need to talk to him pretty soon.

After Detling the pattern around London gets complex and we need to know his routing, if we're going to offer any protection."

"Got it, standby, transmitting."

There was a pause as Flash clicked off his open microphone.

"London Mil, Mission 01, are you in contact with Ascot 4386?"

"Affirmative Sir, he's working this agency on 134.9."

"Roger Sir, am I clear to switch frequency?"

"Affirmative, switch to 134.9 and check in. If no contact, return to this frequency."

Razor acknowledged instantly, and Flash selected the new frequency on the radio box in the back cockpit before transferring his attention immediately back to the target on the scope.

"134.9's up. Come starboard, standard turn."

The intercept would not wait. The two aircraft were closing at over 800 miles an hour and any delay in turning would mean they would roll out way behind the target. Razor eased the control column over and the sluggish jet responded, the numbers beginning to track around the compass rose towards the new heading.

"London Mil, Mission 01 on handover. Level at Flight Level 230 beginning a starboard turn."

"The target's 30 right, range 10, keep that turn going," Razor heard from the back seat, the voice of his navigator urgent and confident, overriding the response from the air traffic controller. "Hold your speed at Mach Point 85. Target is at Mach Point 8. That gives us 50 knots overtake. We'll slow down once in behind. Any visual contact?"

Razor shifted his head, staring around the ironwork of the canopy frame, searching for the elusive first contact, acknowledging the controller's greeting.

"No joy, keep talking."

"Thirty right, range seven miles, two degrees high."

"Still nothing."

"Coming to the nose at four miles, ease the turn."

As Razor scanned ahead, his eye line tracking once again through the gunsight, he picked up the familiar sight of the VC-10 transport, partially hidden by the intrusive ironwork in the front windscreen. It was a reassuring view he had seen many times before, as he had joined up in formation to take on fuel. This time, the VC-10 carried passengers not fuel and his job might be more sinister.

"Visual."

Although he had practised radar identification procedures hundreds of times before, the fact his pilot could see their quarry made life much more predictable for the hard pressed navigator. His patter would continue as the blip tracked down the radar scope, the back-seater constantly refining the approach, but knowing they had sight of the huge airliner meant he could relax. His corrections of a few degrees here, and a few knots there, gave confidence to the pilot, who in turn tweaked the stick and throttles; inexorably closing in. They dropped into the well oiled routine.

"OK level it there and speed back 20 knots," the back seater intoned as the huge fin of the VC-10 loomed large above the canopy arch, dominating the near horizon. The Phantom stabilised alongside, edging slowly forward into the Captain's field of view.

"London Mil, Mission 01, in company. Is Ascot 4386 on this frequency?"

"Affirmative Sir, all other traffic has been cleared to an alternative frequency."

"Ascot 4386, this is Mission 01, how do you read?"

"You're loud and clear Mission 01," came the refined tones of the VC-10 Captain, remarkably relaxed given that the British Prime Minister was sitting just feet behind him in the cabin, and that he must have been warned of a potential threat to his charge. She would, undoubtedly, by now have been warned of the situation and was not known to be indecisive. A back seat driver might be a challenge.

As Razor eased out onto the left wing of the massive airliner, still holding close formation, the additional lateral separation allowed him to relax a little. It would be impossible to miss the grey bulk of the Phantom from the airliner's cabin and it would not be lost on the passengers that the Phantom meant business, it's weapons hanging menacingly from the missile pylons. Razor was sure the PM must have enjoyed an armed escort on previous occasions as she had visited the Falkland Islands and been welcomed by a flight of the resident Phantom Squadron. For him it was a first.

"Ascot 4386, Mission 01, loud and clear also. Have you been briefed on the situation?"

"Negative Sir, your arrival came as something of a surprise. Go ahead with the details."

There was a momentary silence in the cockpit as the implications dawned. Razor and Flash had been asked to ride shotgun for a pilot who had no idea of the threat he faced. His aircraft may soon come under hostile fire but he was, sublimely, unaware of the potential risk he faced. He was certainly, not practised in any type of tactics to prevent a surface-to-air missile guiding on the heat from the Rolls Royce Conway engines that sat at the rear of the airliner, just yards from the Phantom's canopy. The shimmering of the jet efflux behind underlined how much heat emanated from the four massive engines. The pretty looking efflux would be an inviting target for a SAM when set against the surrounding cold air.

Flash cut in, stabbing the transmit button.

"Ascot 4386, Mission 01, are you familiar with "Tesseral" procedures?"

The hush that followed spoke volumes as the crew aboard the VC-10 assimilated the information, their internal discussion stretching the silence.

"Affirmative Sir, but only broadly. Are you suggesting we need to employ them?"

This discussion was drifting into the bizarre and at odds with the routine tactical discussions on a fighter squadron.

"That's affirmative 4386, we have credible evidence of an imminent threat. "Tesseral State Red" has been declared. Stand by."

"What's that fancy electronic kit the VC-10 carries Flash?"

"It's called Matador but it's not the best piece of kit in the inventory. I wonder if these guys even know how to switch it on?"

"You'd think they might have read the workshop manual if they knew the PM was going to be down the back end today."

"Let's hope so, stand by, transmitting."

"Ascot 4386, check your gadget state."

The lengthy pauses were not building confidence and they began to realise the enormity of the challenge. Not only was the airliner unmanoeuvrable but its crew seemed less than competent in operating their own self-defence equipment.

"Where's it mounted?"

"It's behind that glass window mounted in the housing under the rear fuselage. It's a lamp-based system that pushes out a jamming signal that's designed to confuse the tracking algorithms in the seeker head. The good news is that it's optimised against the SA-7 so at least we have that going for us."

Razor thanked his lucky stars that he had a navigator in the back seat. Electronic warfare was a black art in every sense of the word. The description he had just absorbed may have been delivered in ancient Egyptian.

The continued silence over the frequency suggested that a debate was going on in the cockpit alongside, although the crew were probably taking a renewed interest in the, previously ignored, self-protection equipment.

"Thank goodness all they need to do is switch it on," breathed Flash.

The tranquillity was broken by the air traffic controller.

"Ascot 4386, London Mil, start your descent now. Descend initially to Flight Level 50 and report level. Continue inbound via Bravo India Golf and the initial approach fix. You have priority clearance for your approach to Runway 28 Left at London Heathrow."

"Descend to Flight Level 50, cleared inbound, Ascot 4386."

"It must be nice to be Prime Minister," muttered Razor distractedly. No one received a direct feed in from this range. Normally, airliners would orbit in the Heathrow stack for at least 10 minutes before approach clearance was granted.

"OK, maestro what's our plan?" his pilot prompted, refocusing his attention on the task in hand. Flash was already mentally rehearsing the options.

"If a SAM is out there were not going to get much warning. The time of flight of that thing is, maybe, five or six seconds at most. There'll be a visual plume once it leaves the launch tube but we'll need to be lucky to see it at the instant it's launched. Hopefully, it's one of the older SA-7a's. That's a rear-hemisphere weapon so we'll need to tuck ourselves in-behind to act as a decoy, positioning between a potential launch point and the VC-10. We'll need a constant weave to clear the 6 o'clock because, even if we get a lucky pick-up, we'll need to get flares out the minute we see it inbound. Our lookout had better be good. Whoever has first sight pops the flares, OK?"

"Are the flares we're carrying effective against this thing?"

"That's one thing we do know. The SA-7 doesn't have any counter-countermeasures so if it sees the flare it will be seduced. It would chase a lighted cigarette. Our job is to make sure we are in the way once it launches. It's got a narrow field of view so we need to be in its line of sight."

"Why does that not sound like the best place to be?"

"Have faith. A lot of effort has gone into developing these flares so that they look more attractive than a Rolls Royce Spey. Trust me!"

"Yes I know, you're a vicar," Razor muttered, unconvinced.

"They still have the Matador to act as backstop if our flares fail."

The reassurance seemed hollow.

The airliner began its descent, the noise reduction as the engines throttled back, audible, even in the noisy Phantom cockpit over the drone of the Speys. Razor eased back on the throttles in sympathy, matching the descent. In tandem, the airliner and its human shield began to descend slowly.

"Ascot 4386, Mission 01, keep your engines throttled back and carry out a fixed-throttle approach if you can. That'll keep your engines chilled," called Flash.

He was prompting an, increasingly, nervous VC-10 captain.

"Roger that," came the terse reply.

The man was beginning to sound almost tactical.

"It'll be more important once he gets down into the threat zone but the cooler his engines are, the better. If he pumps the throttles, or keeps his power settings high, he's giving the missile the best chance of detection and tracking."

You know that, and I know that, but does he know that?"

"Let's bloody hope so," breathed the, equally, nervous back-seater.

The graceful lines of the VC-10 lay silhouetted against the bright blue sky as it passed overhead the historic fighter station at Biggin Hill - Bravo India Golf - and commenced a gentle turn, homing in on the initial approach fix for the distant international airport. As the altimeter wound down slowly, the features along the River Thames to the north began to emerge from the haze. Razor cranked on more bank, dropping the right wing, prompting Flash to crane his head over his shoulder to clear the airspace below, and behind, the jet. At this stage his efforts were, probably, ineffective as the formation was, as yet, too high to be seen clearly from the ground.

"Tail's clear," called Flash more confidently than he felt.

CHAPTER 53

An Office Block, Six Miles West of London Heathrow Airport.

Heike Brandt parked the rental car, enjoying the silence as the noise of the engine was replaced by the gentle clicking noise from the heater as it cooled. A lone vehicle drove past as she took in the surroundings. To call her technique counter-surveillance was to give her more credit than she deserved, surprising given that, tucked under an unobtrusive rug in the boot, lay a surface-to-air missile, packing enough high explosive to bring down an airliner.

Removed from its rugged carrying case, the SA-7 Grail was hard to disguise, and for that reason, she needed to make sure she was unobserved once she made her move towards the building. A small cafe over the road was open, its steady trickle of customers pushing in through the door, seeking respite from the bright sunshine outside. A young mother pushed a pram down the road stirring a brief, and unexpected, pang of motherly concern that she might become wrapped up in events if plans went wrong. As the woman turned the corner, the road fell quiet and Brandt prepared herself to move.

Whipping open the hatchback, she reached inside and withdrew the bulky missile wrapped in its protective cocoon. The nondescript carrying bag might have contained an item of sports gear or a tent rather than a destructive weapon of war. Wrestling with the object, she pushed the hatchback door closed, the bang jarring her nerves. The disturbance was perfectly normal in the urban setting and she willed herself to relax a little. The road was still clear as she covered the short distance to the multi-storey building, the strengthened glass in the door testament to the tensions in the neighbourhood rather than security. Social stresses here in urban London was the last thing occupying her attention.

Moving hurriedly, she bundled the shrouded object through the door frame, allowing the door to close behind her, shielding herself from scrutiny from the road. Now invisible from casual observers, she finally allowed herself to relax a little. A rank smell assailed her nostrils causing her to retch, involuntarily. She could only imagine the reason for the stale odour of urine. The short climb up the foul-smelling stairwell to the roof seemed endless, the bulky missile heavy and unwieldy. She stumbled occasionally as the efflux port banged against the floor, jarring her slight frame. Grasping the gripstock more firmly, she steadied the launcher against her hip and pressed upwards towards the roof.

Emerging onto the flat expanse, the London skyline stretched into the distance, the panoramic view stunning in the crisp air. A slight breeze kissed her face as she breathed in the fresh air, glad to have escaped the odorous stairwell. She looked across the flat expanse over a small dividing wall, the succession of airliners heading towards Heathrow airport just to the west, visible above the lip and offering instant orientation. In just a few minutes, one of them would become the focus of her world.

CHAPTER 54

The Operations Room, No. 56 Squadron, RAF Wattisham.

The telebrief repeater clicked into life, the strident attention tone achieving its aim.

"Wattisham this is Neatishead, bring Q3 to cockpit readiness."

The call was unexpected and generated a flurry of controlled mayhem.

"I need Q3 bringing up to Readiness 5 chief, the Duty Authoriser snapped at the comms box on the operations desk. I'll alert the Q3 crew."

"Hang on Sir, I'll need to look at that. I don't have anything serviceable at the minute so I'll need some time to work out the best airframe. It'll need pre arm checks and a BF so we're looking at a couple of hours."

"That's the wrong answer chief. This is not an option, it's an order from the SOC. I need that jet and I need it well inside the 60 minutes. Like now! I'll be right over."

He set off at a trot heading for Engineering Control, ignoring the urgent buzz of the direct line.

*

Entering the engineering control room, a reassuring flurry of activity met him. The Senior Engineering Officer, or SENGO, was already in heated discussion with a small group of NCOs and was clearly in control.

"Relax John," grunted the taciturn Scottish officer, his manner instilling a welcome impression of confidence. "I've had a word. You'll have Alpha as soon as it's prepared. The prep team is on its way now. We're still suffering after yesterday's merry go round."

"That's as maybe Sir," replied the harassed Duty Authoriser, deferring to the senior officer's rank, "but you don't have Neatishead breathing down your neck."

"Maybe not but I've already had the discussion with the Boss and he can be just as persuasive."

Mollified, the aircrew officer reversed his tracks, ready to return to the operations desk. He could only imagine how many calls he had missed in his short absence. The engineer had not finished.

"We're not out of the woods yet John. What Chiefy Macintosh didn't tell you is that the nominated Q jet went unserviceable with a hydraulic leak. It'll be down for at least two hours for investigation. We've been scratching around working out which jet we can get on state soonest. It's tight but they are just wrapping up an avionics job on Alpha and they'll do the paperwork straight away. Once that done, it's a before flight service and armament prep."

"How long Sir?"

"Should be 20 minutes and then the load. I've got missiles on the way over from Missile City."

"OK, I'll get back to the desk and hurry the crew along. Let me know when they can walk. This'll be tight."

"We'll also struggle with armourers Sir," responded the harassed engineering controller. "With the pre-arming checks and a weapons load, there's no spare plumber to do the seat checks on Echo and Delta. I'm relying on those for the next wave."

"Don't worry about that chief," replied the aircrew officer. "Q takes priority over normal ops until we've got this one on state. Drop everything."

He turned to leave.

"But don't get used to that concession. It'll be off the table as soon as they crew into Alpha!" he muttered as he pushed through the door, almost bowled over by a departing flight line mechanic.

CHAPTER 55

The Air Defence Operations Centre, RAF High Wycombe.

Boyd was confused, a feeling that he was neither used to, nor comfortable with, but it seemed to be the norm today. There had been times in the cockpit of his Lightning when the hieroglyphics presented to him on the radar had meant little but that had been a tactical problem. A dearth of information was not the problem here as he stared at the unfolding picture. What worried him was that it was impossible that the events could be unrelated, and if they were indeed being orchestrated, then he faced a challenge of a magnitude greater than he had ever experienced.

The hijacked airliner was making steady progress along the airway and, to a certain extent, was the least of his problems, albeit the one which stood to make the biggest news headline. The Prime Minister's VC-10 was now in its descent to London Heathrow and, surely, was safe from attack? For a fighter to threaten it, France would need to be adopting a more aggressive posture than even Mitterrand had displayed towards Margaret Thatcher. Short of a terrorist camped out on the final approach he hoped that he could concentrate on the hijack.

His next biggest worry was the light aircraft that had been flagged up by the irate controller at London Military. Talking to no one, the pilot was rapidly closing on the London Traffic Movement Area and, unless it deviated, would need to be interrogated. With recent security scares, he could not afford the luxury of hesitancy. He had only two armed Phantoms available to him at the moment and was relieved that the Master Controller had got them into the air. The aircrew would not mind an abortive intervention and, from his own experience, he knew that it was better to be in the air and in close proximity than to be struggling to arrive on task, in time. Now might be a good time to have the Q3 bird available. It was the last armed aircraft on call unless he pulled the hooter and called a Station generation. It was within his gift as Duty Air Defence Commander to do that and, out of hours, would be the only way to achieve a timely response. That said, there was nothing more likely to catch the attention of the C-In-C than an unplanned exercise. He'd hold back for the time being. So, until Q3 was up he had two fighters and three targets. How to prioritise?

The PM seemed to be the ace up his sleeve. Having a Phantom alongside would send the correct messages both to the Cabinet Office and to the media who were almost certainly primed by now. He could see the duty "bod." in the MOD Press Office in his mind's eye. It would not be pretty as the journalists wheeled, sensing a story. Putting Q2 alongside the hijacked airliner was really a no brainer but it was a question of timing. He needed weapons on call should, heaven forbid, he be forced to intervene. A few 20 mm cannon shells might add the persuasive power he needed to focus the mind of a hijacker.

The light aircraft had yet to penetrate controlled airspace and was very slow so he had time to react. It would be the easiest of the three problems to solve so maybe he should sort that out first? If he put a QRA jet alongside, the mere presence should be enough to show the general aviation pilot the error of his ways.

Decision taken. He'd allocate Q1 to the PM's aircraft and Q2 to the "puddle jumper". He hoped that was the right conclusion because things were moving rapidly. He also hoped, fervently, that the hijacker believed that an interceptor was closing on his position.

Picking up the direct line to Neatishead, the next move was to check on the fighters. Where were they now?

CHAPTER 56

Over Central London.

Ashworth steadied his nerves. The Lycoming engine was ticking away smoothly, although there was a slight odour of exhaust fumes. The thought of what he was about to do was alien to every instinct. He was not a bad person but he was about to commit an act with the risk that his action may cause a loss of life. Is that what he wanted? He wavered.

The city landscape below was familiar. Up ahead, the River Thames snaked away into the distance following its meandering course back towards its source in Gloucestershire. The city landscape of Docklands stood out from the surrounding urban sprawl, the tall buildings of the financial district sprouting from the concrete jungle. At the Greenwich peninsular, the area was being cleared for a building project. The tableau was intimately familiar.

He cross checked his heading thumbing along the hastily re-planned track, monitoring his progress towards his new goal. His hands were damp on the control yoke, a sign of his mood not his effort.

Overhead, a steady stream of airliners marked an invisible path from the holding patterns over Ockham and Biggin Hill, joining extended finals for the final approach into Heathrow. He could see a bright red fin with a white Kangaroo identifying a Jumbo belonging to the Australian national airline, Qantas. Out on the beam a helicopter clattered down the course of the river, avoiding the built up areas, its course a safeguard against the risk of engine failure over the densely packed city.

"Golf Alpha Sierra Oscar Echo, this is London Centre on Guard. You are flying in controlled airspace. Squawk "ident" to acknowledge and contact me immediately on my initial contact frequency, 124.05. I say again . . . . "

The radio call came as a surprise, waking him to a new problem.

"London Mil, Mission 02 is vectoring 240 inbound. Currently level at 1,500 feet on the regional QNH. Back to operating frequency."

The blunt message steeled him. Who the hell was Mission 02? If it was who he thought it might be, he was about to see a Phantom somewhat closer than usual. They were onto him but it was too late. Right or wrong the die was cast and he would live with the consequences. Pushing the throttle up, the speed crept up to 150 knots, approaching the "never exceed" limit for his tiny Piper Warrior. He could not outrun a Phantom but, whatever way this panned out, he was committed.

CHAPTER 57

Over the Suffolk County Border.

John Sharpe finally settled down, his chest still heaving from the exertion, his leg restraints finally clipped into the snub housings in the ejection seat. In the panic of the scramble, the blue cords were always the last things to be sorted out. Designed to stop his legs from flailing in a high speed ejection, the risk of not being fully strapped in and needing to eject from the aircraft on takeoff, was a risk he accepted. Just getting the Phantom in the air was the highest priority.

With his heart rate returning to something more normal, he scanned the instruments, the first opportunity to check that the jet was functioning normally. The harness chafed his shoulders where the pads were unseated and he adjusted the straps. Although uncomfortable, the harness was doing its job and now held him securely in the seat. He would worry about creature comforts later. There were other priorities to worry about and his eyes returned to the instruments and gauges in a second housekeeping check. All seemed normal. Engines spooling at 95%, temperatures good, pressures all normal and fuel flowing from the external tanks. He relaxed a little more. The selected light stared back at him from the weapons control panel. Not something he normally dwelt upon, the events of the last day had caused him to consider its significance more deeply. Only the Master Arm switch stood between the present dormant status and oblivion. Flicking the switch to Arm, a ready light would signify that the weapon, the Skyflash semi-active missile, was tuned and ready to fire. Locked to its target, the weapon would destroy it and anyone onboard. He hoped that he would not be called upon to unleash its destructive power today.

"Doesn't that vector take us right overhead London, Jim?" he asked his navigator who was still breathing heavily over the intercom, the rigours of the short dash across from the Q Shed, wearing the cumbersome protective clothing, still evident.

"The vector takes us to the east somewhere around the Dartford Crossing," the portly navigator wheezed.

In front of Sharpe, the radar display flicked sporadically into life as his navigator sampled the occasional target. The electronic range bug stabilised at various ranges on the scope and the locked symbology flashed briefly before the radar drifted back into search mode while the harassed navigator moved onto the next target of interest. The smudges on the tube were barely visible to the pilot. That they represented hundreds of tons of airborne metal seemed unreal.

"What speed was our target?"

"The scramble message said slow. . . . . Standby."

There was a pause as the navigator stabbed the transmit button.

"Neatishead, Mission 02, bogey dope."

It was time to identify their quarry.

"Mission 02, your target shows 250 degrees, range 50, slow speed, heading away. Buster. Make max subsonic and await further instructions."

Without further prompting, Sharpe pushed up the throttles watching the airspeed indicator creep towards the magic figure of Mach 1, the speed of sound. Below the Phantom, the Essex countryside flashed past and, at this speed they would rapidly overhaul a slow mover. He checked the needle's progress at Mach 0.98, just below the unseen but mysterious boundary. Without clearance, he had no desire to drop a "boom" over the sedentary English countryside. The supersonic shockwave that travelled ahead of an aeroplane flying at speeds beyond the Mach would cause untold damage. The Phantom powered towards the Capital.

An unvoiced tension lingered between the cockpits. Used to intercepting wayward light aircraft during their time in Germany, the fact that they were vectoring towards the heart of the Capital city, chasing an as yet unidentified light aircraft, was ominous.

"There's no way I'll find this guy on radar in a long tailchase," muttered the frustrated navigator. For a target to appear on his radar scope in pulse Doppler mode, a large closing velocity was needed. In theory, in a long tailchase running down a slow target, the large opening velocity achieved the same aim but it was an area of operation in which neither crew had much experience and even less confidence. They would need to rely on the controller on the ground for vectors but his radars were trained over the North Sea looking for marauding Soviet bombers, not overland. That task normally fell to the air traffic agencies who relied on secondary surveillance radar which, in turn, relied on the cooperation of the pilots by transmitting friendly electronic responses which identified the aircraft. The crew had already been warned that this particular pilot had turned off his IFF equipment, so was largely invisible to the civilian controllers. From discussions on frequency, the errant pilot popped up occasionally as he passed close to an airfield surveillance radar but, for the moment, his presence was masked. They would need a lot of luck and extremely good eyes.

The green fields of Essex gave way to the urban sprawl of the suburbs and the Phantom dropped lower. By now they were down at 1,000 feet, tracking rapidly over housing estates and the commercial landscape of outer London. The noise on the ground in their wake was deafening as the airspeed tickled the Mach and more than one London resident gazed up at the skies trying to identify the culprit. With the high speed over the ground, by the time eyes were elevated skywards, the Phantom had passed.

The town of Ilford hove into view and the calls from the controller increased in urgency. Whether he was predicting the course of the light aircraft or acting on more solid radar data was unclear to them in the cockpit but the range to the target wound down swiftly. In the back, the navigator finally gave up on the radar, instead craning his neck to peer around the ironwork between the two cockpits. In the front, his pilot searched his own area of responsibility intently. Without a radar lock Jim's telescopic sighting system was useless and it was down to good old visual detection techniques. First contact was a source of pride but spotting a slow moving light aircraft over an urban sprawl was hit and miss to say the least. Two heads moved rhythmically left and right.

"I'm going to ease it down to try to skyline this guy," the pilot announced, concentration evident despite the solitude of individual cockpits. Already spreading its noisy wake, the local residents were about to be even more disrupted by the Phantom as it eased, ever lower, to only 500 feet over a small suburb.

"Tally, eleven o'clock, range two miles," shouted the suddenly energised navigator excitedly as both heads swung around onto the bearing.

"Got him," the pilot grunted bringing the nose instantly around.

"Don't go nose-on," warned the navigator, knowing that to draw the tiny, elusive contact into the cluttered gunsight risked losing visual contact amongst the ironwork. Holding the nose off would also give the back seater a chance of maintaining sight from his cluttered vantage point in the back cockpit. More importantly, with such a huge speed differential, the gap between the two aircraft would close rapidly, with potentially fatal consequences.

Sharpe flicked out the speedbrakes, prompting a violent shudder as the huge slabs of metal bit into the dense air at low level, slowing the Phantom's passage. The airspeed wound off quickly as the jet drew a wide arc around the flight path of its smaller brother. Dropping the left wing, Sharpe watched the light aircraft below, the small airframe suddenly emerging from the background, its bright livery standing out from the grey buildings beneath.

"OK, I'll do a long left hand turn and come up on his left hand side. That'll keep the sun behind us so he should be easier to see."

"Copied."

The pilot craned his neck as he flew the long, lazy turn, both sets of eyes fixed on the indistinct spot at the limit of visual acuity. Occasionally disappearing as it flitted over the terrain, the bright colour scheme was, alternately, highlighted and camouflaged against the flickering but varied backdrop. The aircrew jockeyed for position in the cockpit, hauling against unrelenting seat harnesses, unwilling to take their eyes off the target, worried at losing the fleeting contact. The controller had gone silent and the frequency was eerily quiet. Only the wind rush in the cockpit hissed in the background interrupting the dialogue.

"What is it? Do you recognise it?"

"Hard to make out but I'd say it's a Cherokee," replied the navigator. "We'll need to be sure once we're alongside."

They were both regretting not having paid more attention during the aircraft recognition lectures at the last ground training session.

"At this speed I can't stabilise so make sure you clock the registration as we fly past."

"Roger."

"Have you got the camera out?"

"Not sure there's any point but I'll try. With this overtake, we'll be past in an instant. At best it'll be a fuzzy passing shot but I'll do my best. If I'm peering through the lens, make sure you get the registration number."

The Phantom, by now, had slowed to its minimum manoeuvring speed and Sharpe dropped half flap, the airspeed indicator hovering at around 250 knots. Unorthodox, the move would make the lumbering warplane a little more manoeuvrable but the Phantom immediately signalled its displeasure, the airframe buffeting and tetchy.

As the tiny airframe ahead grew in size, the crew braced for the pass. Sharpe, with the better view from the front cockpit first to respond.

"Neatishead, Mission 02, identifies one Piper Cherokee, Golf, Alpha, Sierra, Oscar, Echo."

He immediately pushed open the throttles, the speed increasing in response, the Phantom resuming a more manageable attitude. The navigator grunted as the jet performed a majestic wingover, flying directly over the now oscillating light aircraft. The gesture was more for effect than of necessity but allowed the flaps, which still extended into the airflow, to retract slowly. Despite the dramatic manoeuvre, pulling g during the pass would have been ill-advised; in fact impossible.

The crew gazed down as they repositioned, the visual battle continuing.

"On this track he's going to pass well north of the Dartford Crossing and, if he doesn't deviate, he's heading for central London," the pilot warned the fighter controller, who had been obvious by his absence during the unfolding scenario.

The lazy turn put them back into the stern sector about a mile behind their victim and they struggled to keep sight. As they watched, the tiny craft jinked violently to the right and descended even further towards the urban landscape.

"Target is evading, now heading 300," he called more urgently, trying to prompt a response from the absent fighter controller. Still the frequency was quiet and the silence stretched out. Where was he?

To the south, the Isle of Dogs protruded into the River Thames and below, Docklands stretched out, mingling with its less affluent neighbours. At least the errant light aircraft pilot was no longer heading directly for the Capital. In its descent, the Cherokee pilot had banked away, picking up a diverging course. Sharpe pulled around to follow.

"Neatishead, Mission 02, instructions," he prompted yet again, his frustration becoming belligerent.

"Where does that new course take him Jim?"

"He's headed for the northern outskirts now, roughly towards Bentley Priory. At least he's not headed towards Westminster which takes the pressure off."

"Mission 02, this is Neatishead, how do you read?"

"Welcome back," muttered the irritated navigator.

"Mission 02, loud and clear, did you copy the ident?"

"Affirmative, understand a Cherokee?"

"Affirmative, Piper Cherokee, Golf, Alpha, Sierra, Oscar, Echo, request instructions."

"What is wrong with this guy?"

The situation was approaching boiling point, the pilot only barely maintaining control of his emotions. The intruder, clearly, had no desire to be intercepted, witness his evasive manoeuvre. The reality of the situation was dawning on the harassed fighter crew. The possibility of intervention began to register. To do so would have significant implications and it would be far harder to bring down a light aircraft than it would to engage a typical target against which they trained during practice QRA interceptions. Without a radar lock they could not use a Skyflash missile and an unlocked guns pass, against a slow moving target, would need luck not judgement. Equally, with a limited infra red response from the tiny piston engine, the Sidewinder was useless. Their options were limited.

"Best you let them know sport," the navigator muttered. "Time to earn your flying pay."

A hurried exchange ensued, the controller on the ground obviously engaged in a two-way conversation with an inaudible superior. The regular breaks in the dialogue stretched out further adding to the tension. Finally, a decision was apparently taken and the frequency sparked into life once more.

"Mission 02, Neatishead, your instructions are to intercept, interrogate and order the pilot to divert from his present track. He is to clear London airspace to the east, acknowledge."

Sharpe read back the instructions precisely, speculating on how they differed from what he had attempted just moments before.

"Looks like we have one option left then," he muttered to no one in particular.

"A high speed pass," his navigator confirmed, reading his thoughts precisely.

With their limited weapons options, they would be forced to resort to brute force to make the errant pilot comply. After a final check on the international distress frequency, which elicited no reaction, the pilot dragged the nose around and placed the reticule on the fleeing target. With the range closing rapidly, the tiny airframe growing under the pipper, he began to track the target. Just when it seemed that an impact was inevitable, Sharpe broke the collision and pulled ahead of the target's extended flight path.

Flashing across the nose of the Warrior, which had started a gentle turn in response, the needle on the airspeed indicator firmly passed the Mach. The Phantom shattered windows in its wake. Below and behind the jet, the sonic boom left a trail of devastation along the banks of the Thames. Had the intercept occurred over the more sparsely populated area east of Docklands, the toll may have been lessened but with the Warrior over the outer limits of the City, swathes of glass skyscrapers were left in ruins as the supersonic air cast a footprint over the suburbs.

*

In the cockpit of the Warrior, Ashworth struggled with the controls as the light aircraft bucked viciously in the wake turbulence from the familiar aircraft that flew across his nose. The Phantom showed its full weapons load as it reversed its course leaving no doubt that it was a QRA aircraft and its flight had originated from the same base that Ashworth had left just a few hours before. The windscreen grew dark as the bulk of the fighter masked the sky beyond, before initiating a violent reversal, passing within yards of his extended track. Bracing for the inevitable shock wave, he yanked the control yoke as the wings rocked violently reaching the limits of control. The airspeed fluctuated alarmingly and, as the nose rose, dropped rapidly to below 70 knots in an instant. In the turbulent airflow, the wing dropped in sympathy as the Warrior approached the stall. Ashworth was unable to hold it up. The stall warner sounded and the nose whipped viciously in response as the tiny aircraft entered an incipient spin to the left.

ULTIMATUM

The altimeter began to unwind, the height dropping rapidly as the river below replaced the Phantom, its dank flow now filling the windscreen.

CHAPTER 58

The Air Defence Operations Centre, RAF High Wycombe.

Boyd was not his usual ebullient self. In fact he seemed almost broken, his head cradled in his hands. As a former fighter pilot turned fighter controller, he had often pondered the difference between air traffic controllers and his new brethren. Although each worked to a highly complex and stringent rule book, the former spent their lives coordinating the daily rush of airliners to and fro across British airspace, a smooth flow of air traffic, into and out of airports, their priority. Their purpose in life was to prevent mishaps in the sky. His own community, in contrast, whilst embracing the same principles, had entirely the opposite purpose. Their aim was to bring aircraft together. Rather than engineering separation, the goal was to direct formations of fighters towards their prey, often setting up collision courses and close-aboard passes and to deposit the hunters into the mêlée. The choreography was, in fact, organised chaos. Add to the conundrum, the fact that civilian agencies used vastly different terms to their military colleagues and, indeed, at times, it was almost as if they spoke a different language. What should, in theory, achieve the same aim in the air, might have significantly different outcomes depending on the instigator. The difference this time was that he needed both communities to pull together.

He sat back and rehearsed the possible scenarios once more, silently playing them out in his mind. The old adage applied to this situation; no plan ever survives first contact with the enemy, but he must be ready with his answers, formulated to out-think the terrorists. There would be little time to deliberate as the situation developed. He had to be ready. His first clue might be the hijacked airliner diverting violently from its track. The move might not be immediately obvious to him on his synthetic tote but the air traffic controllers were, normally, quick to spot such diversions from a planned course. Even so, he could not rely on others; he would need to anticipate. He suspected that whoever was onboard the Britannia flight might broadcast their intentions soon, well before such an eventuality, but he could by no means rely on that fact.

What else was he missing? Would a deviation be his main indicator? If not, which of the disparate reports he had read this morning could he believe? Was the information timely? What was the source? Was it credible and verified? If this really was a threat to the Prime Minister he would need radical action, delivered in an instant. It might be a decision of epic consequences. Could he really take the decision to ground all civil air traffic over the UK? Did he even have the authority as Air Defence Commander? He was about to find out if events went wrong. He was, after all, charged with the defence of his country and, for once, it might be more important than intercepting an intruding Russian Bear and he might be called upon to deliver. The concept of responding to the red hordes crossing the FIR boundary was relatively easy to comprehend but his response would be entirely different in the context of an airliner targeted against a key installation or a threat to the PM's plane. Heaven forbid he would be forced to ask for authority to engage. The approval channels were, in theory, clearly identified but, in practice, might be less well oiled. If the nightmare scenario unfolded, would he have the moral courage to order the destruction of an airliner carrying passengers? Was that indeed the right outcome? The checklist said it was. But life was not a checklist and most decisions were not black and white. This was real people, with real consequences and outcomes and people might die. What if the hijacker's aims were more sinister? What if in ordering the destruction, he was sacrificing more people on the ground when the airliner fell to earth, than would die in the air? Was it a valid trade-off? Even then it was not simple. What if the bulk of the airliner fell into a populated area? There could be a massive loss of life on the ground and he would condemn completely innocent civilians to a terrible demise. What was abundantly clear was that there was no simple answer.

He blinked, realising that his machinations had distracted him. The two symbols marking the VIP flight and the airliner, continued to plod steadily towards London. Their slow, rhythmic progress belied the urgency he faced. Where was that light aircraft and what was the idiot pilot doing?

He had to get into the minds of the hijackers. Let's be frank; the terrorists. This was no simple hijacking. Airliners had been hijacked and flown to the desert before being destroyed. They sought outrage but they never repeated a simple plan. There must be more to this than he was seeing and, surely, it could not be a coincidence that the threat to the PM was closely linked in time to the hijacking? It was inconceivable that the two events were not linked. He was looking at a coordinated plot.

What was becoming increasingly clear was that, today, his actions would come under the microscope and he still could not predict the outcome. He hoped that his reading of the situation would be accurate but, if he got it wrong, his actions might be "a day late and a dollar short", to coin the American saying.

Focus. What was the target? If it was him intent on a showdown, bent on fomenting a clash of politics and cultures, what tactics would he choose?

Suddenly the answer was staring him in the face. Oh my God.

Parliament!

CHAPTER 59

Over the Outer London Suburbs.

If the choice had been to protect life over property, the decision to spare the errant pilot's life might have incurred tremendous cost. The verdict would be dissected endlessly for months to come but, for now, the Phantom crew had little insight into what devastation had followed, and even less interest. As they pulled around for a second pass, Jim in the back cockpit strained against his shoulder straps looking for the light aircraft. . . . Nothing.

"Mission 02, haul off, I say again, haul off."

"What did we do wrong?"queried the bemused pilot, more to himself than his captive audience. "What else did they expect us to do? A high speed pass was the only way to divert the guy and that's exactly what we did."

The navigator, ignoring the rhetorical question, continued his visual scan of the ground around their flight path, looking for signs of the brightly painted Warrior.

"Ahh Jeez," he breathed. "Smoke plume in the eight o'clock. It looks like it's gone down."

The hasty Mayday message delivered in a harsh monotone, highlighted the plight of the light aircraft to the ground controller but now was not the time to adopt the role of search and rescue coordinator. Instructions followed rapidly. The plight of the light aircraft was, seemingly, history.

"Mission 02, Neatishead, vector 100 and climb Flight Level 100, further trade bearing 120 range 50 miles, inbound. Interrogate. Your target is squawking 7600."

Interrogate was an ominous and rarely used term. More ominous was the identification code. The prefix 76 meant that an airliner had been hijacked. Sharpe quickly dialled the electronic code into the airborne IFF interrogator control panel in the front cockpit. The red LED symbols winked back.

"Code set," he called to the navigator. When Jim pressed the interrogate button on his navigator's hand controller, he would now see a symbol on the radar scope from any pilot who was transmitting the anti-hijack code.

With events escalating rapidly, Jim called in the smoke plume to the controller, his thoughts barely acknowledging the fate of the Warrior pilot. Sharpe engaged the burners once more and began a rapid climb through the congested London airspace. Unbeknown to the crew, airliners were being cleared out of their path as they climbed, causing carnage amongst the usually ordered recovery flow into the London airports.

The Phantom rolled inverted and Sharpe dragged the nose back to level flight before turning upright, the altimeter pegged at 10,000 feet. He scanned the horizon. In the back, his navigator transferred his attention back to the radar screen, his equilibrium restored after the violent manoeuvre. The display was immediately flooded with contacts. Which one was his? He eased the sodden rubber seal of his immersion suit away from his neck and a waft of overheated air emerged. It did little to ease his discomfort in the warm confines of the cockpit. He gulped back a slight feeling of nausea wishing he had gone easier in the bar the night before.

"Mission 02, instructions, you are to intervene and divert the target to land at Echo Golf Sierra Sierra. I say again, intervene and divert the track to land at Echo Golf Sierra Sierra,

"Roger Neatishead, understand intervene and divert my target to Echo Golf Sierra Sierra, stand by."

"Authenticate: Juliette Mike," replied the navigator, instantly.

He was already well ahead of his pilot and had dragged his authentication codes from his classified noddy guide anticipating the need to verify any instructions. Thumbing through the matrix he identified the response, waiting with bated breath for the reply. Nothing would be left to chance because events had taken a distinctly ominous, not to say expensive, path. Scapegoats would be demanded and they had no intention of volunteering.

"Alpha," came the response from the ether.

"Is that right?"

"Affirmative!"

"Where the hell is EGSS?"

"Stansted. It's the nominated airfield for dealing with a hijacked airliner. I hear the boys from Hereford know it well."

"Ah shoot, this is serious!"

Neither registered the unintended significance of the jargon.

CHAPTER 60

Over Kent.

Utter panic had broken out aboard the Britannia flight, the orderly monotony of a short flight home, disrupted by rumour. Only one passenger had seen Steinbach enter the cockpit but, already, a relatively concealed forced entry had morphed into armed intervention. At least in the minds of the nervous passengers.

From his seat, Hammond felt reluctant to intervene just yet, realising that anonymity, for now, was his friend.

All down the cabin there were signs that normal discipline was breaking down. A woman in row 7 had succumbed to a panic attack. Remonstrating loudly to her irritated husband, she complained of nausea and feeling faint. The harassed man, seemingly more embarrassed than concerned, muttered suggestions which, clearly, were not helping. Fearing that the woman was about to vomit in his lap, an adjacent traveller excused himself and moved to a free seat some rows ahead, attracting instant retribution from the harassed flight attendant who was struggling to restore order amidst the chaos. The frightened woman had now stretched herself out along the row of seats and was groaning loudly, her husband's insistence that she should "not be stupid", attracting an enraged response. A flight attendant appeared with a wet towel, offering words of encouragement, damping the stricken woman's head.

Some rows back, a flustered mother tried, unsuccessfully, to quieten her screaming infant, wishing she could resort to a similar response. With bulging eyes and with tears flowing freely, the child belted out an overture at maximum volume. Generous hugs could not quell the raucous signs of distress as she rocked the baby slowly, its tears soaking her chest.

Further down the cabin, a flight attendant attempted to restore order, coaxing a man back to his seat, urging him to relax. Apprehensive and increasingly red in the face, his corpulent frame rattled the seats as he slumped backwards. Having lost any semblance of military bearing, only firm entreaties from his wife persuaded him to calm down. The flight attendant moved on to fight the next fire.

With the efforts of the flight attendants failing to calm the rabble, the senior passenger, finally, stood up and turned to face the cabin. His resonant bark exuded authority instantly, persuading the discordant passengers to pause. His speech, recently rehearsed in his head, was delivered at the opportune moment and a tenuous tranquillity fell over the disturbed herd.

Only the drone of the jet engines and the low moaning of the woman in row 5 disrupted the quiet.

With the prospect of order returning, Hammond held back.

CHAPTER 61

The Roof of the Office Block, Six Miles West of London Heathrow.

The tube of the SA-7 Grail missile launcher seemed out of place against the weathered concrete of the roof, its matt, dark green paint applied as camouflage for the woods of central Europe rather than urban London.

Brandt took in her surroundings as she crouched in the lee of the stairwell, shielded from view from potential observers in the adjacent high rise buildings. Out of sight from the ground and satisfied that she was not overlooked, she pulled the squat battery from the knapsack and placed it alongside the launcher. Once clipped onto the gripstock and activated she had only 60 seconds of power to the seeker head during which time she had to acquire her target, achieve a lock on and fire the weapon. Timing would be critical.

A Boeing 747 Jumbo flew past, its undercarriage extended ready to land, its velocity deceptive. Given its enormous bulk it appeared to pass slowly but in reality it was moving at almost 200 miles per hour. She gauged the rate of movement, assessing the aspect and the point at which she was likely to have the strongest infra-red response from the engines. Her actual target was smaller and the VC-10s engines were grouped in a tight cluster around the tail fin. Add to that, the older engines on the aging airliner would be hotter and offer a more attractive target.

Hefting the tube onto her shoulder she flipped up the iron sight on the forebody and squinted through the tiny reticule. The tube was heavier than those with which she'd practised, as the bulk of the slender SA-7 missile now sat snugly within, its guidance fins folded back until its release. Running through the engagement sequence in her mind, a sequence she had rehearsed a million times in quieter moments, she took in the urban sprawl, orientating herself and watching the next airliner in the endless stream of arrivals. The favoured aspect would be as the target offered its tail to her when she would have a clear view and plenty of time to sweeten the shot. With the target above the horizon, the seeker head had a clear view, uninterrupted by background emissions. The Airbus she was now tracking slowly merged with its surroundings as it descended on short finals, the sighting picture, and with it the heat signature, degrading rapidly. Assessments made, she scribed a small chalk mark on the ground, hopefully the only indication of her presence once she made good her escape. If she had the capacity to glance at the marker at the critical time, it would show her the optimum bearing for the shot.

She allowed herself the luxury of another rehearsal confident that she could not be seen, the passengers in the passing airliner blissfully unaware that they had escaped oblivion only because, today, they were not her target. The launcher tube tracked relentlessly around the arc, the engines of the target airliner fixed in the iron sight. A gentle squeeze of the trigger and her deadly payload would have been unleashed. She could not suppress a surge of adrenaline. The feelings she was experiencing were primeval and, to a more sane person, would be shocking

The "Doors" time for her target, the VC-10 carrying the British Prime Minister was little more than minutes away. Allowing the time to taxy off the runway and onwards to the Executive Terminal, plus the short six miles to Heathrow, flown at 180 knots, the VC-10 should pass her position imminently. She wondered, idly, whether the military planners realised how much easier their precision would make her task. She could predict her prey's position almost precisely and, given that the VC-10 was almost unique in the skies, with its elegant graceful lines and high mounted tailplane, she would have little difficulty identifying her quarry.

Until now she had focussed almost exclusively on the main event but self preservation was kicking in. As she waited, patiently, her thoughts turned to the diversionary plans wondering how the back-up teams had fared. If Steinbach failed in his efforts to hijack the flight it would be a setback but not serious. Her plan should work in isolation. Hopefully, the chaos the hijack would cause, would buy her time to clear the area which, coupled with a few more surprises, would keep the authorities busy.

Checking her watch, she sat back to wait. A louder, more intrusive, engine tone built in intensity.

CHAPTER 62

Final Approach to Heathrow.

Heathrow, 14 miles west of Central London, with its two parallel, east–west runways, sits between the mundane suburbs of Hounslow and Staines. Following instructions from ATC, the sleek, white VC-10 lined up on the southerly of the two, Runway 28 Left. As the airliner settled down on its final approach, the Phantom crew could hear the rise in the note of the massive engines through the thick Perspex canopy that separated them from the huge Conways, spooling up to approach power. The formation had joined extended finals 10 miles from the airport, the runway just visible in the distance. Massive flaps slowly extended from the leading and trailing edges of the wings as the pilot configured the jet for landing, offsetting the increased drag with power. It was exactly the opposite effect that Flash, in the back cockpit of the Phantom, would have preferred. To counter a heat-seeking SAM the engines should be kept as cool as possible, limiting the telltale infra-red emissions on which the tiny seeker head would track. At this stage the transport crew had little choice and it meant that, from now on, until the wheels were on the ground, the VC-10 was completely vulnerable. Matching the slow approach speed, Razor was leaving his Phantom with little excess power if threatened. It was uncomfortable.

"What sequence have you programmed in?" he asked, his eyes scanning the zone immediately around and ahead of the weaving Phantom. He was sitting below and behind the VC-10, trailing by about 500 yards. Choreography and timing would be critical if attacked. Behind him, and with the radar now in standby mode to avoid radiating the hapless passengers with the powerful beam, his navigator was craning on the restraining straps of his seat. His eyes scanned the area behind the lumbering formation, the more likely avenue for a shot if one was to come.

"It's all or nothing me old mate," Razor heard back. "No point in finessing this one. We've got 15 flares in each dispenser. If we get a sighting of a launch I've got it ready to dump three sequences of six flares at 250 millisecond spacing. That should give a pretty much continuous line of flares that should confuse any heat seeker. Once we get onto short finals, if we still haven't seen anything, I'll reprogram it to put out single flares at one second spacing all the way down until the VC-10 is on the ground. You'll need to keep the gear up or the safety interlocks will operate and the flares won't deploy. That means you'll need to weave in behind at minimum manoeuvring speed on short finals, otherwise you'll be spat out in front and we won't provide any protection."

"No challenge then," muttered the pilot, laconically, as the enormity of the threat sank home. For once he was thankful for his navigator's electronic warfare expertise. Without it, the VC-10 might already be compromised.

As they made yet another ponderous weave behind the lumbering airliner, necks craned on gimbals, each man searched the ground below for the elusive puff of smoke that might signify a missile launch. The Phantom protested at the outrageous demands Razor was exerting through the stick, the wings rocking in protest at the high angle of attack.

Flash focussed on a point in the near distance, his eyes screwed up against the glare.

CHAPTER 63

The Roof of the Office Block.

With three minutes to go to the scheduled arrival, it was time to prepare for the finale; the culmination of years of planning and preparation. Brandt was as ready as she would ever be and an eerie calm had settled over her. Looking around vigilantly, she scanned the area one final time. All seemed quiet and the few windows she could see were empty of people and absent of movement.

The launcher appeared harmless, laid out in readiness, its stark angular lines and green camouflage blending with the dark blanket she had arranged on the floor, it's deadly capabilities impossible to comprehend. The components she would need were readily to hand. The gripstock was already in place underneath the barrel and the thermal battery within easy reach. Two clicks and the weapon was assembled. The tube of the launcher pointed westwards, taunting the stream of airliners tracking inbound to the airport nearby.

A noise! The reverberation of a door moving; the hinges protesting. Her heart responded instantly, the shot of adrenaline sharpening her reactions. She dropped to a crouch and the handgun, secreted at her hip, snapped to the aim. The door to the stairway swung slowly open, creaking but barely ajar. Poised for action, she visualised the torso that would, inevitably, emerge. Whoever was about to come into view onto the roof had a pitiful sense of timing but she had no choice. She had to prioritise. The sight trained on the door handle, she elevated the barrel to the point where she could take a shot at the centre of mass. The take down would need to be quick because the shots would inevitably attract attention, jeopardising her subsequent escape. She cursed her luck. So near and yet . . . .

The door swung wider and she tensed for the shot, her breathing steady, her hands rock solid.

The ginger Tom seemed completely disinterested in the Makarov that pointed in its direction as it ambled, casually, out onto the roof unaware of its role in shaping history.

CHAPTER 64

Final Approach to London Heathrow.

Razor eased the Phantom into loose formation, uncomfortable at slow speed in such close proximity. He positioned wide enough that he could manoeuvre rapidly if needed, wary of being too close where both aircraft would be struck if a missile came from outside the formation. Conversely, too wide and a seeker head would differentiate easily between the smaller heat signature of the Phantom and the hot efflux spewing out behind the four Conways. Any electronic subterfuge would rely on precise positioning. He eased lower, the VC-10 looming above, casting a fleeting shadow, conscious that an attack might come from either side of the formation. Like a close protection officer, he placed themselves between the VIP and the threat, praying that he had chosen the correct side if an attack was imminent. To have to cross sides would cost valuable seconds of what would be an extremely short reaction time.

Flash was completing another scan of the repetitive urban landscape behind when his eyes focussed on a tiny plume of smoke. The warning died on his lips before he had uttered any words. Choked back. Redundant. The plume of smoke drifted, harmlessly, skywards from the dirty stack of a chimney in a waste disposal site some miles distant. A false alarm!

The silence was palpable as he resumed his methodical visual scan, knowing Razor was equally active in his own area of responsibility, forward of the formation. For the pilot, however, the demands of holding position, even in loose formation, on the unwieldy VC-10 distracted his effort. Thankfully, if it really was an SA-7 loose on the streets, the more likely attack vector was from the rear and Flash had, infinitely, more spare capacity right now.

As the formation closed on the threshold, hope sprang that the dire warnings might have been a false alarm. Nevertheless, as the height dropped off the threat heightened. To spot a launch plume, to deploy flares and to pick up enough speed to make a defensive reaction, required skill and even more luck. They had practised similar manoeuvres on Spadeadam Electronic Warfare Training Range but executing an effective defensive counter to protect your own jet was hard. To draw off an attack against the massive airliner alongside would be a miracle. Flash glanced at the Matador infra-red jammer at the rear of the VC-10, hoping that it would do its job if their efforts failed.

Eyes scanned constantly left and right, backwards and forwards looking for an elusive smoke trail.

CHAPTER 65

The Roof of the Office Block.

Brandt hefted the missile launcher onto her shoulder taking the weight and adjusting the balance. She snapped the battery into place under the gripstock and adjusted for the sudden increase in weight, rebalancing the long launcher tube.

"Ascot 4386, outer marker inbound," she heard in the ear bud pressed into her ear. The frequency scanner had been a sensible precaution. Confidence building she knew that there could be only one RAF flight inbound to Heathrow today, thanking the gods that the flight had not been diverted to Northolt, well to the North of London. The flight path into the remote RAF airfield was miles from her current position. All the careful planning would have been for naught. The distractions must have worked.

"Ascot 4386, glide path descending."

Not long now. The call put the VC-10 just five or six miles on the extended centreline.

A British Airways 747 Jumbo droned past on short finals, its gaudily painted tail standing out vividly as it dropped towards the runway in the distance. Her prey should be the next aircraft on finals if the calls were to be believed. Slewing the iron sight on the tube around in the direction from where the Jumbo had approached, she trained the launcher on the pre-surveyed arc. The flash of a landing light caught her attention and she lined up on a bright pinpoint, recognising immediately the distinctive high tail of the VC-10. Her research had not been wasted. Onboard was the British Prime Minister, steadily approaching a rendezvous with destiny.

She relaxed into the shot. Timing was critical. The engagement had to come from the stern hemisphere so she would need to bide her time until the missile seeker head sensed the heat efflux of the four jet engines. Too soon and there would be insufficient infra red energy to acquire the target, too late and the missile might dish as it left the launcher, striking the ground before it made its terminal approach. The elevated position on the roof top should avoid that eventuality. It was not only trajectory that held her attention in the final moments because there was also the issue of battery life. The tiny "Grail" surface-to-air missile relied on battery power to provide launch commands to the missile. Once initiated, she had just seconds to acquire the target and launch the projectile. Any longer and the battery would expire and the seeker head would power down. Timing was everything.

The VC-10 descended, the rear aspect opening up, inexorably presenting the perfect angle to the terrorist on the anonymous rooftop. She tracked the target unerringly. With the target perfectly framed in the sight, she fired the battery, squeezing the acquisition trigger, taking up "half-action" which uncaged the tiny seeker head in the launch tube, prompting the electronic tracking circuits into life. The infra-red response from the VC-10, still distinct above the horizon, registered as a hot spot against the colder background, prompting the tiny seeker into a rhythmic sequence. A light illuminated on the missile body followed by the acquisition buzzer in her ear. Remembering her briefing, she eased the sight forward taking lead on the lumbering airliner and raised the launcher tube giving "super elevation", refining the launch trajectory. Hold steady. . . . .

Trigger press!

There was a pop and the missile lunged from the tube, powering into the air amid a plume of smoke. Brandt felt the launcher tube go light, empty now. The projectile powered away, exhaust gasses condensing in the atmosphere as it sped towards the receding target following a corkscrew, spiral course. She lost sight as it disappeared above an office block, tracking well ahead of the receding target. All she could do now was trust the electronics.

Her job done, her priorities shifted rapidly. Brandt dropped the launcher tube back onto the rug, folded the material over the hardware, once more concealing its identity. She hefted the indistinct object onto her shoulder using the gripstock as an expensive carrying handle and sprinted for the stairs. The missile expended, the tube was much lighter than it had been on the way upstairs and, with little effort, she dragged open the door to the stairwell and disappeared into the gloom. She could dismantle the launcher later.

CHAPTER 66

Short Finals to London Heathrow.

Flash eased back towards the VC-10, the Phantom still distinctly ungainly at approach speeds. They were in the end game. He would, on any normal occasion, have dropped the gear and flaps by now but he had been warned that in these circumstances it was not an option. To do so would set the armament safety locks and inhibit their ability to launch flares. Even the half flap setting he had selected was a luxury he could barely afford. With the countermeasures dispensers mounted on the missile pylons under the wings and the flares dispensed rearwards, he ran the risk of the flares striking the trailing edge flaps, if the trajectory was anything but true. Errant flares were a routine phenomenon and dispensing in the current configuration had rarely been trialled. They were in new territory nor was it lost on either he or his back seater that they were acting as cannon fodder for the Prime Minister. Like the selfless personal protection agents who followed her every move, their role was to place themselves in harm's way, if the unthinkable should occur. Furtive eyes scanned the surrounding urban landscape, only occasionally allowing a quick glance at the runway, tantalisingly close ahead.

Their job was nearly over.

"Plume, four o'clock range two miles! Gate!

Razor plugged in the burners unquestioning, but there was a nagging doubt in the back of his brain. They needed speed to respond, so the response was unavoidable but counter-intuitive. The massive reheat plumes that flared behind the Phantom were manna to a heat seeker. He realised, with apprehension, that he had just become a beacon and it was not a good feeling.

There followed a lull as fuel was pumped into the annular rings around the burner cans of the Spey engine, primed and then lit. It was some seconds before he felt the reheat bite and the Phantom responded, the speed slowly building up. Choreography was all. If he pulled too far ahead, the VC-10 would be unprotected. The threat was in his four o'clock and he had to hold position yet he needed more speed to manoeuvre. A conundrum! He had 300 knots; barely enough.

In full afterburner, they were already a more attractive target and would shield the massive engines of the transport aircraft, throttled back at approach power.

"Chill," he heard from the back seat, prompting him to drag back the throttles, again unquestioningly. Flash, acutely aware of the effect of superheated fuel burning fiercely in the reheat cans was a move ahead but Razor had to keep this jet flying. Even as he weighed the options, he recognised there was no alternative. Unless they dropped into military power, the seeker would home on the huge reheat plumes, infinitely more attractive than the tiny flares Flash was about to deploy. The thrust died as he retarded the throttles.

From the back seat, Flash tracked the plume as it snaked skywards, his gloved hand poised over the dispense button. The missile flight time, from its position little over two miles away, would be mere seconds and he had no time to lose.

"Flares," he called over the radio frequency, hitting the dispense button immediately, yet knowing that no one else in the formation could influence events. Watching the snaking projectile, he kept his thumb firmly over the dispense button and, an instant later, he commanded a second sequence. Unsure of whether the first sequence had done its job or even left the dispenser, he kept his thumb depressed, willing the tiny expendables into the airflow. Flares left in the dispenser with a missile inbound were as much use as a chocolate fireguard.

Still fighting the reluctant Phantom, Razor felt the thump of the deployment as a sequence of flares left each dispenser left and right. Chaff was redundant. There was no way that this missile, launched from a distant rooftop was guided by a radar beam. What's more, the radar warning receiver was eerily quiet, pinging only occasionally as the search radar, close by on the airfield at Heathrow, passed through on it endless rotation. Its calming ping was in stark contrast to the mayhem in the cockpit.

The threat at the head of the smoke trail was guided by the heat of their engines. In the slipstream, a ladder of pyrotechnic decoys shimmied in the airflow and rapidly ignited, reaching peak radiance only milliseconds after emerging from their cartridges. The incandescent core burned fiercely emulating the heat of the engines, a bright tail of smoke enlarging the effect. Fired at a diverging angle, they registered in the tiny electronic brain of the incoming missile causing the intended confusion. Two engine responses became three, then four, requiring the missile seeker to make a choice.

A second sequence followed the first, describing another perfect line of flares behind and away from the Phantom. Beyond the fighter, the VC-10 continued its descent, moving ever closer to the ground and safety, its crew in the cocooned cockpit oblivious to the drama unfolding. At the rear of the airliner, the ancient Matador infra-red jammer blinked its deceptive codes. Only if the missile should break the newly formed cordon would the geriatric jammer be called upon to act in anger. It was a fallback option that no one wished to put to the test.

"Break starboard," Flash called, prompting what he knew would be another automatic response from his pilot. They had to keep the Phantom in between the VC-10 and the approaching projectile, and a turn towards was the only way to stay within the missile's field of view. Razor winced, even as he dragged on the controls, his eyes glued to the airspeed indicator. The jet responded sluggishly, starved of assistance from the reheat. With only 300 knots on the gauge it was desperately slow for the manoeuvre and it let its displeasure be known as the angle of attack increased alarmingly.

For what seemed like a lifetime but, in reality, lasted only a handful of seconds, the "Grail" missile closed the distance on the Phantom. Already outside the field of view of the heat seeking sensor, the VC-10 tiptoed away. Inside the missile head, the simple reticule had begun its journey locked to an attractive heat source which may, or may not have been its intended target. With its lack of any countermeasures, and the complex subterfuge of the Phantom crew, the rapidly blooming flares proved simply too attractive to ignore. Its rudimentary tracking circuits stepped, methodically, down the line of decoys, slowly edging away from the latest target, the Phantom. In its electronic brain, the carefully crafted, chemical output from the decoy flares appeared remarkably similar to a jet engine, and infinitely brighter. The seeker head, in its confusion, sent increasingly spurious manoeuvre commands to the autopilot, veering away from the Phantom, despite its ungainly defence. By the time the missile reached the first flare in the sequence, the pyrotechnic squib had burned out and the core had extinguished. Starved of a target for the willing fuse, the seeker head merely opened out, staring into a now blank space. Outside of its mechanical gaze, the Phantom slowly gathered energy as Razor coaxed the reluctant jet through the turn, holding the persistent missile on the beam. It was readily apparent that the aggressor had lost lock, its corkscrewing motion damping down. It flashed past the Phantom, well outside the lethal radius of the fuse and warhead. The subsequent explosion had nothing to do with detecting a target, rather the missile fuse, with no further candidates for its attention, had sensed failure. A timer, reacting to the excessive time of flight, activated the self-destruct command, terminating the engagement.

From the core of the ensuing fireball, shards of debris, as the missile broke apart, rained down on the shops and offices below. The most significant damage was caused when a pellet from the warhead, designed to pierce the skin of a combat aircraft, shattered the windscreen of a parked car as it fell to Earth.

Brandt had failed.

The drama over, Razor pulled alongside the VC-10, gingerly, and waggled his wings, the universal signal that the pilot could proceed. The co-pilot in the right hand seat acknowledged the gesture enthusiastically, the extended thumb impossible to miss.

The VC-10 flared over the piano keys and settled onto the main runway at London Heathrow and, as it touched down, the wheels kissing the tarmac, a plume of smoke was released from the tyres. The collective sigh of relief, not only from the VC-10 cockpit but from the fighter alongside might have been sensed in the Capital.

The Prime Minister was back on terra firma.

As Razor eased the throttles forward, cleaning up the airframe, with the speed increasing, he rapidly overtook the slowing jetliner, dropping the wing to watch the roll out. The VC-10 dropped behind and out of sight.

"Job's a good 'un," he murmured to no one in particular. "Let's go home for tea and medals."

"Mission 01, instructions from your operators, contact London Mil on 134.9 for further instructions."

CHAPTER 67

Central London.

Across London, in a precisely planned sequence, a series of, apparently, unconnected events were set in motion. Sleeper agents, loyal to the Red Army Faction cause, were primed for mischief. A series of incidents had been set up in advance as diversions, to allow Brandt to escape. Most were unremarkable in their own right, but in the context of the attack, were meticulously planned to divert the emergency services and the authorities.

At East Ham underground station a package, surreptitiously, dropped into a waste bin began to smoulder. The small fire spread to the waste paper that had accumulated during the morning rush hour and, rapidly, a vigorous blaze developed. The thick black smoke drew staff from across the station concourse and calls for a fire engine were issued by at least two of the over-stretched staff adding to the confusion. The gates to the station slammed closed, preventing commuters from either entering or exiting the station. Although the heavily smoking bin dissuaded sightseers, a rapidly expanding crowd formed along the adjacent pavements preventing both commuters and regular pedestrians from moving around. With the roads slowly clogging up, a frustrated fire crew barged their way, unceremoniously, through the snarled traffic, towards the incipient bonfire.

Aboard a London Transport bus, two youths headed for the upper deck began jostling each other. Voices were raised and, soon, the wrestling worsened and the pair barged into seats, knocking passengers bags to the floor, prompting strident objections. A steroid-pumped passenger joined the mêlée intent on separating the combatants, earning a blow to the head which demanded instant retribution. Fists flew. The fracas that ensued alerted the driver who immediately pulled into a bus stop, cursing his luck. No hero, the man flagged down a police constable who had hoped for a quiet afternoon patrolling his urban beat. His urgent message for back up was acknowledged and, in seconds, sounds of sirens split the air as patrol cars in the vicinity responded, converging on the bus stop. Within minutes two police cars sealed off the road, isolating the bus and bringing the traffic to a standstill. The road, a major arterial route through the suburb, ground to a halt and traffic began backing up on both sides of the incident. The two youths jumped from the middle doors which had wheezed open as the bus came to a halt and sprinted into the surrounding back streets.

The youth who entered the small newsagent in Wanstead seemed nervous, his hands constantly touching his face. As he reached the front of the queue, he faced the shopkeeper, but only after pulling a mask over his face. The item in his hand looked remarkably like a 9mm Browning handgun. His demand to empty the cash register spawned no resistance. The register pinged as the drawer whipped open and a wad of banknotes swapped hands. The youth immediately turned and raced out of the shop, the incident over in seconds. The flustered shopkeeper's hands shook uncontrollably as he picked up the phone and dialled 999.

The driver of the stolen Audi selected his victim, an ancient Vauxhall waiting, patiently, to turn right across traffic on the busy A4 near Heathrow. As he approached the junction in the adjacent lane, he eased right just enough to straddle the white line. The contact with the rear of the Vauxhall was perfectly judged, just off centre. The inertia jolted the smaller car forwards, skewing it across the road, directly into the path of an oncoming car. Unable to avoid a collision the driver braced himself just as the two cars collided. Airbags deployed, horns blaring, a following vehicle rammed into the back of the car that had been struck. The driver of the Audi backed swiftly clear of the carnage, swung back into his own lane and sped off. The car would be found some hours later abandoned in a car park in Hounslow. Back at the scene, the traffic lights continued their sequence of, endlessly, changing colours. It would be some hours before the three vehicles could be prised apart and, in the meantime, the A4, the main artery out of London, was reduced to gridlock.

The boiler-suited figure who erected the road barriers attracted no attention. The signs, stolen from the back of a council maintenance truck some hours earlier, were genuine. The hastily applied decals on the side of the van that announced its allegiance to the local water authority, would not have passed close inspection but the man had no intention of dawdling. Pulling up the inspection grating, revealing the large stopcock, his actions would take only a minute. Rather than resolve a water problem as the red warning signs implied, the large hammer that he aimed at the stopcock, sheared the rotary valve from the union and water began to surge into the drain. Replacing the cover, he threw the warning signs back into the van, closed the door and drew out into the traffic. It would be only five minutes before the water flooded the main road cutting off the traffic flow.

Each incident had been carefully planned to magnify the chaos in a number of specific areas. The combined effect was that each of the emergency services began to receive callouts across the capital city, drawing units towards the East End. Normally quiet routines descended into chaos as the artificially engineered emergencies magnified a normally busy schedule of events. Reinforcements were called from across the Capital, with a raft of blue lights slowing traffic even further. Very quickly the services were swamped and the East End, slowly, closed down. The effects would be felt for hours.

In the meantime, an anonymous black VW Golf slipped through the outer suburbs, already clear of the ensuing chaos and heading for Suffolk. What its driver could not know was that each camera that it passed in the newly established "Ring of Steel" snapped away silently, reporting the car's presence to a control room in central London.

A net was closing.

CHAPTER 68

On the A12 Heading Out of London.

Brandt fiddled with the rotary tuning knob, the background static clearing as a local radio station blared out from the tinny door speakers. It was nearly time for the hourly news. The outer suburbs had receded and she had emerged from the urban sprawl back into green countryside. As the announcer rattled through the headlines, it was somehow odd to hear the incidents recounted as matters of fact. The incidents matched their carefully plotted script exactly. By all accounts, the East End of London had shut down and anyone who had thought to follow her path would be severely delayed by the chaos.

"Breaking news", the detached voice announced over the air waves. Brandt's attention peaked.

"Reports are coming in, confirming that an airliner has been hijacked over London and is being diverted to Stansted airport in Essex. It is not known at this time, if there have been any casualties onboard or whether demands have been made. We'll bring you updates as the news comes in."

That should cheer up the families of those people on the flight she thought. They should, even now, be rushing to make panic phone calls to the airport, trying to get further details of casualties. If we'd decided to take it down, there would have been no doubt about casualties, she mused. Despite the crass stupidity of the sensationalist news flash, it was not the headline she had hoped to hear. The hijack was the supporting element and, although it was diverting attention, she had expected another headline. Her attack had not hit the news. The silence could only mean that the missile must have lived up to its name and missed. An airliner carrying the Prime Minister coming down on short finals to the Capital's major air hub could not be covered up by even the most determined Government clamp down.

The aftermath would be visible across the city. People would babble to the media. It would be carnage. That had been the master plan after all; to cause confusion and panic. It should have struck at the very heart of western democracy. The rest of the plan was working but what of her contribution? Whatever the truth, the babble would be that it must have been lacking. Failure was not a word used often in the secretive meetings of the Red Army Faction. It was a word that, normally, preceded an enforced divorce from the group.

She forced herself to calm down but there could be only one conclusion. She had not downed the airliner. She had failed. Her thoughts turned to retribution.

As she pulled out to pass a dawdling motorist, she noticed a dark car coming up fast in the outside lane. It rapidly overhauled her, tailgating for a short distance before she was able to pull back into the inside lane. Anonymity was the key for now. Accelerating away ahead of her, she should also have registered that it took up position only a few hundred yards ahead, slowing down for no obvious reason, to match her pace. The final error was failing to register the unmarked white van behind which, had her senses been more attuned, she would have identified as it joined the A12 at the previous junction. But for the tinted glass in the cabin windows, the van was no different to the other commercial traffic that plied the road and, if she could have seen him, the nondescript driver at the wheel appeared perfectly relaxed. The invisible radio set in the cab had been in constant use for the last few minutes, relaying information between units.

The ability to run a vehicle check would not have alerted the authorities because the registration number of the rental car did not appear on any public database. But the number had indeed been flagged up and a coordinated operation was in train. The net was closing further.

She drove on unawares, the diesel engine of the VW Golf rattling its tune under the bonnet, relieved that, at least, she had extricated herself from a, potentially, tight spot. She was confident in the contingency arrangements and her withdrawal had gone to plan so far. The signpost for Romford flashed past but her destination, back in the wilds of Suffolk, was still some way off. Later that night the same light aircraft in which she had arrived would run the gauntlet once more, this time heading east back to Germany. She almost allowed herself to relax.

As the dark car that had passed a few minutes before slowed to a stop, it slewed across the carriageway blocking progress. She reacted instinctively but slowly to the unexpected development, a collision seemingly inevitable. Yanking the wheel over, her car lurched drunkenly across the hard shoulder striking the safety barrier hard, sparks trailing behind the vehicle as it slowed to a halt. The white van followed behind but halted, skewed across the inside lane, now lying at right angles to her path. Already, steam was issuing from the Golf's radiator but she recognised, in the confusion, that it was time to leave. Pushing the door hard, it resisted, buckled under the impact and would not move. The airbag had fired and billowed, uselessly, in front of her, impeding any movement. Climbing over the gearstick she reached for the passenger door handle and pushed. The door popped open and she tumbled out, emerging from behind the passenger door. Behind her, on the road, the rear doors of the white van had sprung open, a commotion preceding the cluster of bodies that tumbled out onto the tarmac, instantly setting up a perimeter along the roadside. The squat automatic weapons needed no interpretation as to their purpose.

Unharmed so far, it might be a temporary luxury. She assessed her only obvious escape route, calculating the distance from her position by the road to the trees beyond the barrier. The open fields offered a poor escape route. As her mind assessed the fading options, a harsh voice decided her next move for her.

"Armed police officers, stay still, raise your hands."

The decision was uncomplicated. With no plans to commit martyrdom; at least not yet, she was almost resigned as a pair of black-suited officers forced her to the ground, whipping her raised hands, painfully, behind her. The steel handcuffs felt ice-cold as they bit into her wrists.

She lay still, stunned at the speed of her detention. What now?

CHAPTER 69

The VIP Arrivals Lounge, London Heathrow.

Margaret Thatcher marched towards the door of the Arrivals Lounge, oblivious to the drama that had unfolded on short finals, her aide in tow. She would learn all too soon of the attempt on her life but for now she had more pressing business. The official car was stationary on the tarmac, the cavalcade in place, blue lights flashing in unison. She grimaced at the sight of a second aide rushing towards her, clearly intent on diverting her from her trajectory. He hustled her inside the building much to her annoyance.

"Prime Minister, welcome home."

"Thank you," she muttered unconvincingly, knowing that the respite from the relative calm she had experienced aboard the airliner had been too short. There was barely a pause in tempo as the aide pressed ahead, his words tumbling out.

"We have a developing situation, Prime Minister. An airliner has been hijacked over Belgium and is heading towards the Capital as we speak."

"Surely, that must have been just behind us as we made our approach?"

His nods confirmed her appreciation, her heart sinking. The words he omitted were as telling as those he offered. It was her worst nightmare. Despite the resolute exterior, an image she staunchly cultivated, the prospect of casualties to the hands of terrorists was an anathema. Losses in the air haunted her even more. Since the early days of radical terrorism, the perpetrators had become increasingly bold and, seemingly, immune to suffering. At first, the threat of violence had been enough to persuade less robust governments to yield, thereby avoiding casualties. As stances had hardened, so had the willingness to wreak havoc, and innocent lives began to be traded for attention on the world stage.

"Give me the details," she began, listening intently as the aide conveyed the few hard details that had emerged. It became apparent that facts were few so, in her indomitable style, she took up the offensive.

"Where is the airliner now?"

"Still over the Channel, heading inbound towards London, Prime Minister. Its destination is London Heathrow, and it's due to land in just 20 minutes."

"Have we launched fighters against it yet?"

"Yes, QRA was launched immediately, as soon as the electronic identification signal, signifying the hijack was seen. They're vectoring inbound as we speak."

"Do we have contingency plans for this eventuality?"

"Yes of course. The norm is to divert a suspected aircraft to Stansted Airport."

"The flight path into Heathrow is directly down the Thames, as I have just witnessed. Every single high value target in the Capital lies along that route. In the absence of any hard intelligence, we cannot risk a rogue airliner passing so close to vital installations. Pass on these instructions to the Master Air Defence Controller at Strike Command. He's at High Wycombe, is he not? Verbatim mind. Intercept the airliner and, if it refuses to comply with instructions, he is authorised to engage and destroy the airliner."

"But Prime Minister, the flight originated from one of our own airbases in West Germany. It's a trooping flight carrying service families home for holidays and it's scheduled to land at Luton."

"I would have preferred not to know that but my instructions stand. If the Captain of the hijacked airliner refuses to divert from his course, I will not live with the risk to the Capital when the terrorists' intent is unknown. What if they intend to use the airliner as a flying bomb? Tons of unspent aviation fuel would wreak havoc to buildings around the city."

The aide consoled himself, relieved that the weight of responsibility lay elsewhere. For once, he felt sympathy for the "Iron Lady", a feeling normally absent.

For her own part, she steeled herself, knowing that there could be no deviation from the long-held stance that there would be no negotiations with terrorist groups. At least that part of the decision had come easily.

"Do we know which faction is involved?" she asked, almost reluctant to hear the answer.

"Yes Prime Minister, it's the Red Army Faction, the Baader-Meinhoff Gang."

Her expectations reached an all time low..

CHAPTER 70

Over Kent.

"Mission 01, Neatishead, your target bears 120, close range, are you visual?"

The hope of a return to base had been short lived for the weary crew.

"Mission 01, affirmative," Flash replied, squinting against the sunlight as the shape of the passenger jet emerged from the surrounding blue sky, the stubby fuselage and under-slung engines gradually forming the familiar shape. The stylised logo depicting the figure of Britannia complete with trident, proudly worn on the fin, seemed to taunt the Phantom crew as they closed in. Normally a symbol of national pride, with the airliner having been seized by armed terrorists as it went about its usual business, the emblem had switched loyalties. Inside the cabin were innocent families returning to the UK after a tour of duty overseas; relatives going home after visiting loved ones serving in Germany; soldiers returning for ceremonial commitments in the capital city. They were united in a single strong belief, that they would land safely at Luton airport.

In the back cockpit, Flash knew precisely where the flight had originated because he had used it himself, taking his wife, an RAF air traffic controller, on their new and exciting posting to Wildenrath some years before. Yet the situation he now found himself facing was too close to home. Their actions over the coming minutes might affect his wider "RAF family"; and in fundamental ways.

The detail was best unacknowledged between the two cockpits for the time being.

Strident directives intruded on his reverie but he could not miss the critical words,

". . . . . contact me on Guard," the detached voice initiating what would be an unstoppable series of events. The voice was familiar. There was no pause. The words came from his own front seater.

"Britannia 24, this is Mission 01 transmitting on Guard; come up 121.5 for instructions."

In the front, listening to the commands from his back-seater, Razor adjusted the final approach towards the airliner, the barked commands overriding the external chatter from air traffic control. The Boeing was holding a steady height as he closed in gently, tweaking the throttles to stabilise alongside, the Phantom locked in position on the wing. The radar scope camera would be recording the relentless approach into the final position, so, should there be any recriminations during the inevitable aftermath, there would be an indisputable record of the outcome. Whatever that might be. It was not lost on the crew that their only means of recording the voice communications was through an obsolescent Walkman device, plugged into the intercom through a jury-rigged adaptor. Their conversations and those from the ground might be critical. All ATC communications were recorded but they were adept enough to make sure their backs were covered. Despite its limitations, it would have to suffice.

The long wait before the frequency crackled into life, left both aircrew on tenterhooks, apprehensive should their demands go unheeded. The airliner pressed on; its drive towards the Capital, apparently unhindered.

"Mission 01, Britannia 24 on Guard."

At last.

"I'm heading 290, about to begin our descent into Luton."

"The heading's all wrong, Razor. That takes it across London not into Essex."

The response from the front was tentative; probing.

"Roger Britannia 24 copy your squawk, I understand you are unable to comply with normal directions."

"That's affirmative. I am under directions to follow a reassigned course, approaching Luton from the south."

"Understand you're approaching from the south?" he queried, the implications immediately obvious.

Normal routing to Luton would have the Boeing head out over Essex, initially on a more northerly heading before approaching from the southeast. To the south lay London and the congested approach patterns into Heathrow. If the Boeing descended unchecked into the middle of the busy arrivals pattern there would be mayhem.

"That's bullshit Razor." the navigator's concern superfluous. "There's no reason to reroute to the south other than to cause mischief . . . . . or worse."

The pilot was already attuned to the repercussions.

"Neatishead, Mission 01, did you copy Britannia 24's intentions?"

"Affirmative 01, standby."

"He'll be on the line to the Air Defence Commander."

"So would I!"

Both aircrew, dark visors dropped against the glare, stared at the airliner, their gaze never faltering, willing it to divert from its flight path.

The wait stretched out.

"Mission 01, Neatishead, instructions from Sunrise."

"Who the hell's Sunrise?"

"It's the ADOC! As you said; the Air Defence Commander."

"Straight from the horse's mouth then?"

Almost before the conversation had stilled on their lips, the airliner began a slow descent, the manoeuvre unannounced. Razor dragged the throttles back to stay in formation, the height dropping off only slowly.

"Neatishead, Mission 01, target descending," he reported to the controller, the pressure ramping up. The use of the word target was not lost on anyone. The airliner, carrying RAF personnel was suddenly a threat. Their fears were merging with reality. If unchecked they would become their worst nightmare.

"Roger, Mission 01, standby, seeking instructions."

The voice was harassed. The subsequent delay was interminable.

When the response finally materialised, the edgy aircrew might have wished the frequency had remained quiet. Suddenly, any timidity had evaporated from the controller's voice. A new steel was apparent.

"Mission 01, Neatishead, you are authorised to make a single guns pass to divert the airliner from its path. If the warning burst fails you are authorised to engage. I say again, if the warning burst fails you are authorised to engage. I authenticate, Charlie Alpha."

"Check that mate," breathed Razor, digesting the instructions they had just been passed. Such an order could not be followed blindly. There were strict procedures to make sure that the order had come from the command authority. Flash fumbled on his kneeboard, checking the complex matrix of letters, seeking authentication. Secretly, he knew there was little doubt as he knew the voice was the same controller who had been talking to them since check in.

"Affirmative, the authentication is valid."

The quiet was broken only by the background noise in the cockpit as the two aircrew stared across the small gap towards the airliner flying alongside. Faces pressed to the windows, watching the Phantom jockeying in close formation, enjoying the spectacle. Although many onboard had enjoyed the sight of a Phantom alongside, some as they made their approach to the tiny South Atlantic dependency in the Falkland Islands, few could know the threat they now posed. For the Phantom crew, the innocent faces amplified the enormity of the decision they now faced and the enormity of the consequences if the hijackers did not capitulate.

"Listen Flash, I know I'm Captain of this tub but this is not a decision that I should take alone. What are your thoughts?"

"It's easy mate. We've had an order and it's been authenticated. Now is not the time to question years of training. We can't know why engaging this aircraft is so important but someone way higher up the chain than us knows and has decided for us. We just pull the trigger."

"My thoughts as well but I had to ask."

"That's what your flight commander would say back on the ground."

"But you are my flight commander. . . . . Ah, never mind"

The cockpit lapsed back into silence.

"Weapons checks," prompted the businesslike rejoinder from the back cockpit. Endless hours of training kicked in. Razor began the familiar routine.

"Coolant's on, tone set, CW, remaining off for now, guns selected, Master Arm to arm, LCOSS uncaged."

The checks were perfunctory and stark. The weapon system was now live and, as the gunsight gyrated on the collimator lens directly in the pilot's sightline, he tensed. Used to tracking a compliant banner fluttering behind a Canberra bomber, a warning pass against an airliner was a more complex and challenging profile. The reticule, as the gunsight was known, its red symbols dancing on the sight glass, moved gently in concert with his control movements. He eased the Phantom out from its close formation position on the airliner's wing and, instantly, the radar fired up once more as his navigator locked up the target. Now fed with ranging and positional information, the gunsight responded instantly, computing its revised but deadly trajectory. It calculated how far ahead of the Boeing the pilot would need to aim, to ensure the cannon shells from the SUU-23 gun pod and the target coincided in space. Throughout the pass it would update its deadly calculation. Only three hits from the high explosive incendiary shells the gun carried were needed to bring down a fighter. Fighters were designed to be more resilient than the soft target presented by a vulnerable airliner. For this pass, however, Razor would need to aim way ahead to avoid the deadly calculation being accurate. He would have to lead the target by a considerable margin or the result would be catastrophic.

He tipped-in, dragging the gunsight onto the airliner's cockpit before reversing the turn and pulling the gunsight well ahead. Although the SUU-23 gun pod was loaded with high incendiary rounds, it did not contain tracer ammunition, so the fall of shot would be invisible to the Phantom crew but, hopefully, not to those occupying the airliner cockpit. It would be a finely timed manoeuvre, and for much of it, the airliner would be invisible below the nose of the fighter. It would need to be close enough to ensure that the hijackers were under no illusion that they would be threatened with deadly force, if they persisted. It had to be far enough ahead of the flight path that there was no risk of striking the airframe with a stray round. Just one hit from a 20 mm high explosive incendiary round could be enough to destroy vital flight systems aboard the thin-skinned aircraft. As a minimum, a hit would cause a rapid decompression as the pressurised cabin air vented to atmosphere. One thing was certain, it would be impossible for the terrorists in the cockpit to miss the sight of a gun pod being emptied at the rate of 6,000 rounds per minute. With only one pass authorised, there was little point in holding back. It would be a long trigger press. If they failed to comply, the gun would not be the next weapon used.

Razor pulled the gunsight ahead, the roll tabs matching his angle of bank precisely. The radar ranging bar marched around the periphery of the sight, its shortening length signifying the rapid closure. The Phantom ate up the separation between the aircraft rapidly, despite the fact that the undeviating, predictable path of the airliner through the sky was not an easy profile to track. Used to fighters that manoeuvred hard to avoid a shot, the compliant airliner was a sitting duck, its bulk taunting, yet Razor felt an almost mesmerising urge to allow the sight to drift backwards towards the cockpit. It was how he had been trained and the urge to comply was strong. What he was doing felt wrong. In the nick of time, as the pressure on the stick relaxed, he snapped back to reality. Resuming the pressure on the controls, pulling far ahead, his mind focussed. With the bulk of the airliner now masked by the belly of the Phantom, he squeezed the trigger and the whine of the six barrels penetrated the cockpit, the noise of the gun drowning out the ambient cockpit noise as it spooled up, rapidly, to its full rate of fire, in an instant. Unseen, the cannon shells erupted from the barrels, a wave of spent cases left in the wake, a stream of lead filling the air ahead, the density of the burst causing a haze. From the cockpit of the airliner, the gout of flame from beneath the QRA jet was dramatic, lethal, its intent unmistakeable.

Stabilising the turn, breaking out hard and away from the airliner's flight path, Razor returned to the perch position to the left of, and above the wing. He waited, urging compliance.

The radio was quiet.

Surely there could be no chance that the intent of the pass could have been misconstrued or even unobserved? The intent was unmistakeable.

"Britannia 24, Mission 01, you have one minute to comply with my instructions and follow me to Stansted or I am authorised to engage. I repeat, I am authorised to engage, acknowledge."

Silence.

*

In the cockpit, Steinbach had watched the Phantom break out following the guns pass. He had to admit, the sight of a fully loaded Phantom, its afterburners cooking, vortices streaming off the wingtips, was impressive, if not slightly chilling. The sight of the radar-guided missiles hanging menacingly in the belly, gave no room for doubt. Maybe he had underestimated the Brits? Had he pulled the tiger's tail. Or should that be the Lion?

*

Razor and Flash resigned themselves to the inevitable. This was the moment for which they had prepared. All their training had been focussed on developing their ability to deliver a lethal weapon but, how could it be that the object for their efforts would be their own countrymen? Hostages in a deadly tit-for-tat.

"We need to drop back outside minimum range. I suggest we use Skyflash as it has a bigger warhead to get the job done," came the quiet, confident tone from the rear. The throttles responded without further prompting, words superfluous.

The Phantom drifted back into weapons parameters.

"Skyflash selected, CW is On," intoned the pilot, making the final weapons selections. The "Selected" lights flashed on the weapons panel signifying that the semi-active missiles had re-tuned to the radar frequency, ready for their terminal, and, undeniably, deadly mission.

The Phantom slipped back into a loose trail position, the radar tracking the airliner, its commands relayed to the electronic circuits in the Skyflash missiles below the fuselage.

Razor flipped the Master Arm switch back to "Arm", his heart heavy. He checked the weapons panel for one last time, stalling for time, hoping for a final reprieve. His finger tightened. "Selected" and "Ready" glared back at him, showing the Skyflash missile was ready for its ominous task. In combat, such delay would have been terminal. His finger hovered, yet again, over the trigger. Ready to apply the killing pressure.

Why was he hesitating?

*

"Locked up, in range, clear to fire."

Back to the recurring nightmare. Razor was about to consign 94 souls to a premature grave and there was no way out. He had rehearsed the moment endlessly on exercise. The monotone from the back seat repeated a familiar litany. He had listened to the patter so many times and responded automatically. Thousands of simulated missiles had left the rails and destroyed exercise targets. The difference was that, up to now, it had been simulated. This was real.

There was no choice.

The order had been given.

He pulled the trigger.

The thump from below his feet signalled the start of the launch sequence, as the hydraulic rams on the launcher thrust the Skyflash missile downwards into the turbulent airflow beneath the Phantom. A thin lanyard attached to the missile body, umbilical like, extended from the launcher as the separation between airframe and payload increased. At the limit of its travel, a clip separated, initiating motor launch. Already, the seeker head, primed by the radar and its electronic guidance circuits, locked to the electronic response from the airliner. The head, cocooned within a tiny protective radome, shifted its attention along the new bearing, its circuits primed to track the velocity of its victim. The motor ignited, the hot gasses accelerating the slim body, instantly, to supersonic speeds. The Skyflash surged ahead, enveloping the Phantom in a suffocating cloud of vapour. In the cockpit, its departure was like the noise of the passage of an express train. In its wake, the radar in the nose of the Phantom stared fixedly at a point in space.

At its focus, Britannia Flight 24.

*

The Captain turned his head towards the hijacker, slumped, inanimately, on the rumble seat. The man stared fixedly ahead. How old was he, this young man? He looked as if he was barely out of school. Certainly, barely old enough to have graduated from university. What had brought him to this point? Where did political dogma trump humanity?

"You know they will do it, don't you?"

"Quiet!" the man snapped. "Let me think."

"They will engage. Those were Skyflash missiles strapped beneath the Phantom. I used to fly Jaguars in the RAF. Would you like me to explain its potential? Look-down shoot-down capability against fast-jet targets. Looking up against a sky background is a walk in the park. It has a 40 Kilogram blast fragmentation warhead. It can take down a Bear bomber."

"Quiet!"

The ensuing silence was a chink in the armour; if only a small one. The Captain paused, anxious not to press his luck.

"If we divert to Stansted as ordered, you'll have more time to negotiate. If not . . . . ."

The pause stretched out ever longer, allowing the hijacker to complete the thought.

*

The tension as the missile guided on its short trajectory was shattered; the voice over the radio calm but authoritative.

"Britannia 24, requesting vectors to the ILS for Runway 22 at Stansted."

The hijacker had capitulated!

Action.

Razor's hand moved, instantly, to the switch controlling the continuous wave radar, even now passing guidance signals to the missile ahead.

He flipped it off.

The notation "Safe" did not yet reflect the real situation.

"Break lock," the pilot shouted as his hand moved, instinctively, back to the throttles but his back-seater was already reacting to the message. Both had been living in hope. Flash squeezed the acquisition trigger as if life itself depended on it.

It did!

Interrupting the tracking signal, even before the urgent call had faded from Razor's lips, the radar thumped against the mechanical end stops as it reverted to search mode. The time base on the green radar scope in the back cockpit was once more scanning left and right.

Surely normality had resumed?

The green blip ahead, hitherto the focus of the radar's attention, was less than two miles away.

Still boosting, the smoke from the Skyflash missile tracked towards its prey, the rocket motor powering the deadly payload towards the doomed airliner. The trajectory was inked in the sky, marked by the curving smoke trail, at the apex, a steel cylinder carrying 94, unsuspecting, souls.

Razor tensed, knowing he had done all he could to prevent the carnage, his eyes locked to the trail. The path seemed inevitable. He had been too late.

Starved of information, the inanimate, tracking loops registered the loss of the vital guidance data and began to scan the velocity spectrum for an alternative victim. Without a substitute, the autopilot locked the stubby control fins on the missile body into a neutral position and the missile went ballistic. Eating the distance between itself and the target at a speed well above Mach 2, the gap closed swiftly. The missile was programmed to follow a course to its last known intercept point, a guard against Soviet jammers, intent on deception on a future, electronic battlefield. It homed to a point in space where its prey had last been seen.

From the cockpit Razor watched mesmerised, unable to influence events, the choreography set. If the missile passed the airliner within range of its radio fuse, it would still detonate, programmed to respond to any lump of metal that passed inside its malevolent radius. The seconds seemed like hours but the smoke trail, marking the path of the still boosting missile, shot past the left wing of the plodding airliner and disappeared into the blue skies beyond. The, now distant, trail extinguished as the boost phase ended, the missile disappearing from view. Coasting and blissfully invisible, it self-destructed, its target gone. The ball of smoke that blossomed in the distance marked a reassuring finale.

The shattered crew exhaled, almost in unison. The hijackers had capitulated. They would not know why, but the fact that the airliner was still flying was enough. It began a gentle turn back to the east, heading slowly towards East Anglia, the height beginning to drop off, immediately.

The standoff might not yet be over but a crisis had been averted.

"Britannia 24 descending."

"Britannia 24, Mission 01, acknowledged. Follow me."

Words were inadequate.

Razor stared at the, seemingly, innocent switch controlling the continuous wave radar. He would ponder the significance many more times over numerous very large beers.

Flash stroked the acquisition trigger. Had he not broken lock, the Boeing would, by now, have been confined to a fiery end.

*

A red fire truck held at the threshold of the active runway, ready to follow the airliner on its landing run, its blue lights flashing out a beat.

As Razor eased open the throttles, accelerating above and ahead of the airliner, he watched over the lip of the canopy as the Britannia Airways airliner flared and settled onto the runway. A brief puff of smoke from the undercarriage heralded its safe arrival back on terra firma. It had been the second time today he had watched the same scene.

He allowed himself a brief moment of hope that the bodies, tightly strapped into the cabin, would survive the ordeal. They had narrowly avoided oblivion but they were not yet safe.

"Mission 01 overshooting."

CHAPTER 71

Canon Row Police Station, Central London.

The figure slumped before Hawkes was a shadow of the firebrand who had been arrested in the wilds of Suffolk just a few hours before. Brandt had visibly deflated during the drive back to London, the presence of two bulky policemen hemming her in on either side and the manacles that secured her wrists and ankles, guaranteed acquiescence. The highly visible weapon, toted by the firearms officer who had accompanied her, was positioned well out of her reach, its presence the final guarantee of compliance. All the brash, bluster was gone.

Even though the terrorist looked defeated, Hawkes knew better than to believe that she was spent. The woman was a viper and he trusted her not one iota. She had to be pinned down and the link between the spent missile launcher secreted in the boot of the Golf, and her evident co-conspirator was the key. "Dancing around the handbag" came to mind as the policeman grilled his reluctant suspect. She had been avoiding the truth for some while and it was time to revert to the direct approach. It was time to confront her with hard evidence.

"Look, let me lay it out for you," he began gently. "Maybe I can show you that cooperation is the only way to limit your pain. You and I both know that we found the missile launcher in the boot. The fact that it has Cyrillic script blazoned all over it is no coincidence. If it didn't come direct from Moscow, the Soviet Union is, certainly, its origin. We've had you under surveillance for days and the fact you've spent a few happy hours with a Soviet agent is no coincidence. We know just how much you have been doing to cause mischief. Or worse!"

The English understatement was lost on the German, the word mischief not part of her vocabulary. Two pictures slid across the table into her sightline, Hawkes watching closely as her eyes dropped downwards. The look of apprehension was unmistakeable. It was her first sign of weakness. Dmitry Guskov was not a stranger. Any trained interrogator knew that once that threshold was breached, progress could be made. He probed for the weak spot.

"We know you have strong links to the Red Army Faction. You're an activist and your background is well known to us. I've got you and I can put you away for a long time but I want Guskov."

The inscrutable mask had been reaffixed but her body language had changed. The nervous inflections were evident to the trained eye.

"Look, you know he would kiss you off as much as look at you." He fought to maintain an even delivery. "Guskov's motive was purely political, designed to foment a rift between the western allies and aimed at stopping reunification. It's obvious to anyone who has taken even a passing interest in Cold War politics. He's KGB through and through. No one gets in his way and no one will divert him from his goal. You were just the scapegoat."

The pause was carefully timed. He sensed the breakthrough before her lips even moved.

" I can help," he hinted.

The conflict between self interest and revenge was brief and barely counter-balanced by a failing loyalty to the cause. Her self interest won out. Ultimately, she preferred self preservation over morality.

"I can give you Guskov but I want assurances."

The offer hung, enticingly. Hawkes was tempted to respond immediately, the relief overwhelming, but a rash acceptance was not in his nature. There was still more to gain but he had breached the dam. His stock response would be that the UK Government does not negotiate with terrorists but what was said in press interviews, was in stark contrast to discussions behind closed doors. The potential prize was tantalisingly close. To take down an active KGB agent and to remove him from the streets would bring not only kudos to him and his small team but it would make national headlines.

"What do you want?" he probed, the negotiator dominant.

"I'm not going to prison," she replied baldly. "I doubt I'd survive."

How she planned to avoid that fate and whether she would succeed, would rest on the coming discussion.

"I know when and where Guskov plans to leave the country and, before you put out warnings to the airports and seaports, you'd be wrong. He won't be using any of the obvious routes out. He's much more subtle than that and you know it."

The bravado was gone. The pitch was simple. She was fighting for her future and he believed her.

"If we can find a way to avoid you facing trial, how can I be sure you'll cooperate?"

"You may not have that luxury. The timings are such that if you don't act quickly he'll be gone. If you want him, the window is quite short. Delay and he's home free."

As Hawkes pondered his predicament, his mind raced. She was the epitome of duplicity and gut instinct said that he should tie her down. But, damn it all, she was right. Guskov would not linger.

"He leaves tonight but I want assurances before I tell you where and when."

Hawkes had begun to rehearse the difficult conversation he would have with the prosecutor from the Crown Prosecution Service when he tried to sell him the deal. It would not sit well with the lawyer allowing a known terrorist back onto the streets, whatever the prize. Maybe he could shift her to a safe house or arrange an extended stay at a detention facility? It would bide time. The Prime Minister's view was well known and, given that she had been on the wrong end of a missile launcher just a few hours before, her attitude would have hardened. She would have to know eventually, but If it came out in the press that a deal had been struck, there would be a national outcry and even the Iron Lady was not immune to public opinion. His advantage in the debate would be that, if he could give the PM both Guskov and Brandt, she could play the "Evil Empire" card, so eloquently played by Regan recently. The Soviet agent was, after all, the mastermind behind the plot, not Brandt. Despite the PM's respect for Gorbachev, the antics of the KGB eclipsed even his rising star.

Hawkes was, above all, a practical man knowing that the West German Secret Service, the Bundesnachrichtendienst, would want a say in her fate. For that discussion he would need Chisholm. Nevertheless, if she walked free from Canon Row Police Station today, she was marked. The terrorists had engineered her complicity in a direct attack on the Prime Minister. They would know that she had been apprehended when she failed to meet her rendezvous. If she did not, subsequently, stand trial for the crime, it would be only a matter of time before retribution was meted out. For Hawkes, whether that trial was in London or Bonn, he cared little. Either way, he needed the information she held and torture was hardly an option.

"I need to make a call but I'm sure we can come to an accommodation. Give me ten minutes."

There was no need to parrot the usual caveat for the tape as the device had been switched off long before the loaded conversation had begun. No one would ever hear the sordid details of the deal he was about to negotiate.

Escaping the foetid atmosphere of the interview room, breathing in the relatively fresh air in the dingy corridor, his conscience was remarkably clear. The mental checklist grew as he framed a potential deal.

CHAPTER 72

Stirling Lines, Hereford.

The SAS officer, clad in disruptive camouflage kit, seemed out oddly of place in the drab office at the rear of the Headquarters building. Framed pictures ringing the wall hinted at an illustrious career that could never be acknowledged outside the confines of the elite organisation. On closer inspection, the pictures captured events that might have hinted at minor celebrity. A younger facsimile of the officer behind the desk, was captured with a minor Royal pinning a decoration to a proud chest. The ceremony would not have made headlines at the time and the celebration was, evidently, sparsely attended. Whilst his appearance might have seemed incongruous, his attitude was the polar opposite. He wasted no time. His manner was all action.

"Sarn't major!"

A similarly clad NCO emerged in the doorway filing its frame.

"Sir!"

"Get teams two and three to the briefing room right now. Operation 'Limit' has been called. Have the standby A-109 fired up and get the Tiger Team underway right away. We'll brief them when they land on. Have the Quartermaster draw weapons before we brief and get them aboard the helo. It's a counter-terrorist op so make sure it's the right load-out. Briefing in ten."

"Sir!"

The warrant officer withdrew from the room, returned to his own office and rifled through the drawers, pulling out a lanyard holding a single key. A call to the Boss had set in motion a well rehearsed series of events and, merely the mention of the word "Limit", signified that the destination would be the civil airport at Stansted. It was a codeword, intimately familiar to the whole squadron.

The remote airport in the heart of the Essex countryside was the designated landing ground for any airliner suspected to have been hijacked. A small resident, civilian team, was nominated to coordinate with his own specialist, anti-terrorist team and would be the first unit to be alerted once the airliner was ordered to land. That the squadron received the warning simultaneously, and was already making preparations to respond, was no coincidence.

The SAS officer walked across to his own filing cabinet, twisting the Manifoil lock in a series of random gyrations, pulling out a blood-red folder, the operation name "Limit" emblazoned across the front cover. A key slotted into a smaller security container within the can and, scooping up the sealed contents, he moved urgently back to his desk and scanned the contents rapidly. The instructions, direct from the outer office of Number 10 Downing Street would provide some light reading for the short flight he was about to make.

A series of briefing slides were already prepared and he penned in some last minute detail from the scribbled notes he had taken during the phone call. There would be a constant dialogue between the headquarters and Number 10 over the next hour but what he had was enough to get them started. They needed to be in the air, and quickly. Scant minutes after taking the call he was heading to the briefing room where ten troopers of No. 22 Special Air Service waited patiently.

The air in the briefing room was calm, yet the inscrutable faces ranged before him gave no signs of the underlying tension that must have been present. It was no surprise to their commander. Short notice briefings were a feature of life on the squadron and were rarely called for anything other than a major crisis. It came with the job. Planning and rehearsal were the key to success and, everyone was intimately familiar with what was about to occur. Well rehearsed, almost every man present in the room had practised every last element of the plan endlessly. Nothing was left to chance intentionally, but terrorists had a bad habit of posing unexpected challenges that no end of scenario rehearsals could predict.

The officer tapped the lectern and the low murmurs faded away. His briefing would provide essential, degradable, information only. The overhead projector snapped on revealing a schematic diagram of an airfield dispersal. Key points were highlighted gled identified.

"Stansted International Airport in Essex. About twenty minutes ago, Britannia Flight 24, a trooping flight from RAF Wildenrath, an airbase in West Germany, was hijacked over Belgium. There are 94 souls onboard, mostly service families returning home on leave or returning to the UK at the end of their tours of duty. No demands have yet been made but expect those before we go in. We know that policy dictates that there will be no negotiation with terrorists and, the PM has made that clear to me on more than one occasion, so I doubt she will be inclined to change her mind this time. The jet has been ordered to land at Stansted and we expect to find it on the allocated parking apron here, on the western side of the main runway. A Phantom from the UK Quick Reaction Alert was in company but I have no information of its whereabouts. I doubt it will have landed as there would be little it could do on the ground."

He stabbed the overhead projector, highlighting the dispersal and reminding the group of the assembly points.

"There's no suggestion as to who the hijacker is. We think it's one man, operating alone but that may change as we get eyes-on. Assume that we'll find more and be prepared. There's no inkling how an armed man got onboard through a secure RAF checkpoint but that's for others to investigate. Let's focus on what we can change. Operation Limit is underway. Our job is to end this hijack without loss of life and as quickly as we can. This is personal gents. These people might be our own families. Our job is to change the terrorist's mind."

His rare, emotional lapse registered within the group. It would not affect how they responded to the emergency. Professionalism would prevail but the flinty stares had hardened measurably as the briefing broke up.

CHAPTER 73

Stansted International Airport.

The atmosphere inside the Boeing cockpit was becoming uncomfortable as the sun streamed in through the cockpit windows. In the cabin, despite the fact that the auxiliary power unit had been spooling away since the engines had been shut down, the conditions were deteriorating. The steady flow of conditioned air was fighting against the mass of sweaty, nervous bodies.

The first exchanges over the radio had ended, replaced by a tense standoff. Steinbach was showing his nerves and feeling isolated, reluctant to risk tipping his hand by calling Hammond to the cockpit. It may yet prove more useful to have someone in the aft cabin, temporarily anonymous, should bravado amongst the passengers win out over nerves. Should the doors be breached, it was unlikely that Hammond could influence events but, for now, his compatriot had managed to keep his anonymity and may yet prove valuable.

Steinbach keyed-off the microphone after another seemingly open ended discussion, fuming at the dulcet tones of the hostage negotiator. The replies, littered with short pauses, specifically designed to ramp up the stress and control the exchange, were exasperating. The negotiator's arrogance was working, building a feeling of haplessness, leaving him incensed. The subsequent spiel was utterly predictable, seemingly to put him at ease, but in reality closing down the options. The offers, the delays and the noticeable prevarication was a variation on the "good cop - bad cop" theme and masterly delivered. Steinbach recognised the technique and had been coached in counteracting the impasse, not that knowledge seemed to be helping his predicament.

The increasingly edgy terrorist took stock. Rather than having landed at Heathrow, he found himself sequestered on a remote dispersal at a rural airport in Essex, separated from the mainstream airline traffic. It was the very volume of traffic that he had been relying upon to wreak havoc had he been able to land at Heathrow. He knew that stopping all traffic into the main London hub would have been impossible, whereas he had been denied the buffer, Stansted being much easier to control. At this stage, assurances of free passage were worthless and, unless he could trade bodies for fuel, he would be trapped on this isolated dispersal until the episode reached an inevitable conclusion. He had hoped that the "bodies" he had in mind could have remained alive, but he was steeled for the possibility that he might need to make an example of at least one of them if his will continued to be questioned. He would start with one of the cabin crew rather than one of the innocents. In all likelihood, eventually, he may have to resort to threatening one of the children if the stupid bastards continued to believe he would not follow through. Although not his primary option, he was under no illusions that he would, if needs be. He would be reliant on Hammond to intervene in the cabin if that proved necessary. Thank goodness for back up. This was one twist of the scenario that they had not war-gamed back in Erklenz and it might have been the plan's downfall. How to snare the flight attendant? If he stepped out of the cockpit, he had little doubt that the crew would make sure that he did not step back inside, but how to signal his intent to Hammond in the back? At some stage dialogue would be vital but, at present, he would resort to cryptic announcements over the public address system and hope that his co-conspirator would recognise his plan. He would hold back as long as possible not yet wishing to show his hand.

*

"Golf Bravo Mike Echo Lima overhead Foxtrot."

To the clusters of enthusiasts ranged along the airport perimeter fence, ears glued to portable radios monitoring the air traffic control frequencies, little could be gleaned from the routine radio call. Around the airport it set in chain a pre-arranged sequence of events. Airliners were held in the holding pattern some miles distant in the Stansted control zone. An airliner that had just touched down on the main runway followed the barked instructions from the Ground Controller, turning off and making its way without delay to the jetway. There would be no further movements on the airfield for at least the next hour.

Within minutes a pair of outwardly commonplace Augusta Bell A109 helicopters flew over the perimeter fence at well below tree top height, their approach trajectory precisely choreographed to remain invisible from casual watchers but, specifically, from the designated concrete apron which now housed the Britannia Airways Boeing 737. The dark blue airframes clattered to a halt some distance from their final objective, the rotors braking to a standstill, the whine of the turbines dying away. As the doors sprang open, bodies emerged from all sides, pulling ruggedised equipment cases in their wake, moving without delay towards a screened-off section of the apron.

With the dispersal once more quiet, only the distant sound of the auxiliary power unit disturbed the eerily still airfield. One man split from the group and made his way towards a knot of bodies. Decorum once more established after the mayhem of the arrival, the officers brushed dust, thrown up by the helicopters, from ruffled jackets. The insignia marked them out as Metropolitan Police officers but only the well informed would know that they were from the elite counter-terrorism squad.

The identity of the new arrival, clad in a tight fitting black jumpsuit was concealed by a sinister facemask, the anonymity intentional. He approached the obvious leader of the group and a short exchange ensued.

"What's the situation Chief Superintendant? Do we have an execute order?"

"No Sir, not yet but I have been instructed to hand operational control over to you."

There was no rancour.

"No change from the prebrief?"

"None."

"Is the dispersal locked down?"

"Affirmative. No unauthorised movements, all arrivals and departures suspended and I have a perimeter established by the local police force."

"Any exchanges with the crew?"

"I've only been in contact with the chief hostage negotiator so far. He's had the first demands and, not surprisingly, they refuse to negotiate at the minute. He's not optimistic. He reckons that they're following one of the classic patterns."

"What's his take? Has he established a definite allegiance?"

"That's easy. Red Army Faction without a doubt."

"At least that should make it easy for our political masters. We know that they have no compunction in taking lethal action. I hope the politicians don't dither."

The silence was hardly reassuring, nor was the evident concurrence.

"I have control Chief Superintendant. My comms man has two-way contact with the decision maker in Whitehall. We'll take it from here."

"My team is at your disposal."

The offer fell on deaf ears as the military officer moved back towards his team. Help from an outside party, even one as accomplished as the counter-terrorism team, was not part of any plan.

Behind the screens, although each and every weapon in the formidable arsenal had been cleaned and oiled to extinction, team members had disassembled their personal weapons once more and were applying a light sheen of gun oil. It was not necessary but calmed frayed nerves. Not one of the battle-hardened veterans would admit to such a frailty as nerves. Equally, there would be no delay when called upon because every single man in the group could reassemble his personal weapon in seconds, the drill automatic and second nature. The light anti-tank weapon that lay casually in the grass looked incongruous on a civilian airfield. It seemed hardly appropriate to storm an airliner, presumably, a weapon of last resort.

The target was invisible from behind the brightly painted screens, strategically placed for the very purpose. Ostensibly, blast deflectors, they had never been used as such, indeed, requests to use the remote dispersal for engine runs had always been robustly refused. Their purpose was to conceal motion, not to contain noise.

The temporary standoff would soon end.

"Boss! Decision maker coming on frequency, stand by."

The remote earpiece which the officer clamped to his ear, linked him direct to a secure room in the Cabinet Office on Whitehall. Unseen, a highly specialised and extremely high-ranking party had assembled in minutes. Only convened in extremis, the group contained experts in every field of hostage response and were equipped and prepared to make decisions. The man listened intently, expecting questions and prevarication but he was heartened to receive an instruction consisting of a single, well rehearsed codeword. He turned back to the troopers clustered alongside the blast shield, his face concealed behind the mask, impassive.

"Sarn't Major. Execute!"

The response instant.

"Stand by for time hack."

Each of the black-clad bodies stared intently at G Shock watches, cuffs drawn back, ready for the synchronisation.

"Five, four, three two, one, hack. Thirteen zero seven."

"Go, go, go!"

*

Steinbach was uneasy. It was too quiet.

Since his first demands for fuel and safe passage had been issued, the radio had been, jarringly, silent. His opening gambit had been bluff. He had no intention of flying the airliner elsewhere. His role was to shock the decision makers and to divert attention away from the major event which was going ahead many miles distant in Central London. Had his plan worked, he would have been much closer to that event but, even though his original destination had been London Heathrow, Stansted could suit his purposes just as well. His goal now was to extract himself from this unexpected predicament and he had 94 reasons why the authorities would provide a vehicle in which he could escape from the airport. Although their much vaunted position was that they would never negotiate with terrorists, he knew that in the past, albeit unacknowledged, demands had been met. Murky deals had been endorsed and he felt sure that once bodies began emerging from the airliner, either alive or dead, a vehicle would arrive. The transport would be marked of course to make sure that its progress could be tracked but he did not plan to stay with the vehicle for long. A switch would be made and then he would make his escape. Stansted was a complication but being in a more remote location might yet be to his advantage. He was sure that, by now, his back up team would have spotted the change in venue and be responding. A hungry media would have broadcast the hijack almost as soon as the airliner had been commandeered. The plan could still work.

*

The special forces team had split into two groups and the trooper leading the first team darted into place behind the nosewheel of the Boeing, the remainder of his team fanning out around him. Looking back he watched the second team position below the trailing edge of the wing. Both groups had advanced from directly behind the airliner, the avenue of approach carefully calculated to ensure that they were invisible from either the cockpit or from the passenger windows. Two of the troopers, one in each team, carried a small pistol, similar in appearance to a Verey gun, normally used to fire warning flares. Adapted to fire a small grappling hook or a lead weight, a rope fired over the top of the fuselage would give access to the boarding doors at each end of the airliner. Their method of entry would be far from conventional.

The stifled thump of the pistol firing was drowned out by the whine of the auxiliary power unit at the rear of the tail cone, although the muffled clang as the rope straddled the fuselage must have been audible inside.

There was no time for hesitation.

*

Inside the cockpit, Steinbach seemed perplexed, his eyes widening briefly before the side of his head exploded in an eruption of gore. The .308 Winchester round from the L96A1 sniper rifle passed though the instrument panel behind the Captain's seat in the blink of an eye, the only evidence of its passing, a starred bullet hole in the side screen of the cockpit window. The round had barely deviated from its trajectory. The sniper was invisible behind a strategically placed screen only metres from the airliner, the view to the cockpit unhindered. Such a short range shot was academic and the feckless target had done nothing to shield his profile.

Steinbach slid to the floor at the precise moment another muffled thump sounded from beyond the interconnecting cabin door. The obstruction lifted from its hinges shortly before a wraith-like body, shouting at screaming pitch, appeared in the void, the noise immobilising the occupants, acquiescence guaranteed. His warning was redundant; everyone within the confined space froze without question. Steinbach was already bleeding out on the floor.

The dead terrorist would never know but Hammond had chosen the easy route. Whether he would be able to explain away his presence onboard would depend on his guile and how well he could justify his presence, given his former life as a Navy officer. With chaos all around, he placed his hands on his head and adopted the brace position along with the other passengers in the cabin. The shouted commands were extremely compelling.

CHAPTER 74

Over London.

Many miles to the south, Ashworth felt an extraordinary calm. The close encounter with the Phantom might have been fatal, the Warrior bottoming out of the dive only feet above the surrounding cityscape. The angular contours of a gaudy office block, its mirrored walls a luminous blue, were still etched in his mind. It had taken a robust pull on the controls to avoid his premature demise.

With his confidence slowly recovering, he fought to regain control over events. Whilst the tiny light aircraft was flying along straight and level, its engine once more beating out a rhythm, his grasp on events had slipped and his mental attitude was shot.

Looking across the wing, it was hard to accept that he was flying through the most congested airspace in the world. Above, the skies seemed empty, yet there would be a brace of airliners within close proximity, threading their way along precisely defined air corridors into the London airports. A stream of helicopters would be following the route of the Thames, ready to deposit their highly paid businessmen and celebrities on adjacent rooftops, in time for their impending appointments. His presence seemed out of place.

The massive jet fighter had disappeared shortly after the pass, its outbound course masked from view, the crew seemingly losing interest in his progress. Despite his reprieve, he realised how close he had come to failing, the consequences slowly sinking in. Nevertheless, he was so close now, within striking distance of his goal, that he could not allow himself to fall at this final hurdle. He recognised his target.

Easing left and selecting his aiming point, he grasped the release lanyard in his left hand, simultaneously pushing the throttle fully open. With one final look over his shoulder at the improvised weapon strapped to the makeshift launcher, a feeling of calm settled over him. Satisfied, he returned his focus to the flight path.

At that moment, fixated on his target, he realised his mistake. The rectangular windows of the building filled the windscreen.

CHAPTER 75

Downing Street, London.

The Prime Minister winced involuntarily as the door latched into place, the echo resonating around the room. The reaction was untypical. It would not do for the "Iron Lady" to be seen to falter.

Glad that she had been alone, she began analysing each of the momentous events of the last few days, methodically. The significance could not be starker. It did not take her legendary, incisive, analytical powers to know that she had enjoyed a lucky escape.

Determining how the attack had been mounted and by whom would be her first action and she already had the intelligence community on alert. More importantly, she doubted the Red Army Faction had the wherewithal to mount such a high profile attempt against her on British soil. That meant that there was a greater power behind the challenge to her leadership. A nagging doubt tickled the edge of her subconscious. and would not go away. Surely the KGB could not sponsor such a blatant venture under the noses of her intelligence services? She suspected she knew the answer but hoped that she was wrong. If she was proved right, the very substance of perestroika was at risk. The investigation was underway and answers had best be provided; and soon.

Discipline re-imposed, her pathetic reaction of a few moments ago was deeply troubling. It demonstrated an uncharacteristic vulnerability that even the IRA had been unable to tap when they had launched an attack on her hotel at the 1984 Party Conference. Once more her mortality had been threatened and it had been a close run thing. What if the missile - and it was already proven that it had been a Soviet surface-to-air missile - had struck home? The brazen effort, described so vividly just moments ago by her aide, was pure malice. There could have been no survivors aboard the VC-

10 but, even more chilling, there would have been mass casualties in the suburbs. The headlines would have been ruinous to the country. A Government unable to protect even its leader, never mind its people.

She shuddered, involuntarily.

More information was trickling in. That the attack seemed to have been coordinated with a series of other, smaller, incidents was equally alarming. Such intricate planning was not the work of an amateur cell and, hitherto, the Red Army Faction had been considered more as a group of disruptive hippies than a player on the world stage. That view would have to be reconsidered, whatever the outcome of investigations. The ongoing hijack at Stansted needed to be brought to a safe conclusion, and quickly. Now was not the time for weakness.

She slumped back in the chair, needing a few minutes alone to enjoy the solitude and regroup but it could not be for long because the Nation would demand her personal intervention. She would need to show firm leadership. Nothing less would do.

There were loose ends to tidy up and a robust discussion with the Head of MI5 would be next on the agenda. Terrorists will not commit atrocities openly on the London streets. Not only did it reflect badly on her image, it represented a challenge to the wave of patriotism that had emerged following the conflict in the South Atlantic. She needed that tide to flow not ebb and, after all, there would soon be an election campaign to fight.

The Cold War was never predictable.

In the meantime, a number of trusty servants had done well and they should be applauded. She drew out her fountain pen and began to write.

CHAPTER 76

A London Suburb.

Chisholm and Hawkes emerged from the police vehicle. The journey had been heralded by flashing blue lights to within a few miles of their hastily nominated destination but the mad dash had still taken almost an hour and the cramped interior had become claustrophobic.

The conditions inside the support van were, arguably, worse and the cramped bodies range along the length of the van had raised the temperature and humidity to a suffocating level. The surveillance officers stared at a bank of video monitors, the drab facade of the house of interest giving little back. There was no movement.

Chisholm gestured silently to the, evidently, disconcerted policeman, pointing to the rear doors. Without waiting for acknowledgement he slipped through the narrow gap and eased the door ajar.

It would have been safer to stay in the van but both men were frustrated at the lack of activity, particularly after the hectic journey across town. If reports were correct, events would come to a head very soon. Walking a short distance, staying out of sight of the target house, they avoided conversation, words elusive after the time cooped up in the car. With a self imposed deadline approaching, it was a last minute opportunity to stretch cramped limbs. The time to intervene was imminent. Chisholm stamped his feet, more to reinvigorate his circulation than to warm himself. The tension was palpable.

The brick-faced, semi-detached house around the corner looked like any of the other bland residences in the leafy suburb, the Edwardian features typical of the area. What made this one different was, that If reports were correct, a maverick Soviet agent was at this very moment biding his time, waiting for some faceless contact in the Soviet Embassy to arrange his extraction.

Looking back at the anonymous, white panel van parked opposite the support van, a casual onlooker might assume that it had been parked up for the night. Appearances were deceptive because, inside, six black-clad figures made final checks on their weapons, anticipating the order to move. It was a situation they had faced many times before but, if the edge ever wore off, it might be the time that they made the ultimate error. Their targets were, invariably, not nice people.

"Do you think Guskov is in there?" Chisholm asked, his voice hushed.

"My analyst at "Q" seems to think so. He promised to keep me updated."

The stilted conversation was cut short by a ringtone. Hawkes had finally conceded and accepted a new mobile phone that now protested its presence in his pocket. Its intrusion was unwelcome. He made a mental note to work out how to turn off the ringtone. Thankfully it had not gone off within hearing distance of the house. Putting the bulky device to his ear, he grunted a reluctant greeting, nodding occasionally, his responses monosyllabic.

"What did he say?" Chisholm asked, the tension plain.

"The chatter has stopped. They were monitoring a known communications channel and, until a few minutes ago, it had been flooded with heavy traffic. It's gone quiet. He couldn't say much else over this thing. They're completely insecure. He was talking in a code that a five year old could crack"

"So what now?"

"He thinks something is about to happen. It's the calm before the storm. His words, not mine. I guess I get to make the big decision on when to send the team in."

"Not much to go on."

The statement of the blindingly obvious earned Chisholm another grunt.

Hawkes was in a quandary. He had no certainty that the Soviet agent was inside the house. What if Brandt was lying? The only other evidence was a few decrypted snippets from communications monitoring and a report of strange "goings on" from a local resident. But if Brandt was correct and Guskov was inside; and more importantly, Hawkes didn't make a move, the wily old Soviet agent would spot something amiss and be gone. Guskov had proved time and again that his tradecraft was as good as it comes; indecision was not a good idea. How had it come to this point? He was trusting a known terrorist to plan an arrest. Even if everything went perfectly, Guskov would claim diplomatic immunity the minute he was taken and would be repatriated to the Soviet Embassy within hours. Convention would not let them hold him. He was a "legal". The best they could hope was to make a public fuss during the deportation process. That, however, was up to his political masters, not him.

It was decision time.

*

Guskov was invisible to all but the closest scrutiny. From his vantage point along the street, he watched the pair of men intently, harbouring no doubt about their intentions nor the reason for their presence. There could be only one conclusion. He had been sold out. He also knew that there could be only one culprit because only one other person involved in the plot knew his identity.

Brandt.

Reaching into his pocket, the tiny control box slipped into his palm, its bulk insignificant, its destructive power enormous. Inside the house, just across the street, his carefully prepared surprise lay ready.

Almost inconsequentially he squeezed the button. From this moment on, he was on borrowed time.

*

The decision was never made. As Hawkes turned back to face the bland semi-detached house, the front of the building lit up, momentarily, before the windows blew out, showering debris in a wide arc. The flash of the explosion lit the surrounding streets, followed by the thump of the accelerant and the sinister sound of the blast that followed. As the glass fragments rained down on the street, peppering vehicles along its length, the noise rolled down the leafy avenue. The grating and crashing of beams and bricks followed, thrown in a wide radius from the seat of the blast, littering the surrounding gardens.

In an act of self preservation, Hawkes dived for the cover of a low wall, narrowly avoiding the force of the shock wave that stormed overhead. Chisholm was not so lucky. Facing away from the house, he failed to sense the impending risk and took the full force of the shock wave at his back which bowled him over, launching him headlong into a brick wall. Slumping to the ground, immobile, his arm twisted out at an impossible angle; it was clear that the limb was broken. Blood seeped from a gaping head wound.

Two blocks away, a nondescript rental car fired up its engine, the occupant checking the surrounding area briefly in the rear view mirror before pulling away. His departure went unnoticed.

Hawkes looked horrified at Chisholm, his distorted body testament to the massive force of the explosion. The semi-detached house was burning fiercely, the flames encroaching rapidly on its neighbour.

In the distance, sirens from an emergency vehicle wailed ominously.

"The bastard!"

CHAPTER 77

Headquarters Strike Command, RAF High Wycombe.

The Commander-in-Chief Strike Command leaned back in his chair feeling, if he might allow himself the luxury, a little smug. The Wattisham boys had done well and not only had the Chief of the Air Staff called to offer his congratulations, the letter that had been hand-carried from the Prime Minister's office was a source of some pride and a good deal of satisfaction. She must have penned the letter the moment she had arrived back in Downing Street for it to have arrived so quickly.

The QRA crews had yet to debrief so his scant information had come second-hand from the military air traffic control centre at West Drayton. It seemed that the crews had responded well, protecting the VC-10 from attack, despite the lack of warning. He knew from his own time flying Jaguar fighter-bombers in Germany that there was little warning of an inbound SA-7 missile if, indeed that was what had been fired.

He may have to call the Chief of the Metropolitan Police to give him a little ribbing. He had shared a course at Staff College with the avuncular police officer and the man had a well developed sense of humour but he doubted whether he would find this one amusing. His officer had tracked the terrorist but had not picked her up until after the missile had been launched. But for the Phantom alongside the Prime Minister's aircraft, the outcome might have been vastly different. One up to the Air Force.

The senior officer glanced through the briefing pack, reviewing the flags, each meticulously and symmetrically tagged at the top of the page. Such attention to detail was expected in his office. At times, presentation overrode content. The story was not over yet. With such a high profile target it was only a question of time before a request for an interview from the BBC was lodged. Whitehall, and particularly their own people in MOD

Public Relations, would respond to the media frenzy. Nevertheless, he would be prepared if called, his photographic memory storing each relevant detail, noting in parallel which classified sections to avoid. He wanted to be credible during his moment of glory but not at the expense of a security breach. The RAF Police were equally renowned for their lack of humour.

In slower time, the security services would need to go over the defensive contingency plans again. It was impossible to seal every rooftop in London but there were only so many that gave an open aspect across the approach paths to the airports and they needed to know them intimately. A terrorist had worked out arcs of fire so the intelligence community would need to do likewise. Next time, there may not be the same advanced warning and, if the budget cuts continued to bite, he may not have appropriate forces to intervene.

Turning his attention to the immediate action report from the SAS Commander at Stansted, his mood warmed. It made good reading and Director Special Forces would be pleased with the content. Operation "Limit" had been an unqualified success and the airliner had been retaken without casualties and within an hour of landing. The media was already having a field day, interviewing relieved service families as they emerged through Customs at Stansted. It was a public relations coup so far but questions over how security had been breached at Wildenrath would follow, and that would fall to him; or at least to his counterpart in the RAF Germany Headquarters at Rheindahlen. He would speak to his own staff soon and find out why the errors had been made but it was a sad day when you had to screen your own people in order to weed out terrorism. How a member of the Baader Meinhoff gang could even get on Station was horrific in its implications. That a bomb had been smuggled into the hold of a trooper flight was shocking and someone would have to answer for the consequences. Things would have to change and he suspected that the days of carefree travel were well and truly over. The Provost Marshal at HQ RAF Germany would already be tap dancing, trying to respond to the inevitable criticism. Overall though, they had executed a complex joint operation and succeeded. A coordinated attack had been foiled and they could be happy with the contribution.

An urgent knock broke his conceited reverie as his personal staff officer barged in.

"Sir, I'm sorry to interrupt but I thought you should know. Breaking news on the BBC. A light aircraft has just hit the Ministry of Defence Main Building. It approached from the Thames side and hit the southern facade on the Embankment. There was a secondary explosion on impact although it's not clear if that was just fuel igniting. First reports are that there have been a number of fatalities, bizarrely enough from shrapnel injuries. It's almost as if a weapon had exploded from first reports. We're not yet sure if the events are linked but a light aircraft has been reported missing from the RAF Wattisham Flying Club. The registration matches that of an aircraft that penetrated the London Control Zone earlier and was intercepted by QRA. Of more concern, the description of the missing aircraft matches that of an eye witness who was on the Embankment and saw the impact. He also said that it seemed like the light aircraft was making a "bombing run". Those were the words he used."

The aide's words flagged. The C-in-C's face sagged, his pallor ashen. The change in his demeanour was subtle but manifest and the aide knew that it would be a good idea not to interrupt his thoughts. When he finally spoke his tone was hushed.

"These acts were, unmistakably, interrelated. This was not the product of a tinpot German terrorist cell. Whoever was behind it has sent a message and it has everything to do with reunification. Whoever is responsible. . . . ." he hesitated momentarily, "and I suspect I know who without fear of contradiction, he or she has delivered an emphatic . . . . . Ultimatum!"

EPILOGUE

Hawkes watched as Brandt was ushered into the room, stilling his natural urge to stand. She was, after all, a terrorist without principles. She would have taken lives without even a thought, innocent bystanders embroiled in the carnage of an aircraft crashing into the London suburbs.

He had travelled to Suffolk that morning, arriving at the secluded cottage in the early hours. Ironically, he was only a short distance from Little Seething, the airfield from which Brandt had launched the ill fated attack on the PM, although such details had yet to emerge.

"How are you settling in?" he asked as Brandt dropped into the seat, the tension between them blatant. It was not their first meeting since she had been detained.

"How do you think? This wasn't what we agreed in London. I might just as well be in prison for all the freedom I have here. We're miles from anywhere, the warders watch me every moment and the routine is identical every day."

Hawkes gauged his response warily. He was stalling.

"Look, there's no easy way to break this. The negotiations with the Public prosecutors hasn't gone well. They've been resistant from the outset. I've tried to agree any number of compromises but we keep getting back to the hard-line position. As they see it, having a go at the British Prime Minister cannot go unpunished. If word got out, we would have a stream of nut jobs all intent on wreaking havoc."

He made eye contact as he used the derogatory term, sensing success. The point had struck home.

"Then you'll need to approach the problem from a different angle," she murmured, her accent heightened by the evident stress.

"I'll be frank. The Germans want you back to face trial. They want you extradited, not only for your efforts in London but for your attacks in Germany."

"How did they know you have me?"

It was a mistake.

"That's irrelevant now."

"But you promised me freedom in return for Guskov. You lied. . . . ."

*

Guskov walked briskly across Red Square, the familiar views of his regular morning commute following his return to the Lubyanka. The air was turning crisp in the early morning autumn sun and he detected the first hint of the approaching winter. It was his favourite time of the year but it did little to improve his foul mood.

His contacts in England had scoured the countryside looking for Brandt, to date with no success. The woman had disappeared, although it was no big surprise. If he had her in custody she would disappear more permanently. What he had gleaned from his Embassy contacts was that she had sold him out. She had resisted interrogation for only a few hours before offering him up. Since then, counter-surveillance in London, from the MI5 "watchers", had been at record levels for some days. It had been almost impossible for the KGB operatives to move without close surveillance.

Customs checks at airports had been stepped up leading to unprecedented queues in the departure lounges across the country as passports had been scrutinised thoroughly. Thankfully, his departure had been via another less public avenue. His journey home had been far from comfortable but risk of detention aboard the tramp steamer had been minimal. It had still been a blessed relief to disembark in Estonia.

The familiar facade of the secretive, headquarters building loomed ahead and another day tied to the desk beckoned. His boss had been firm in his direction. Guskov's tail feathers had been clipped. He was warned off venturing into the field for the foreseeable future and he doubted if he would ever see London again. The warning had been short of a rebuke but he doubted that the oft heralded promotion would figure in the future plans now.

Far from generating a rift in the western alliance, NATO nations seemed closer in their collective posture than ever. The media in Moscow, rather than criticise the unrest in East Germany, was selling it as an awakening. The political apparatus was beginning to sell Glasnost as the future. Given that the press apparatus was entirely driven by the Politburo party line, he could see the future clearly.

Brandt.

The name was burned into his psyche. His mind was set on revenge, however long it took.

*

The Prime Minister pinned the medal onto Flash's lapel, patting the ribbon down and settling it properly in place. Alongside, Razor stood rigidly to attention through the formalities. Given the threat to the mandarins in Whitehall from the IRA, both flyers wore lounge suits, a sop to personal security. The gleaming military medals seemed incongruous, set against black pinstripe.

The PM thanked each in turn for their heroic actions, making it perfectly clear that she felt that her continued presence on the planet was due entirely to the two of them. Razor almost blushed. Almost.

"I'm sure you will appreciate the reasons why this matter has to remain classified. There are elements which, if released to the general public, would cause unrest. I can never be seen to be negotiating with terrorists, and any deviation from that line has to be stringently policed. You'll understand why."

The gentle expression of only moments ago had vanished, replaced by the familiar facade of the hard-bitten politician, so well-known on television. Her words might have been taken from a quote on the TV news but for its devious undertones.

Both men murmured assent. There would be no coffee and no further fanfare. The ceremony was short, the PM, after a final word of thanks, immediately ushered away by a harried aide. Within minutes she would be beset by today's national crisis, her legendary schedule brutal in its intensity. They were, politely ushered out of the elegant reception room.

*

Flash placed the foaming beer mug in front of his pilot and eased onto the bench seat. The Clarence pub was only a two minute walk from No.10 Downing Street, even if they had been ushered discretely out of the back door, safe from the eyes of the prying media who were, as usual, camped out on the doorstep.

"It's an odd world isn't it?"

He looked at Razor, the youthful looks on the face opposite fading; the stress of the last few days clearly evident.

"I'll drink to that," he replied, offering up his own tankard. As the beer glasses clinked over the table, the conversation stilled, the silence easy, the clamour of the busy pub almost drowning out their unsaid thoughts.

"The newspaper headlines have been filled with speculation over what went on. Ever since the bloke in Hounslow found the carcass of a SAM-7 on Datchet High Street, speculation has been rife. You don't have to be Sherlock Holmes to fit together all the pieces. Even a three year old could work out that it was a coordinated plot but our part has to be a state bloody secret. How come?"

"That's the system Razor. You know how it goes. If we tried to say a word we'd have the RAF Plods on the doorstep inside ten minutes. I for one, don't want to spend time in Colchester prison just for five minutes of glory. The Official Secrets Act is draconian if they decide to apply it rigidly."

"It's a shame, the terrorist who tried to down the PM's jet isn't in Colchester," the sullen pilot responded. "They'd be delighted to welcome him there!"

It was hardly the celebration either of them had planned during those brief, heady moments immediately after the attack, as they had headed back across Essex towards Wattisham, the VC-10 safely on the ground at Heathrow. The medals were stuffed unceremoniously into jacket pockets, the plaudits from the PM almost forgotten. The accolades hollow.

*

At the very moment the pair were draining the last drops of beer ready to head home, a black car pulled up in front of a chocolate box cottage in Suffolk. A woman was bundled without ceremony into the back seat.

Her destination?

Bonn and a questionable, or perhaps inevitable, future.

AUTHOR'S NOTE

When writing novels, I try to stay as close to reality as I can but I hope you'll forgive me for a little artistic license in my interpretation of the political facts surrounding the fall of the Berlin Wall that form the basis of the plot. Reagan, Gorbachev and Thatcher were, indeed, the key characters influencing the momentous changes and Regan's speech in Berlin proved to be history in the making. Thatcher was less enthusiastic at the prospect of a reunited Germany but, in particular, President Mitterrand of France was highly sceptical, and was equally happy to slow the pace of developments. Gorbachev saw Glasnost, which means openness in Russian, as a way to introduce democracy into the highly bureaucratic, and reluctant Soviet political machinery. He saw the Russian people as the best means to implement change and felt a free media might become a catalyst to achieve the goals. Nevertheless, resistance from both the Communist Party Central Committee Secretariat and the Politburo meant he was thwarted throughout the process. Obviously, the events in the novel which capture these enigmatic leaders in action are purely fictional.

Negotiations in 1987, when the action in the book takes place, centred on limiting the proliferation of Intermediate Range Nuclear forces and German opinion was, not surprisingly, concerned at the effect and potential consequences of the presence of such destructive power within its borders. Conversely, reaction was necessarily muted in the east where the populace was heavily controlled. A Soviet initiative sought to persuade a nervous German Government to move towards "denuclearisation". Far from supporting reunification, it engendered a tense and nervous atmosphere, prompting Thatcher to urge further caution to avoid disrupting the delicate Cold War balance. In the end, rather than terrorist acts as portrayed in the novel, influencing political thinking, it was liberalisation, starting in Hungary and progressing to East Germany, Czechoslovakia and finally Romania which shaped history. Indeed, such terrorist atrocities would have been more likely to stiffen resolve than force capitulation. An inability to match the, hideously, expensive US "Star Wars" initiative, rather than the Greenham Common peace camps, ultimately dictated change. I took liberties with history but I hope it helped the plot.

To protect the innocent, there is no flying club at RAF Wattisham although the airfield was the home to the Anglia Gliding Club, one of the earliest organisations to occupy the airfield after it returned to RAF control. RAF flying clubs are an important adjunct to operations allowing those who might, otherwise, not be able to fly to enjoy the thrill of aviation. Hopefully, the carefully supervised way in which flying is conducted at modern RAF flying clubs prevents anyone taking such drastic action as that plotted by Ashworth in the story. Equally, the real G-ASOE was a Hiller helicopter registered to a well known international company, not a Wattisham Flying Club based Cherokee Warrior, so its use in the story is entirely fictional. I should also like to make it clear that there is no suggestion that the owner of Sanctuary Farm just outside the village of Little Baddow would contemplate being involved in the nefarious activities of the disaffected airman Ashworth and the involvement of the farm and its owner is also entirely fictional.

Some may have wondered why I included the quote from the Bluebird project leader at the start of the book. The McDonnell Douglas Phantom, the central them of my Phantom air combat series, undoubtedly had soul. Just ask any of the thousands of aircrew who were privileged to fly the aircraft over its operational life.

As always. my thanks to Phil Keeble and Paul Pike who helped me edit the book and to Dean Crawford who produced another great cover.

I hope you enjoyed the story.

GLOSSARY

ADMISREP. Air Defence Mission Report.
ADOC. Air Defence Operations Centre.
Angels. Codeword for height. Angels 05 is 5,000 feet.
ANPR. Automatic Numberplate Recognition.
ASCOT. A callsign used by RAF military aircraft on international flights.
Air Support Command traditionally used Ascot. This callsign was replaced
by RAFAIR.
ATC. Air Traffic Control.
Augusta A-109. A helicopter used by the Special Air Service for covert
operations.
Bogey dope. An American radio call requesting information on a potential
opponent. A hostile target is a bogey; dope meaning information.
Buster. To use maximum military power.
"Cock" a jet. To prepare the cockpit for a scramble. This involved setting
switches and straps into the best position for a rapid strap-in.
Coolant. Liquid cooling fluid that chills the infra-red missile seeker head so
that it can detect a hot spot against the ambient background conditions.
CW. Continuous wave radar used to guide a Sparrow or Skyflash missile to
the target. Transmitted by the main radar.
Delta H. An instrument giving relative height of the target once the radar is
locked on.
DDR. The former East Germany known as the Deutsche Demokratik
Republik.
Doors. A term used to identify the time at which a VIP flight will arrive at
the terminal and disembark a VIP.
Duty Authoriser. The officer nominated to supervise the daily flying
programme and to authorise flights when crew could not self authorise.
Flight Level. A height based on the standard altimeter pressure setting.
Flight Level 150 is 15,000 feet.
Gate. To use reheat and make maximum speed.
GCHQ. Government Communications Headquarters. A communications
surveillance centre.
Glasnost. A Russian term meaning "openness and transparency", adopted
by Mikhail Gorbachev to describe his initiative in moving towards
democracy.
GPS. Global positioning system. The American satellite navigation
constellation.
Grail. NATO codename for the SA-7 portable air defence missile.
HAS. Hardened Aircraft Shelter.
ID. The RAF identity card was known as a Form 1250.

IFF. Identification, Friend or Foe. An electronic box transmitting a code to ground controllers identifying the cooperating aircraft.

ILS. Instrument Landing System.

INAS. Inertial Navigation and Attack System. "Nav" was the selection for "navigate", the mode used in flight.

Interrogate. A command requiring the crew to investigate a track normally of unknown identity.

IRA. Irish Republican Army.

LCOSS. Lead Computing Optical Sighting System. The gunsight. A reticule was projected into the windscreen displaying tracking information to aim the SUU-23 gun pod.

LED. Light Emitting Diode.

London Mil. The military air traffic coordination centre in London.

Mandatory. A QRA state reflecting a risk to life or possessions if QRA is launched. Often used in poor weather.

MANPADS. Man-Portable Air Defence System.

Mayday. The international call of distress.

Master Arm. The final arming switch that makes the weapon system live.

Master Controller. The senior controller at an air defence Sector Operations Centre.

MI5. Military Intelligence Department 5. The branch of the security services tasked to protect the Homeland.

Missile City. The nickname for section of the Station Armoury where the air-to-air weapons were stored.

MOD. Ministry of Defence.

NATO. North Atlantic Treaty Organisation.

Operation Tesseral. An operation to authorise the use of anti surface-to-air missile tactics.

Perestroika. A Gorbachev era initiative to make socialism work more efficiently, better to meet the needs of Soviet citizens.

Plumber. RAF slang for an armourer.

PM. Prime Minister.

Provost Marshal. The senior RAF policeman in a major Headquarters.

QRA. Quick Reaction Alert. Fighters held on permanent standby to protect UK airspace.

Q Shed or the Shed. The QRA alert facility.

Q1. The primary alert aircraft. Held on readiness 5 or readiness 10.

Q2. The secondary alert aircraft. Held on readiness 5 or readiness 10.

Q3. The reserve alert aircraft normally held on 60 minutes readiness to launch. In times of tension or heightened activity it was not uncommon to have the whole squadron armed. Additional Q aircraft would be sequentially numbered.

RSBN. Radiotehnicheskaya systema bliznej navigacia. The Soviet radio navigation system.

Safety altitude. The minimum height to which an aircraft can descend without risk of striking a fixed obstacle.

SAS. Special Air Service. UK elite special forces.

SAM. Surface-to-air missile.

SENGO. Senior Engineering Officer.

Sitrep. Situation report.

Solidarity. An anti-communist Polish trade union of the 1980s which fought for workers rights and social change.

Squawk. To transmit an electronic identification code.

Telebrief. A secure communications system linking the air defence agencies which could be plugged directly into the aircraft communications system whilst on the ground.

TMA. Traffic Movements Area. Controlled airspace within which aircraft are under radar control.

Tone. The aural tone emitted by the Sidewinder when it detects a target, heard in the crew's helmets. The AIM9-G emitted a "growl" whereas the AIM-9L emitted a "chirping" noise.

Tourex. The end of a tour of operational duty leading to a posting to a new unit.

Vector. To fly in a direction at a speed and height.

VW. Volkswagen.

VOR. A radio navigation beacon giving a magnetic radial from a point on the ground. Used to fix position.

Weapons Checks: Coolant (chills the infra-red missile seeker head). Tone. The audio tone emitted by the Sidewinder when it detects a target. Master Arm. The late arm switch that makes the weapon system live. LCOSS. Lead Computing Optical Sighting System. The gunsight.

ABOUT THE AUTHOR

David Gledhill joined the Royal Air Force as a Navigator in 1973. After training, he flew the F4 Phantom on squadrons in the UK and West Germany. He was one of the first aircrew to fly the F2 and F3 Air Defence Variant of the Tornado on its acceptance into service and served for many years as an instructor on the Operational Conversion Units of both the Phantom and the Tornado. He commanded the Tornado Fighter Flight in the Falkland Islands and has worked extensively with the Armed Forces of most NATO nations. He has published a number of factual books on aviation topics and novels in the Phantom Air Combat series set during the Cold War.

OTHER BOOKS BY THIS AUTHOR

Have you ever wondered what it was like to fly the Phantom? This is not a potted history of an aeroplane, nor is it Hollywood glamour as captured in Top Gun. This is the story of life on the frontline during the Cold War told in the words of a navigator who flew the iconic jet. Unique pictures, many captured from the cockpit, show the Phantom in its true environment and show why for many years the Phantom was the envy of NATO. It also tells the inside story of some of the problems which plagued the Phantom in its early days, how the aircraft developed, or was neglected, and reveals events which shaped the aircraft's history and contributed to its demise. Anecdotes capture the deep affection felt by the crews who were fortunate enough to cross paths with the Phantom during their flying careers. The nicknames the aircraft earned were not complimentary and included the 'Rhino', 'The Spook', 'Double Ugly', the 'Flying Brick' and the 'Lead Sled'. Whichever way you looked at it, you could love or hate the Phantom, but you could never ignore it.

"The Phantom in Focus: A Navigator's Eye on Britain's Cold War Warrior" - ISBN 978-178155-048-9 (print) and ASIN B00GUNIM0Q (e-book) published by Fonthill Media.

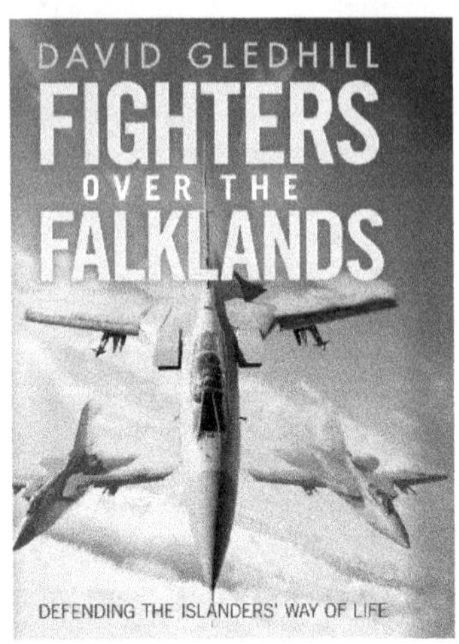

Fighters Over The Falklands: Defending the Islanders' Way of Life captures daily life using pictures taken during the author's tours of duty in the Falkland Islands. From the first detachments of Phantoms and Rapiers operating from a rapidly upgraded RAF Stanley airfield to life at RAF Mount Pleasant, see life from the author's perspective as the Commander of the Tornado F3 Flight defending the islands' airspace. Frontline fighter crews provided Quick Reaction Alert (QRA) during day to day flying operations working with the Royal Navy, Army and other air force units to defend a remote and sometimes forgotten theatre of operations. The book also examines how the islanders interacted with the forces based at Mount Pleasant and contrast high technology military operations with the lives of the original inhabitants, namely the wildlife.

"Fighters Over The Falklands – Defending the islanders Way of Life" - ISBN 978-17155-222-3 (print) and ASIN: B00H87Q7MS (e book) published by Fonthill Media.

The Tornado F2 had a troubled introduction to service. Unwanted by its crews and procured as a political imperative, it was blighted by failures in the acquisition system. Adapted from a multi-national design and planned by committee, it was developed to counter a threat which disappeared. Modified rapidly before it could be sent to war, the Tornado F3 eventually matured into a capable weapons system but despite datalinks and new air to air weapons, its poor reputation sealed its fate. The author, a former Tornado F3 navigator, tells the story from an insider's perspective from the early days as one of the first instructors on the Operational Conversion Unit, through its development and operational testing, to its demise. He reflects on its capabilities and deficiencies and analyses why the aircraft was mostly under-estimated by opponents. Although many books have already described the Tornado F3, the author's involvement in its development will provide a unique insight into this complex and misunderstood aircraft programme and dispel some of the myths. This is the author's 3rd book and, like the others, captures the story in pictures taken in the cockpit and around the squadron.

"Tornado F3 In Focus – A Navigator's Eye on Britain's Last Interceptor" - ISBN 978-178155-307-7 (print) and ASIN B00TM7A80E (e book) published by Fonthill Media.

    The Panavia Tornado was designed as a multi-role combat aircraft to meet the needs of Germany Italy and the United Kingdom. Since the prototype flew in 1974, nearly 1000 Tornados have been produced in a number of variants serving as a fighter-bomber, a fighter and in the reconnaissance and electronic suppression roles. Deployed operationally in numerous theatres throughout the world, the Tornado has proved to be exceptionally capable and flexible. From its early Cold War roles it adapted to the rigours of expeditionary warfare from The Gulf to Kosovo to Afghanistan. The early "dumb" bombs were replaced by laser-guided weapons and cruise missiles and in the air-to-air arena fitted with the AMRAAM and ASRAAM missiles.

In this book David Gledhill explores the range of capabilities and, having flown the Tornado F2 and F3 Air Defence Variant, offers an insight into life in the cockpit of the Tornado. Lavishly illustrated, Darren Wilmin's superb photographs capture the essence of the machine both from the ground and in the air. This unique collection including some of David Gledhill's own air-to-air pictures of the Tornado F2 and F3 will appeal to everyone with an interest in this iconic aircraft.

"Tornado In Pictures _ The Multi Role Legend" - ISBN 978-1781554630 (print) published by Fonthill Media.

The process to deliver a modern combat aircraft from concept to introduction to service is often measured in decades. Described as a weapon system, modern designs such as the Eurofighter Typhoon are intricate jigsaws with a fusion of new techniques and sometimes unproven, emerging technologies. By the time the new weapons system reaches the front line it will have been tested by the manufacturer, evaluated by test pilots and assessed by service pilots. There have been examples of success but some spectacular failures with projects cancelled late in development. This book will investigate why and takes you from the original requirement through the complex testing and evaluation process showing recent examples of the path to declaring a new combat aircraft operational on the front line. It will look at how today's test organisations have matured to meet the task and investigate the pressures they face. It will also look at real-life examples of systems testing. David Gledhill and David Lewis, both experienced test evaluators, will uncover the reasons why some aircraft serve on the front line for years before becoming truly effective in their role.

Operational Test - Honing the Edge - ISBN 978-1781555712 (print) published by Fonthill Media.

The McDonnell Douglas F4 Phantom was a true multi-role combat aircraft. Introduced into the RAF in 1968, it was employed in ground attack, air reconnaissance and air defence roles. Later, with the arrival of the Jaguar in the early 1970s, it changed over to air defence. In its heyday, it served as Britain s principal Cold War fighter; there were seven UK-based squadrons plus the Operational Conversion Unit, two Germany-based squadrons and a further Squadron deployed to the Falkland Islands. Phantom in the Cold War focuses predominantly on the aircraft s role as an air defence fighter, exploring the ways in which it provided the British contribution to the Second Allied Tactical Air Force at RAF Wildenrath, the home of Nos. 19 and 92 Squadrons during the Cold War. As with his previous books, the author, who flew the Phantom operationally, recounts the thrills, challenges and consequences of operating this sometimes temperamental jet at extreme low-level over the West German countryside, preparing for a war which everyone hoped would never happen.

Phantom in the Cold War: RAF Wildenrath 1977 - 1992 - ISBN 978-1526704085 published by Pen and Sword.

Colonel Yuri Andrenev, a respected test pilot is trusted to evaluate the latest Soviet fighter, the Sukhoi Su27 "Flanker", from a secret test facility near Moscow. Surely he is above suspicion? With thoughts of defection in his mind, and flying close to the Inner German Border, could he be tempted to make a daring escape across the most heavily defended airspace in the world? A flight test against a Mig fighter begins a sequence of events that forces his hand and after an unexpected air-to-air encounter he crosses the border with the help of British Phantom crews. How will Western Intelligence use this unexpected windfall? Are Soviet efforts to recover the advanced fighter as devious as they seem or could more sinister motives be in play? Defector is a pacy thriller which reflects the intrigue of The Cold War. It takes you into the cockpit of the Phantom fighter jet with the realism that can only come from an author who has flown operationally in the NATO Central Region.

"Defector" - ISBN 978-1-49356-759-1 (print) and ASIN B00EUYEUDK (e book) and Audiobook ASIN B00WB21MW0, published by DeeGee Media.

Combat veteran Major Pablo Carmendez holds a grudge against his former adversaries. Diverting his armed Skyhawk fighter-bomber from a firepower demonstration he flies eastwards towards the Falkland Islands intent on revenge. What is his target and will he survive the defences alerted of his intentions? Crucially, will his plan wreck delicate negotiations between Britain and Argentina designed to mend strained relations? Are Government officials charged with protecting the islanders' interests worthy of that trust or are more sinister motives in play? Maverick is an aviation thriller set in the remote outpost in the South Atlantic Ocean that takes you into the cockpits of the Phantom fighters based on the Islands where you will experience the thrills of air combat as the conspiracy unfolds.

"Maverick" - ISBN 978-1507801895 (print) and ASIN B00S9UL430 (e book) published by DeeGee Media.

When a hostage is snatched from the streets of Beirut by Hezbollah terrorists it sets in train a series of events from the UK to the Middle East that end in the corridors of power. A combined air operation is mounted from a base in Cyprus to release the agent from his enforced captivity. Phantom and Buccaneer crews help a special forces team to mount a daring raid, the like of which has not been attempted since Operation Jericho during World War 2. With Syrian forces ranged against them and Israeli and American friends seemingly bent on thwarting them, the outcome is by no means certain. As in his other novels David Gledhill takes you into the cockpit in this fast paced Cold War tale of intrigue and deception.

"Deception" - ISBN 978-1508762096 (print) and ASIN B00V8JTE40 (e book) published by DeeGee Media.

 With tensions rising in post-war Europe, the Soviet Union closed the air corridors to Berlin, the former German capital, in a bid to starve the population into submission. The western allies responded by mounting the largest air supply operation the world had ever seen which would become known as the "Berlin Airlift".

Step forward into the 1980s with the Cold War at its height. A NATO reinforcement exercise held at a British airbase in West Germany, brings British, American and French fighter crews together to practice the air corridor policing mission. When a Pembroke transport aircraft engaged in a covert reconnaissance mission is intercepted by a Mig fighter and forced to land in East Germany, events escalate. Will the crew become a pawn in the relentless confrontation as the Soviets increase the rhetoric? Have western military plans been compromised by the unexpected aggression?

Provocation is a fast moving thriller that replays the tensions of the Cold War and its dark undertones. As with his other novels, David Gledhill takes you into the cockpit of the Phantom fighter jet to experience the action first hand.

"Provocation" ISBN 978-1515382584 (print) and ASIN B014GUHGKG (e book) and Audiobook ASIN B018EPFG06, published by DeeGee Media.

Flying the Jaguar bomber in a Cold War West Germany, Nick Gleason is, perhaps, at the peak of his career but he is a loner struggling with his conscience and he begins to question the morality of his role. If war in Europe breaks out, he would be tasked to deliver a thermo-nuclear weapon to a target in the East.

Two British fighter aircraft, one a Phantom, the second a Jaguar piloted by Gleason, converge at low level over the Osnabruck Ridge on the North German Plain. One is armed with a practice nuclear bomb, the other simply conducting a routine training exercise but their flight paths are destined to cross. Events have been far from routine as the crews are drawn towards the encounter that threatens to jeopardise their very existence. Was a mid-air collision inevitable from the outset or could the, seemingly, inexorable chain of events have been broken? Was destruction predestined? The countdown to impact is underway.

"Impact" ISBN: 978-1541371552 (print), ASIN B01N5GUIR8 (e book) and Audiobook ASIN B01MTAXJT8, published by DeeGee Media.

The year is 1986 and the Cold War threatens to turn hot. An agent is sent to join a carrier battle group in the North Atlantic, his covert mission to help the Soviet Union to track British nuclear powered submarines as they set off to patrol the oceans. To mask his bold assignment a complex diversionary operation is launched from the decks of the aircraft carrier "Kiev", the pride of the Red Banner Northern Fleet. The target; British military radar installations on the Scottish coastline.

Commanders respond by deploying Phantom fighters to a remote base in western Scotland to assist Quick Reaction Alert forces where a tense stand-off develops before unexpected events bring the two sides to the brink. Could these be the opening moves of World War 3 or will the intrepid fighter crews foil the Soviet efforts?

As with all his books David Gledhill takes you into the cockpit with unparalleled realism for another high octane adventure in the skies.

"Infiltration" ISBN: 978-1520919133 (print), ASIN B06XTR452Q (e book), published by DeeGee Media.

Visit my website and sign up for updates on my books: http://deegee-media.webnode.com/